In a plague-stricken medieval convent, a nun works on a forbidden mystic manuscript. In rural South Carolina, an alligator named Dragon becomes a beloved pet for a precocious, tough-talking twelve-year-old. During a long, muggy July, an adolescent girl finds unexpected power as her family obsesses over the horror film *The Exorcist*. On the outskirts of a Southern college town, a young woman resists the tyranny of a shape-shifting older professor as she develops her own sorceress skills. And at a feminist art colony in the North Carolina mountains, a group of mothers contends with the supernatural talents their children have picked up from a pair of mysterious orphans who live in the woods.

With exuberance, ferocity, and astounding imagination, Julia Elliott's *Hellions* jumps from the occult to the comic, from the horrific to the wondrous, in eleven stories of earthbound characters who long for the otherworldly.

Hellions

Also by Julia Elliott

The New and Improved Romie Futch

The Wilds

Hellions

stories

Julia Elliott

TIN HOUSE / PORTLAND, OREGON

These stories have previously appeared, in earlier form, in the following publications: "Bride" (*Conjunctions* 63, Fall 2014; *The Best American Short Stories 2015*, ed. T. C. Boyle); "Hellion" (*The Georgia Review*, Summer 2018; *The Best American Short Stories 2019*, ed. Anthony Doerr); "Erl King" (*Tin House*, Spring 2018; *The Pushcart Prize XLIV*, 2020); "The Maiden" (Reactor Magazine, February 2025); "Flying" (*Conjunctions* 78, Spring 2022); "Arcadia Lakes" (*Conjunctions* 80, Spring 2023); "The Mothers" (*Conjunctions* 82, Spring 2024); "Moon Witch, Moon Witch" (*Conjunctions* 70, Spring 2018); "Another Frequency" (*Conjunctions* 76, Spring 2021); "The Gricklemare" (*Conjunctions* 74, Spring 2020); "All the Other Demons" (*The Georgia Review*, Summer 2024)

Manufacturing by Versa Press
Interior design by Beth Steidle

Library of Congress Cataloging-in-Publication Data

Names: Elliott, Julia, author.
Title: Hellions : stories / Julia Elliott.
Description: First US Edition. | Portland, Oregon : Tin House, 2025.
Identifiers: LCCN 2024051365 | ISBN 9781963108064 (paperback) | ISBN 9781963108125 (ebook)
Subjects: LCGFT: Short stories.
Classification: LCC PS3605.L4477 H45 2025 | DDC 813/.6—dc23/eng/20241108
LC record available at https://lccn.loc.gov/2024051365

Tin House
2617 NW Thurman Street, Portland, OR 97210
www.tinhouse.com

DISTRIBUTED BY W. W. NORTON & COMPANY

1 2 3 4 5 6 7 8 9 0

For Eva

Contents

Hellions

Bride

Wilda whips herself with a clump of blackberry brambles. She can feel cold from the stone floor pulsing up into her cowl, chastising her animal body. She smiles. Each morning she thinks of a new penance. Yesterday, she slipped off her woolen stockings and stood outside in the freezing air. The morning before that, she rolled naked in dried thistle. Subsisting on watery soup and stale bread, she has almost subdued her body. Each month when the moon swells, her woman's bleeding is a dribble of burgundy so scant she does not need a rag.

Women are by nature carnal, the abbot said last night after administering the sacred blood and flesh. *A woman's body has a door, an opening that the Devil may slip through, unless she fiercely barricades against such entry.*

Wilda's body is a bundle of polluted flesh. Her body is a stinking goat. She lashes her shoulders and back. She scourges her arms and legs, her shrunken breasts and jutting rib cage. After thrashing the small mound of her belly, she gives her feet a good working over, flagellating her toes and soles. She reaches back to torture the two poor sinews of her buttocks. And then she repeats the process, doubling the force. She chastises the filthy maggot of her carnality until she feels fire crackling up her backbone. Her head explodes with light. Her soul rejoices like a bird flitting from a dark hut, out into summer air.

Sister Elgaruth is always in the scriptorium before Wilda, just after Prime Service, making her rounds among the lecterns, checking the manuscripts for errors, her hawk nose hovering an inch above each parchment. As the sun rises over the dark wood, Wilda sits down at her desk. She sharpens her quill, opens her inkpot, and takes a deep sniff—pomegranate juice and wine tempered with sulfur—a rich, red ink that reminds her of Christ's blood, the same stuff that stains her fingertips. This is always the happiest time of day—ink perfume in her nostrils, windows blazing with light, her body weightless from the morning's scourge. But then the other nuns come bumbling in, filling the hall with grunts and coughs, fermented breath, smells of winter bodies bundled in wool. Wilda sighs and turns back to *Beastes of God's Worlde*, the manuscript she has been copying for a year, over and over, encountering the creatures of God's menagerie in different moods and seasons, finding them boring on some days and thrilling on others.

Today she is halfway through the entry on bees, the smallest of God's birds, created on the fifth day. She imagines bees spewing from the void, the air hazy and buzzing. In these fallen times, bees hatch from the bodies of oxen and the rotted flesh of dead cows. They begin as worms, squirming in putrid meat, and "transform into bees." The manuscript provides no satisfactory information on the nature of this transformation while going on for paragraphs about the lessons we may learn from creatures that hatch from corpses to become ethereal flying nectar eaters and industrious builders of hives.

How do they get their wings? Wilda wonders. *Do they sleep in their hives all winter or freeze to death? Do fresh swarms hatch from ox flesh each spring?*

Wilda is about to scrawl these questions in the margins when she feels a tug on her sleeve. She turns, regards the blunt sallow face of Sister Elgaruth, which nips all speculation in the bud.

"Sister," croaks Elgaruth, "you stray from God's task."

Wilda turns back to her copying, shaping letters with her crimped right hand.

At lunch in the dining hall, the abbess sits in her bejeweled chair. Rubies glint in the dark mahogany. Though the abbess is stringy and yellow as a dried parsnip, everybody knows she has a sweet tooth, that she dotes on white flour, pheasants roasted in honey, wine from the Canary Islands. Her Holiness wears ermine collars and anoints her withered neck with myrrh. Two prioresses, Sister Ethelburh and Sister Joan, hunch on each side of her, slurping cabbage soup with pious frowns. They cast cold glances at the table of new girls.

The new girls have no Latin. They bark the English language, lacing familiar words with the darkness of their mother tongue. One of them, Aoife, works in the kitchen with Wilda on Saturdays and Sundays. Aoife works hard, chopping a hundred onions, tears streaming down her cheeks. She sleeps in a cell six doors down from Wilda's. Sometimes, when Wilda roams the shadowy hall to calm her soul after Matins, she sees Aoife blustering through, red hair streaming. Wilda feels the tug of curiosity. She wants to follow the girl into her room, hear her speak the language of wolves and foxes.

Now, as Wilda's tablemates spout platitudes about the heavy snows God keeps dumping on the convent in March, the new girls erupt into rich laughter. They bray and howl, snigger and snort. Dark vapors hover over them. A turbulence. A hullaballoo. When the abbess slams her goblet down on the table, the wild girls stifle their mirth. But Wilda can see that Aoife's strange amber eyes are still laughing even though her mouth is pinched into a frown.

At vespers, the gouty abbot is drunk again. His enormous head glistens like a broiled ham. He says that the world, drenched in sin, is freezing into a solid block of ice. He says that women are ripe for the Devil's attentions. He says their tainted flesh lures the Devil like spicy, rancid bait. The abbot describes the Evil One scrambling through a woman's window in the darkness of night. Knuckles upon pulpit, he mimics the sound of Satan's dung-caked hooves clomping over cobblestones. He asks the nuns to picture the naked fiend: face of a handsome man of thirty, swarthy-skinned, raven-haired, goat horns poking from his scalp, the muscular chest of a lusty layman—but below the waist he's all goat.

It has been snowing since November and the nuns are pale, anemic, scrawny. They are afflicted with scurvy, night blindness, nervous spasms, and melancholy. Unlike the monks across the meadow, they don't tend a vineyard at their convent. And when the abbot describes the powerful thighs of Satan, the stinking flurry of hair and goat flesh, a young nun screams. A small mousy thing who never says a word. She opens her mouth and yowls like a cat. And then she blinks. She stands. She scurries from the chapel.

After the abbot's sermon, Wilda tosses on her pallet, unable to banish the image from her mind—the vileness of two polluted bodies twisting together in a lather of poisonous sweat. She jumps out of bed and snatches her clump of blackberry brambles. She gives her ruttish beast of a body a good thrashing, chastising every square inch from chin to toes. She whips herself until she floats.

God's love is an ocean sparkling in the sun, and Wilda's soul is a droplet, a molecule of moisture lifted into the air. When she opens her eyes, she does not see her humble stone cell with its straw pallet and hemp quilt. She sees heavenly skies in pink tumult, angels slithering through clouds. She sees the Virgin held aloft by a throng of naked cherubs, doves nesting in her golden hair.

In her melodious voice, the Virgin speaks of Jesus Christ her Son, his tears of blood. The Virgin says her Son will return to Earth in April to walk among flowers and bees.

When the bell rings for Matins, Wilda is still up, pacing, her braids unraveling. Somehow, she tidies herself. Somehow, she transports her body to the chapel, where three dozen sleepy-eyed virgins have gathered at two in the freezing morning to revel in Jesus's love.

At breakfast, Wilda drinks her beer but does not touch her bread. Now she floats through the scriptorium. She slept a mere thirty minutes the night before. She has a runny nose from standing in the freezing wind with her hood down, and she shivers. But her heart burns, a flame in the hallowed nook of her chest.

You are all Christ's brides, said the abbot this morning. *Do not break the seal that binds you to him.*

"I am the bride of Christ," Wilda whispers as she sits down at her lectern. She opens her inkpot, sniffs the blood-red brew. She has a burning need to describe the voice of the Virgin, the frenzy of beating angel wings as the heavens opened to let the Sacred Mother descend. Wilda wants to capture the looks on their faces, wrenched and fierce. But there stands Sister Elgaruth, wheezing behind her. Wilda turns, regards the sooty kernel of flesh that adorns Elgaruth's left nostril. Though Elgaruth is ancient, she is one of God's creatures—magnificent, breathing, etched of flesh and bone.

"Sister," says the old woman, "mind the missing word in your last paragraph."

Elgaruth points with her crooked finger, deformed from decades of working in the scriptorium.

"Forgive me. I will be more mindful," says Wilda.

Sister Elgaruth shuffles off. Wilda eyes the shelves where the unbound vellum is stashed, noting the locked drawer that stores the choicest sheets, stripped from the backs of stillborn lambs.

She has never touched the silky stuff, which is reserved for three ancient virgins who are penning *Venerabilis Agnetis Blannbekin* for an archbishop.

When Sister Elgaruth departs to the lavatory, Wilda tiptoes over to the old woman's lectern. She opens the first drawer, noting a pot of rosemary balm and the twig Elgaruth uses to pick dark wax from her ears. The second drawer contains a Psalter, prayer beads, a bundle of dried lavender. In the third drawer, beneath a crusty handkerchief, is a carved wooden box, four keys within it looped on a hemp ring. Wilda snatches the keys, hurries to the vellum drawer, tries two keys before unlocking the most sacred sheets. By the time Sister Elgaruth returns, Wilda is back at her desk, three stolen sheets stuffed into her cowl pocket. Her heart, a wild bird, beats within her chest.

She turns back to *Beastes of God's Worlde*.

The goats bloode is so hotte with luste it wille dissolve the hardest diamonde.

In the kitchen, Aoife chops the last shriveled carrots from the root cellar. Aoife is sturdy, pink-cheeked, quick with her knife. She sings an odd song and smiles. She turns to Wilda. In the abbot's pompous voice, she croaks a pious tidbit about the darkness of woman's flesh—a miraculous imitation. For a second the abbot is right there in the kitchen, ankle-deep in onion skins, standing in the steam of boiling cabbage. Wilda feels an eruption of joy in her gut. She lets out a bray of laughter. Sister Lufe turns from her pot of beans to give them both the stink eye. Wilda smirks at Aoife, takes up a cabbage, and peels off rotted leaves—layer after slimy layer—until she uncovers the fresh, green heart of the vegetable.

Wilda kneels on bruised knees. She has no desk, only a crude, short table of gnarled elm. Tucked beneath it are sheets of lamb vellum, her quills, a pot of stolen ink. She faces east. Her window is a small square of hewn stone. Outside, snow has started to fall again, and Wilda, who has no fire, rejoices in the bone-splitting cold. She mumbles prayers. Shiver after shiver racks her body. And soon she feels nothing. Her candle flame sputters. She smells fresh lilies.

The Virgin steps from the empyrean into the world of flesh and mud.

The light from her body burns Wilda's eyes.

The words from her mouth are like musical thunder in Wilda's ears.

"My Son will return to choose a bride," says the Virgin, "a pearl without spot."

And then the Virgin is lifted by angel throng, back into the realm of pure fire.

As the snow thickens outside, Wilda sits stunned. She prays. And then she takes up her plume. She tries to describe the beauty of the Virgin. At first, her words get stuck like flies in a spill of honey. But then she begins with a simple sentence in tiny, meticulous script.

Whenne the Virgin descended I smelde apples and oceane winde.

At Prime Service the abbess keeps coughing—fierce convulsions that shake her whole body. Eyes streaming, she flees the chapel with her two prioress flunkies. The abbot pauses, and then he returns to his theme of Hell as a solid block of ice, the Devil frozen at its core. Satan is a six-headed monster with thirty-six sets of bat wings on his back. The Evil One must perpetually flap these wings to keep the ninth circle of Hell freezing cold.

Wilda frowns, trying to grasp the paradox of Hell as ice, wondering how this same Devil, frozen at the center of Hell, can also slip through her window at night, burning with lust, every pore on his body steaming. But it is morning, and the abbot is sober. When he returns for vespers, his imagination inflamed with wine, he will speak of carnal commerce between women and Satan. But this morning his theme is ice.

Today is the first day of April, and a crust of snow covers the dead grass.

The chickens won't lay. The cows give scant milk.

The cellar boasts nothing but hard sausage, ox tails, and salted pigs' feet.

The beets are blighted, the cabbages soft with rot.

But Wilda smiles, for she knows that Christ will return this blessed month, descending from Heaven with a great whoosh of balmy air. She has described the glory in her secret book—trees flowering and fruiting simultaneously, lambs frolicking on beds of fresh mint, the ground decked with lilies as Christ walks across the greening Earth to fetch his virgin bride.

Sunday in the kitchen, Aoife puts two bits of turnip into her mouth, mimicking the abbess's crooked teeth. Crossing her eyes, Aoife walks with the abbess's arrogant shuffle, head held high and sneering. Wilda doubles over. As laughter rocks through her, she staggers and sputters. Her eyes leak. She wheezes. At last, the mirth subsides, and Wilda leans against the cutting table, dizzy, relishing the warmth from the fire. A stew, dark with the last of the dried mushrooms, bubbles in the cauldron. Aoife, still sniggering, places her hand on Wilda's arm. Aoife's smile sparkles with mischief, and the young nun smells of sweat and cinnamon.

Wilda's body floats as she looks into Aoife's honey-colored eyes, irises etched with green. Aoife murmurs something in her mother tongue, but then she speaks English.

"Man is a rational, moral animal, capable of laughter."

Aoife removes her hand and turns back to her bucket of turnips.

The abbess is dead by Tuesday. Her body, dressed in a scarlet cowl, rests on a bier in the chapel. The abbot, fearing plague, sends a small, nervous prior to conduct the service. The chapel echoes with the coughs of sickly nuns. The prior covers his mouth with a ruby rag. He hurries through the absolution, flinging holy water with a brisk flick of his fingers, and departs. Three farmers haul the body away.

That night a hailstorm batters the convent, sending down stones the size of eggs, keeping the nuns awake with constant patter. Sisters whisper that the world has fallen ill, that God will purge the sin with ice. No one arrives from the monastery to conduct the morning service, and nuns pray silently in the candle-lit chapel.

Contemplating the body of Christ, Wilda kneels before her little book, waiting for words to come. She sees him, torn from the Cross, limp in the Virgin's arms. He is pale, skinny as an adolescent boy. His side wound, parted like a coy mouth, reveals pomegranate flesh. Though he has flowing hair and a silky beard, Christ is otherwise hairless, with smooth skin and nipples the color of plums. He has a woman's lips, a woman's soft yearning eyes. Wilda imagines him waking up in his tomb, cadaverous flesh glowing in the cryptic darkness. His groin is covered with loose gauze. His hair hangs halfway down his back, shining like a copper cape when he emerges into sunlight.

The world is frozen in sinne, Wilda writes, *frozen until the Lammbbe descendes to walk among floweres and bees. He wille strewe his marriage bed with lilies. Halleluiah!*

Fifteen nuns have been taken by the plague, their bodies carted off by farmers. Now, not even a prior will set foot in the convent, but the nuns shuffle through their routine, sit coughing and praying in the silent chapel, their hearts choked with black bile. They pine for spring. But the heavens keep dumping grain after grain of nasty frost onto the stone fortress. In mid-April, the clouds thicken, and a freak blizzard descends like a great dragon from the sky, vanquishing the world with snow.

Prioress Ethelburh orders the nuns to stay in their rooms praying, to leave only for the lavatory. Kitchen workers will still prepare food, but the nuns will no longer gather in the refectory for fellowship. Victuals will be taken from door to door to stave off the contagion.

In the kitchen Aoife is bleary-eyed, and Wilda worries that the plague has struck her. But then the poor girl is weeping over a pot of dried peas.

"What is it, sister?" Wilda moves toward her.

"Nothing," says Aoife, "just the sadness of winter and death."

But then Aoife pulls up her cowl sleeve, shows Wilda her arm—pale and finely shaped, mottled with pink blisters.

Wilda jumps back, fearing contagion.

"Only burns," Aoife whispers, "from Prioress Ethelburh's hellish candle."

Wilda allows her knuckles to stray across Aoife's soft cheek.

"I was out walking in the garden," says Aoife, "watching the moon shine on the snow, and she . . ."

Sister Lufe bustles in with a rank wheel of sheep's cheese, and the two women jump apart. Aoife spoons melted snow into her pot of dried peas (the well is frozen). Wilda hacks at a black cured beef tongue (the last of it). Outside the sun glares down on the endless white blight of snow. The trees are rimed with frost, the woodpile obscured, the garden paths obliterated.

Stomach grumbling, Wilda kneels on cold stone. For supper she had three spoons of watery cabbage soup and a mug of barley beer. The crude brew still sings in her bloodstream as she takes up pen and parchment.

The Lammbbe will come again, she writes, murmuring the word *Lammbbe*, reveling in its deep, buzzing hum. She closes her eyes, pictures Jesus hot and carnified, walking through snow. Frost melts upon contact with his burning flesh.

Walking accrosse the barren Earthe, she writes, *the Lammbbe wille leeve a hotte traile of lillies.* When Christ steps into the convent orchard, the cherry trees burst into bloom. *Thirty-sixe virgines stand in white arraye, pearles withoute spotte.* The nuns stand in order of age upon the lawn, ranging from thirteen-year-old Sister Ilsa to sixty-eight-year-old Elgaruth. Jesus pauses before twenty-six-year-old Wilda. He smiles with infinite wisdom. Stroking her cheek, he peers into her eyes to look upon her naked soul. Wilda feels the heat from his spirit. At first she can't look at his face. But then she glances up from the grass and sees him—eyes like molten gold, lips parted to show a hint of white teeth, tongue as pink as a peony.

"My bride," he says.

And the cherubim shreeke withe joye.

The shrieks grow louder—so loud that Wilda looks up from her book. She's back in the convent, hunkered on the cold floor. She gets up, walks down the hallway, turns left by the lavatory. The screaming is coming from the sad room where nuns are punished, but Wilda has never heard a ruckus in the middle of the night. She peeks in, sees Aoife seated, skirts pulled up, hair wild, eyes huge and streaming. Prioress Ethelburh twists the young nun's arms behind her back. Prioress Joan burns Aoife's creamy left thigh with red-hot pincers. This time, Aoife does not scream. She bites her lip. She looks up, sees Wilda standing in the doorway. Their eyes meet. A secret current flows between them. Ethelburh turns toward Wilda, her mouth wrenched with wrath, but then a violent cough rocks through her. She shakes, sputters, drops to the floor. And Aoife leaps from the chair like a wild rabbit. In a flash she is halfway down the hall.

"Surely mockers are with me," says Prioress Joan, casting her clammy fish eye upon Wilda, "and my eye gazes on their provocation."

The next morning, Ethelburh is dead, her body dragged beyond the courtyard by hulking Sister Githa, a poor dim soul fearless of contagion. Twelve bodies lie frozen near the edge of the wood, to be buried when the ground thaws.

Aoife is singing in her mother tongue, the words incomprehensible to Wilda, pure and abstract as birdsong, floating amid kitchen steam. Poor old Lufe is dead. Hedda and Lark have passed. Only Hazel, the girl who carries bowls from door to door, loiters in the larder, bolder now that Lufe is gone, inspecting the dwindling bags of flour.

"Prioress Joan has taken to her bed," whispers Aoife.

"God bless her soul," says Wilda, crossing herself.

Aoife chops the last of the onions. Wilda picks worms from the flour. And the soup smells weird—boiled flesh of a tough old hen.

"Sister," says Aoife, her mouth dipping close to Wilda's ear, "I have heard that the abbess kept food in her chamber. Pickled things and sweetmeats. A shame to let it go to waste, with our sisters half-starved and weak."

Snow falls outside the kitchen door, which is propped open with a log to let the smoke drift out. Even though it is afternoon, the light in the courtyard is dusky pink. Wilda thinks of Jesus multiplying fishes and loaves. She sees bread materializing, hot and swollen with yeast. She pictures fish—teeming, shimmering, salty in wooden pails.

"Sister," says Wilda, "you speak the truth."

The two nuns tiptoe up winding stairs, climbing toward the turret where the abbess once lived. The door is locked. Smiling, Aoife fishes a key from her pocket. She opens the door and steps into the room first. Wilda stumbles after her, bumps into Aoife's softness, stands breathing in the darkness, smelling mildew and rot and stale perfume—myrrh, incense, vanilla. When Aoife pushes dusty drapes aside, windowpanes gleam in a diamond pattern, alternating ruby and clear. The nuns marvel at the furnishings—the spindly settee upholstered in brocade, the ebony wardrobe with pheasants carved into its doors, two gilded trunks, and the grandest bed they have ever seen—big as a barge, the coverlet festooned with crimson ruffles, the canopy draped in wine silk. As Wilda wonders how the crooked little abbess climbed into this enormity each night, she spots a ladder of polished wood leaning against the bed.

Aoife opens a trunk and pulls out forbidden things—a lute, a fur-lined cape, a crystal vial of perfume. They find a bottle of belladonna and a clockwork mouse that creeps when you wind it up. The girls giggle as the mouse moves across the floor. Aoife strokes the ermine cape as though it is a sleeping animal. Wilda leans against the settee but does not allow herself to sit. The second trunk is chocked with dainty food—small clay jars of pickled things, dried fruit in linen sacks, hard sausages in cheesecloth, venison jerky, nuts, honey, wine.

Aoife opens a pot of pickled herring, sniffs, eats a mouthful, and then offers the fish to Wilda. They taste fresh, briny, tinged with lemon. Something awakens in Wilda, a tiny sea monster in her stomach, so weak and shriveled that she hardly knew it existed. She feels it stretching strange tentacles, opening its fanged mouth to unleash a wild groan. Wilda is starving. She gnaws at a twisted strand of venison, tasting forest in the salty meat, the deer shot by a nobleman's arrow, strips roasted over open flames. When Aoife opens a pot of strawberry preserves, she moans as a fruity smell fills the room—a kind of sorcery, the essence of a sun-warmed berry field trapped in a tiny crock. Tears in the creases of her eyes, Aoife eats with her fingers. And then she offers the jar to Wilda. As the monster squirms in her gut, Wilda dips a finger and tastes the rich, seedy jelly.

"Hallelujah," she whispers, smacking her lips. She eats more strawberries. Offers the pot back to Aoife. But Aoife has discovered a stash of sugared almonds. Wilda tries them— butter-roasted with cinnamon and cloves, a hint of salt, some other spice, unfamiliar, bewitching. The nuns sit down on the soft settee and spread their feast on a carved trunk. They eat smoked fish, dried apricots, pickled carrots, and red currant jam. Suddenly very thirsty, they have no choice but to uncork a bottle of wine, passing it between them. After shaving off teal mold with a small, gilded knife, they consume a chunk of hard cheese. And then they discover, wrapped in lilac gauze, a dozen pink marzipan rabbits.

The monster in Wilda's stomach lets out a bellow. She can picture it, lolling in a hot stew of food, the scales on its swollen belly glistening. Wilda pops a candy into her mouth, closes her eyes, tastes manna, angel food, milk of paradise. The young nuns drink more wine.

Aoife jumps to her feet, opens the abbess's wardrobe, examines gowns and cloaks. She pulls out a winter frock, thick velvet, the luminous color of moss, sable fur around the neck and cuffs. As Aoife undresses, Wilda looks away.

"How do I look?" Aoife asks, buttoning up the bodice, posing as though she has pulled on fine frocks a hundred times.

Wilda tries to speak, but words won't come. Her throat feels dry. She takes another swig of wine.

The dress brings out the secret lights in Aoife's eyes, the swanlike curve of her neck.

Wilda feels ugly, small, though she has not seen her reflection in a good, clear mirror in seven years, not since her parents and brother died and her aunt sent her off to the convent.

Aoife chooses a fur cloak from the wardrobe, slips it over Wilda's shoulders. Aoife plucks up the lute, strums a haunting tune, sings a song in her mother tongue that makes Wilda feel like she's dream-flying, her stomach buckling as she soars too fast into whirling stars, the air thin and strange and barely breathable.

Imitating the abbess, Aoife hobbles over to the bed, climbs up the ladder, peeks over the edge at Wilda, who can't stop laughing.

"It's a boat," Aoife says, crawling around like a child. Wilda remembers her brother galloping around on his stick horse. Memories like these stopped haunting her two years ago, part of the earthly existence she has kept at bay. Now she remembers the two of them rolling in the garden, flowers in their fists, singing bawdy songs they barely understood, laughing so hard she thought her ribs would crack. She remembers the way her parents scolded them with stanched smiles, trying not to laugh themselves.

Wilda climbs up the ladder. She sits beside Aoife on the high bed. The stiff fabric of the coverlet smells of must and faint perfume.

"Look!" says Aoife, opening a cabinet built into the bed's headboard. Inside is a crystal decanter encrusted with a ruby cross, a burgundy liquid within it. Aoife sniffs, takes a sip.

"Wine," she says dreamily, "though it might be some kind of liqueur."

Aoife offers the bottle. Wilda drinks, tasting blackberries and brine and blood, she thinks, though she has never tasted blood, for the Sacrament does not transubstantiate until it passes into the kettle of the stomach, where it is boiled by the liver's heat, the same way alchemists turn base metals into gold.

Aoife's hand scurries like the clockwork mouse over the coverlet to stroke Wilda's left wrist. Their fingers intertwine. Wilda marvels at the deliciousness of the warmth streaming between them.

Leaning against thick down pillows, the two sisters sit holding hands, sipping the concoction at the top of a stone fortress, snow falling in the eternal twilight outside—on the monastery and meadows and forests, on frozen ponds and farms and villages. They discuss animals in winter, the burrows and holes where furry and scaly things sleep.

"Do you think their blood freezes?" whispers Aoife, her breath on Wilda's cheek. "Do you think they dream?"

Aoife rests her head on Wilda's shoulder and sighs. Wilda has the eerie feeling that everyone in the world is dead. That she and

Aoife are completely alone in an enchanted castle. That they are just on the verge of some miraculous transformation.

Waking to the clang of monastery bells, Wilda clutches her throbbing head. She tries to sit up, thinking she's on her cot. But then she smells musty perfumes, odors of pickled fish and honey. Her cheeks burn as the previous night's feast comes back to her in patches. How had it happened so fast?

Her swollen belly throbs with queasiness, the sea monster slithering in a mash of wine and food. She leans over the bedside and heaves a foul gruel onto the floor. Sunlight glares through the windows. How long has she been asleep? She turns to Aoife, still dozing beside her. Not Aoife—just the abbess's fur cloak, crumpled, patched with bald spots, sprawling like a mangy bear. Wilda remembers a tale from her childhood—about a fair woman who turned into a bear. Singing with the voice of a nightingale, she lured hunters into deep woods. The bear scratched out the eyes of the lovesick hunters and devoured them whole. The bear, like Aoife, had eyes the color of honey.

Wilda climbs down from the bed, hurries back to her cell, and latches the door. As she paces around the cramped space, she feels the rankness of the flesh upon her bones, the puffery of her belly. Her brow and cheeks are hot. She wants to check on Aoife, see how she feels, laugh about the previous night's feast—a whim, a trifle, nothing—but her skin burns with shame. She pictures Aoife singing in her green dress. She imagines fur sprouting from her smooth skin, yellow claws popping from her fingertips.

Wilda vows to stay in her room without eating, without sleeping, whipping herself until the hideous sea monster ceases to squirm in her belly, until she has purged her flesh of excess fluid and heat and is again a bird-boned vessel of divine love—arid, clean, lit up with the Holy Word. She has a clay bottle of water, almost full, the only thing she needs.

Wilda kneels on the floor, naked, whipping herself for the third time, bored with the effect, not feeling much in the way of spinal tingling, her mind as dull as a scummy pond. She sighs, trying not to think of Aoife, the lightness of her laughter. She contemplates Christ in his agony—hauling the Cross, grimacing as iron nails are hammered into his hands and feet, staring stoically at the sun on an endless afternoon, thorns pricking his roasted brow. But the images feel rote as a rosary prayer. So Wilda hangs her whip on a nail and lies down on her bed. She watches her window, waiting for the day to go dark, the light outside milky and tedious. She hasn't eaten for two days, but her belly still feels bloated. Contemplating the beauty of Christ's rib cage, the exquisite concavity of his starved and hairless stomach, Wilda shivers.

When she hears the giggle of young nuns running down the hallway outside her door, her heart beats faster. And there's Aoife again, knocking softly with her knuckles.

"Sister Wilda," says Aoife. "Won't you take some food?"

Wilda says nothing.

"Sister Wilda," says Aoife. "Are you well?"

"I am," says Wilda, her voice an ugly croak.

Her heart sinks as Aoife slips away.

She lies awake for many hours.

Just as she is about to fall asleep, Wilda hears some kind of flying creature flapping around in her room. A candle flickers on her writing table, her book still open there.

She spots a flash of wing in a corner. A dove-sized angel hovers beside her door like a trapped bird wanting out. An emissary, Wilda thinks, come to tell her Christ is near. Wilda unlatches the door, peeks out into the dark hallway, and lets the being go. The angel floats, wings lashing, and motions for her to follow. The angel darts down the hall, a streak of frantic light. Wilda lopes after it, dizzy, chilled. They pass the lavatory, the empty infirmary.

The angel flies out into the courtyard and flits toward the warming house, where smoke puffs from both chimneys. Crunching through snow, Wilda follows the angel into the blazing room.

The angel disappears with a diamond flash of light.

Fires rage in twin hearths. There, basking on a mattress heaped with fine pillows, is Aoife. Dressed in the green gown, drinking something from a silver Communion goblet, Aoife smiles. Hazel lolls beside her in sapphire satin, munching on marzipan, an insolent look on her face. Hazel is a wretch, Wilda thinks, unworthy of Aoife's company, a slip of a girl who washes dishes and composts kitchen scraps, a girl who sings hymns out of tune, a sinner who has no inkling of Christ's love. Wilda cannot bear to look at them together.

"Sister." Aoife sits up, eyes like sunlit mead. "Come warm your bones."

Overcome with a fit of coughing, Wilda can't speak. It takes all of her strength to turn away from the crackling fires, the smells of almond and vanilla, from beautiful Aoife with her wine-stained lips and copper hair. Wilda flees, runs through the frozen courtyard, through empty stone passageways where icicles dangle from the eaves.

Back in her cell, she collapses onto her cot.

When Wilda wakes up again, her room is packed with angels, swarms of them, glowing and glowering and thumping against walls. An infestation of angels, they brush against her skin, sometimes burning, sometimes freezing. Wilda hurries to her desk, kneels, and takes up her plume.

A hoste of angells flashing like waspes on a summer afternoone. My fleshe burned, but I felte colde.

One of the angels whizzes near her and makes a furious face—eyes bugged, red cheeks puffed. Another perches on her naked shoulder, digging claws into her skin. Wilda shudders, shakes the creature off. As the throng moves toward the door, a high-pitched humming fills the room. Wilda opens the door and follows the cloud of celestial beings down the hallway, past the infirmary, out into the kitchen courtyard.

Wind howls. Granules of ice strike her bare skin as Wilda follows the angels toward the orchard. Her heart pounds, for surely the moment has come, the fruit grove gleaming with celestial light. Wilda can see skeletal trees sparkling with ice, a million flakes of wind-whipped snow, the darkness of the forest beyond. And there, just at the edge of the woods, the shape of a man on horseback.

The angels sweep down the hill toward the woods and wait. They buzz with frustration as Wilda trudges barefooted through knee-deep snow. Now she can see the man more clearly, dressed in a green velvet riding suit, a few strands of copper hair spilling from his tall hat. His mouth puckers with a pretty smile. His eyes are enormous, radiant, yellow as apricots. Recalling the softness of Aoife's pale hand, Wilda pauses. But when she pictures Hazel, bold and mocking, she charges forward into deeper snow. Though she cannot feel her feet, her entire body burns with miraculous warmth.

Flowers, she thinks, *not snow*, for Christ has strewn the woods with lily petals.

Hallelujah!

Hellion

"Put that gator right back where you found him, or I'll pepper your asses with .177s."

I aimed my Daisy right at Butch, the more chickenshit of the pair.

Mitch held Dragon by the jaws while his little brother, Butch, tried to steady his lashing tail.

"Feeding him Atomic FireBalls, I see, which might could kill him. Why you want to mess with an innocent beast?"

"Come on Butter, we just wanna see him fart fire," said Mitch.

"Idiots, put him back."

They couldn't grab their rifles with Dragon thrashing and ready to bite, so they eased him down into his number-two tub, which was getting snug now that he'd grown.

"Put that chicken wire over the top and get them latch-action toggles clamped."

Mitch kept Dragon's jaws shut while Butch crouched with the cover, slamming it down as soon as Mitch let go. Then Dragon went apeshit, snapping at the wire, so mad I knew I wouldn't be able to hold him for a week.

"Was a dumb thing to do, but we did it," said Butch, lighting a cig butt to play it cool. He leaned on his Beeman like John Wayne.

I lowered my gun.

"Do it again and I'll sick the Swamp Ape on you. Promise you won't mess with Dragon again."

"Promise," they said.

"Let's spit on it."

We spit into our palms and did some funky hand jives.

"Y'all heard about the citified pansy at Miss Edna's house?" asked Butch.

"Who?"

"Your third cousin from Aiken, according to our mama. They got a mall there and a nuke reactor."

"Something tells me he's gonna be achin' real soon." Mitch laughed so hard he upped a lump of snot. He spit the loogie in the dirt and slid astride their Yamaha Midget x-7. Butch hopped on back, holding the sport fender as they sped off.

My great-aunt Miss Edna, postmistress of Davis Station and widowed a decade, didn't take crap. She allowed me use of her library, told me I could be a career girl if I applied myself. Tried to get me in a dress and said my towhead was too pretty for a pixie cut, especially since I was almost thirteen.

Hands and face fresh washed, I stood on her porch, waiting for her to answer my knock. When a skink skittered over the steps, I longed for my Daisy—an easy dollar down the drain. Suffering some phobia that went back to her childhood before the Civil War, Miss Edna paid me one buck for every lizard I shot. I'd present them in a shoebox, do a body count while she cringed, and then bury them out back her shed.

"Well hello there, Butter." Miss Edna stood behind her screen door, the boy lurking in her shadow, a pale freckled scrap of male humanity who looked like he'd strain to lift an ice-cream spoon. "Come in and meet Alex. He's just a month older than you."

Alex nodded, led me back to the den, where he had his Atari hooked up to Miss Edna's console Panasonic. Sat right down to play Q*bert, keeping his eyes on that creepy head with feet, jumping it around on a pyramid of cubes—an exercise in mind-less stupidity.

"Come all this way to play Q*bert?" I asked him.

"Nothing else to do," he said.

"You stuck your head out the door since you came?"

"Why bother?"

"Why don't you let me show you a thing or two?"

When Alex pulled away from the screen, I noticed he was long in the neck, with eyes the color of my mother's olive agate beads. A cowlick ruined his strawberry-blond new-wave bangs, preventing them from cascading over his right eye. But his lips pouted like Simon Le Bon's.

"What you got to show?" He looked me over.

"A whole 'nother universe. Teach you how to drive a go-cart, how to shoot an air rifle, plus several techniques for handling a live gator. How to creep up on the Swamp Ape without making him bellow. Show you flesh-eating plants, the plat-eye demon floating over black water, and forest fairies mooching from hummingbird feeders."

The bragging spewed out like I was hexed. I would've kept going if Miss Edna hadn't called me back to the kitchen.

"Butter," she said. "Promise me you'll watch out for Alex, the boys around here being mostly hellions."

"I'm a hellion too, Miss Edna."

"No, Butter, not like the rest. You're my great-niece, after all."

She drew me close so she could whisper, suffocating me with her White Shoulders perfume.

"Alex's mama just had a premature baby boy. Know what that means?"

"Came out before he was cooked."

"That's right. A poor three-pound thing struggling to breathe in an oxygen tank. Alex, being tenderhearted, is taking it hard. Keep that in mind and be gentle with him. You can be a lady when you want to."

Ladies sat still and tormented themselves with stiff dresses and torture-chamber shoes. Ladies held their tongues when men walked among them and fixed them food and drinks. As my mother, who worked the night shift at Clarendon Memorial, said, "I don't have time to be a lady."

"I'll never be a lady," I said. "But I won't let the boys mess with Alex."

The next day was one of those blazing summer mornings—sky blue as a pilot light and birds going full throttle, opening their beaks and warbling, *Glory be.* I had Alex riding shotgun in my Hellcat KT100, a decent yard cart upgraded by my father with thirteen-inch tires and a Titan engine. Wind in my hair, Dr Pepper between my thighs, one hand on the wheel while the other handled a fresh-lit cig butt. Had a mind to race the Hellcat that day, with Alex there to witness my triumph, and we were headed over to the cliffs.

The boys were already there, brown and shirtless, popping wheelies and jumping gullies, flying ass-over-teacup around that eroded moonscape where a feller buncher had plucked pines from the earth like they were dandelions. The second we arrived, Butch and Mitch did donuts around us, spitting loogies and slurs, calling Alex *poontang, gerbil balls, city flower,* and *fagmeat.*

"Your mama's got sweet tits," screamed Butch, who was all of ten. "Ask me how I know."

I eased into a clump of upstart pines and cut the motor. Sat in the shade for a spell, sipping my Dr Pepper.

"Look," I told Alex. "First thing you got to learn is ignore their insults, save your wrath for what matters. Remember that nuclear radiation has endowed you with a Hulk-like condition where you might, any minute, pop out into a raging, muscular mutant."

"What?" Alex chuckled.

"Well, that's what I told them since you live near that nuke plant. Also said you could mind read, tell futures, and levitate."

"Why would you say that?"

"For one, pardon me, you're weird. And two, they would've already snatched you off the cart and whipped your ass if I hadn't. We got to keep up the mystery. Now, if Mitch or Butch mess with you, mention that their mother's got webbed toes. They don't know I know, so that'll spook them. Tell Kenny Walker, a big fool who flunked three grades, that he *will* realize his dream and become a professional wrestler. As for Dinky Watts, the little spaz whose freckles run together, tell him redheads are mind readers by nature and you'll teach him this art like Merlin did King Arthur. Don't even talk to Cag Stukes, the one in the Gamecock jersey, because he speaks the language of fists."

Alex went pale.

"I should go back to Meemaw's house."

"They'll track you there. They'll climb through your window at night and dump fire ants in your bed. Tough this one out and you're home free. Think about it like a video game. Get to the next level."

I drove straight into a cloud of dust that hovered like a nuke mushroom, came out the other side, jumped two gullies, hugged the outer wall of a U-turn, and fishtailed right up to the action. Though it almost killed him, Alex loosened his grip on the side rail, mustering a half-assed appearance of cool. The boys went crazy strutting their stuff: Cag circling with a two-wheeled donut on his Rambler x 10; Butch standing on the seat of their Midget while Mitch popped a wheelie; Dinky hopping the hind wheel of his Hornet while Kenny zipped higgledy-piggledy on his Scorpion 5. I realized how stoked they were to blow this city boy away. They finished their daredevilry, circled us twice, and then stood idling, staring at Alex, half hoping my tales were real—that the boy would float up out of his seat. Instead, Alex staggered from the cart, fell to his knees, and wallowed on the ground like a bass gasping for water.

"Shit," I said. "Looks like he's about to turn."

Clutching his head, Alex stood up.

"I can-not al-low it to hap-pen a-gain," he said. "Too ma-ny in-no-cents slaugh-tered."

Alex twitched as though shaking a winged demon from his back. He tottered and stared up at the sky, croaked out gibberish, pausing between bouts as though taking dictation from God.

"Your mother has mermaid blood." He pointed at Mitch and Butch. "Hence her webbed toes. She swims in Lake Marion on full-moon nights."

The brothers' jaws dropped, and I pictured them creeping around their den at night, their mama crashed on the couch, her feet freed from the Reeboks she wore to waitress, toes moist and pale in the spooky TV light.

"And you." He turned to Kenny. "Blessed with giant's blood. Your name will join the ranks of Hulk Hogan and Ric Flair."

"Last but not least"—Alex pointed solemnly at Dinky—"redheaded elf of rare blood, small of stature but vast of mind, I will teach you the telepathic arts."

With his word magic, Alex struck the boy-beasts dumb. They stood, dreamy eyed in the balmy morning air—all except Cag, who fidgeted, waiting to hear his fortune. But Alex paid him no mind, sank into my Hellcat as though exhausted from divining. And we sped off cackling at our stunt.

After lunch I fetched Alex from Miss Edna's porch, blood thrilling when I saw him smile. The boy was bored with his video games, revved up for real adventure, and I spirited him off into the afternoon. We zipped through three backyards to mine, scooted round the shed, and rolled up to Dragon's den. When I cut my motor, cicadas blared like summer's engine. We scrambled from the cart and hunkered down by Dragon's hole, dug deep by my father back in April, when I'd found the baby gator moping motherless in the swamp. I'd fed him peepers and minnows, brought green life back into his yellowing scales.

Now Dragon pressed against the chicken wire, flaring his nostrils and smacking his chops. He could smell the treats I'd brought, his food bucket bungeed to my Hellcat's rear frame.

"Easy there, Dragon," I cooed, fetching his dinner. I swung the bucket over his head to let him catch the scent of meat. "Hungry, buddy?"

The reptile snapped at the wire, his tub spattered with liquid shit. I prayed those Atomic FireBalls hadn't torn him up too bad.

"He won't bite you or try to run?" Alex backed away from the cage.

"Got him trained," I said, unclamping the chicken wire, relieved to see Dragon creep halfway out onto his rock. He used to perch like an anole there, little and jaunty. Now, hemmed in by tub walls, he slithered, covering the mass of the rock, his tail whisking the tainted water. He stared up at me, gold-eyed, jaws cracked, waiting for the first morsel to dangle in his range.

Alex squawked when the gator jumped to snap a gizzard from its loose-tied noose. But by the third chicken giblet, the fear had left him. When I lowered a bluegill, Alex inched up behind me, so close I could feel his body heat. Maybe that's what flustered me. Maybe that's what caused me to lean in too close and get snagged by a tooth—a jagged red rip right through the meat of my lower thumb. I didn't scream, but Alex did. I had to shush him, tiptoe to secure the chicken wire while Dragon chewed in a trance, savoring the taste of fish splashed with his adoptive mother's blood.

Hot tears burned my eyes, but I didn't let them spill. I grabbed my first-aid box from the cart and doused the wound with peroxide. Watched pink froth sizzle in the cut. Wiped it clean with fresh gauze and covered the ugliness with a Revco jumbo strip.

"**Sure you don't** need stitches?" Alex asked that evening.

"Just a scratch. Put some antibiotic ointment on it at home. Mama works at the hospital, so we got medicine galore."

We lazed in a cypress grove at the edge of the swamp, right where the woods got eerie. Frogs bellowed, down in the dark wet where the Swamp Ape lurked. When darkness came on, along with the glitter of bugs and stars, I taught Alex frog language: the twitter of wood frogs, the bark of tree frogs, the donk-donk of green frogs. Frogs bleated like sheep and rattled like woodpeckers, droned like power saws and bellowed like bulls. Peeper season was over, and I tried to imitate their high warble, like something from beyond the moon.

We stared up at the sky, didn't look at each other, and shared secrets about our lives. I told Alex my mama was a vampire according to my daddy. A pale woman who drew blood on the hospital night shift, she slept through most of the day. I told him about my father's slipped disc, his stunted soybeans and blighted corn, how he'd tried to stay busy after both cash crops failed. But his back was busted, and summer had broken him, driving him to drink when dusk came on.

"My parents' clocks are out of sync," I said. "And their moods never mesh. Mama sleeps in a mask in a darkened room, sun flicking around the edges of blackout blinds, while Daddy lurks through the house like a man held captive by silence."

Alex spoke of his own dad, an engineer who worked the nuke plant, a giant fortress gated off from the world. Alex imagined it glowing on a hill, surrounded by forest, contaminated animals creeping, luminous in the night. He feared his father brought radiation home in his clothes, that it mixed in the washing machine and poisoned them all. Maybe that was why his mom had birthed a preemie, a three-pound bug-eyed baby that struggled to breathe in his incubator.

"His eyes are dark," said Alex, "and you can almost see right through his skin. If they keep him in oxygen too long, he'll get brain damage. But if they stop the flow, he might die of asphyxiation."

"Terrible," I said.

But there were other babies even smaller than Matthew. One of them, a girl called Amy, just disappeared one day. Alex saw a grease spot on her sheet. And then the nurse pulled the sheet off the mini-mattress and gave him a weird look, wadded it up and threw it into a big rolling hamper. Made him wonder how many hospital sheets had been leaked on by the dead. Made him think about all the death mixed up in the washing machines and streaming from the HVAC vents.

We fell silent and listened to the frogs, cricket chirr shimmering over the lower calls. An owl hooted. A chuck-will's-widow cawed its own name. Through this delicate symphony came the bellow of the Swamp Ape, mournful and longing, as though epochs of human misery had mixed together into this one voice, ringing from the deepest dark. I knew where the creature's hovel was, a shack so mossy it looked like a bear's den, part and parcel of the wood. I'd seen pieces of the ape-man in the circle of my flashlight—a crazed red eye, a roaring maw, a hairy arm reaching out to snatch the Slim Jims I fed him.

"What the hell is that?" asked Alex.

"Swamp Ape," I said. "Monster of the forest who only comes out at night. Some people say he's a throwback to ape times, a variety of Bigfoot that's half-aquatic. Others think he escaped from Clemson University, a lab-made species half-human, half-ape. Another faction believes he's a regular man, gone feral from drink and craziness, second cousin and once lover of Sadie Morrison, an ancient lunatic who lives in a mansion that's half-sunk into black water. Alligators, they say, creep right through her living room, and possums suckle litters on her velvet couch.

Birds nest in her moss-festooned chandeliers. Open any closet and a hundred insects spew out."

Though I'd never been able to find her house, I saw Miss Sadie at the Piggly Wiggly sometimes—gray beehive like a crooked wasp nest, polyester dress from the 1960s, and tattered pantyhose. She always filled her buggy with saltine crackers and cans of oyster stew.

"But you've seen this Swamp Ape thing?" asked Alex.

"I have. And I can take you to him." I pulled a bundle of Slim Jims from my rucksack. "He won't hurt you if you bring him a treat."

We set off down a foot trail, flashlight flickering over cypress knees that looked like druids kneeled in prayer. Vines thickened. Trees were smothered with Spanish moss. Mosquitoes swarmed around our force field of Deep Woods OFF!

I felt something damp and knuckly brush against my wrist. It was Alex's hand, reaching for mine, half-scared, half-longing. We twined our fingers together and walked deeper in. I felt a sweet twist of nausea in my gut, and the ground went mushy under my feet.

"This is it," I whispered. "The Swamp Ape lives just beyond the border between wet and dry ground."

We let go of each other. I flickered my light through the trees and spotted the collapsing hovel. Out came a bellow so long and low, so misery-packed and wistful, that I longed to join in, to howl my torments in the muggy dark.

"Mr. Swamp Ape," I said. "Got a treat for you."

I placed the Slim Jims on a stump. And then we backed away, stepping onto solid land. I could hear the man-beast creeping out, the squelch of feet in mud, grunts and thick breathing. I flashed my light in time to see a red-frizzed hand take the Slim Jims. Caught a glimpse of shaggy potbelly. A bulging, baggy eye. And then the Swamp Ape was gone, retreated into his den, tearing into shrink-wrapped meat.

"Did you see him?" I whispered.

"Yes," Alex rasped, his voice ghostly, light as a dandelion seed in wind.

The next morning Alex looked freaked, pale with bluish streaks under his eyes.

"What's the matter with you?"

"Kept dreaming that the Swamp Ape crept outside my window. You think it's a real monster or just a crazy person?"

"A person can be a real monster too."

Alex chewed on that for a minute, then slipped into my go-cart.

Off we drove toward Eb Richburg's farm shed. Eb was laid up at Clarendon Memorial, getting his sinuses drained. Since he'd let me drive his tractor before, I figured he wouldn't mind if I took a city boy for a trip to Ruby's Whatnots. I took the back way, so Miss Videl wouldn't spot us, and parked behind their propane tank.

Mr. Eb's shed smelled of diesel and pesticides. His 4040s, pride and glory, was parked between a riding mower and a no-till corn planter. I smirked when I saw he'd left the key in it.

I climbed up. Waited for Alex.

"Swear you've got permission for this."

"Sorta," I said.

"I don't know." He made a fish face, but climbed up anyway, wedging himself into the big bucket seat beside me.

"Trust me." I slipped my tanned hand onto his pale knee. I sat for a spell, relishing the warmth that flowed between us. I pulled a Camel butt from the pocket of my cutoffs, lit it with a BIC, took three tokes, and tossed it onto gasoline-spotted concrete, where a small puddle flared into flame. I laughed as I watched the fire wane. Alex winced but didn't groan. When I cranked the 4040s, it shuddered to life like a T-Rex.

We lurched toward the sunny doorway and rolled into a bare-dirt lot. After shifting to second, we chugged onto Moses Dingle Road. It felt good to shift to third, driving with my left hand while lighting another cig butt with my right, nicotine buzz coming on just as I upped it to fourth. And then we were cruising, passing the post office, Uncle Henry's store with its stack of watermelons, and Hog Heaven BBQ. We passed houses and mobile homes, crumbling barns and prefab sheds. The sky was cloud-crammed, light streaming through holes in the mass.

"I love to drive," I said. "Calms me down."

"Got to admit," said Alex, "that this experience is having the opposite effect on me."

We passed a neighborhood of sun-bleached shacks and trailers, a cornfield and a metal barn, and I eased into the lot of Ruby's Whatnots. We parked the tractor and went into the cinder-block building. Miss Ruby was a tall, striking woman who'd been to college and had traced her lineage back to Nigeria. She taught history at Manning High School.

Miss Ruby's parents ran the shop during the school year, but she worked it in the summer. The only hippie in Davis Station, she sold carved wood sculptures, a variety of cosmetics and hair products, incense, handmade macramé bags, her father's garden produce, and homegrown herbal remedies she mixed herself, along with fishing tackle, fresh worms, ice, chips, snack cakes, candy, sodas, and beer.

"Hey there, Butter," said Miss Ruby. "I see you've got a pal today."

"His name's Alex. A city boy from Aiken."

"Aiken." She widened her eyes in mock awe.

"It's not that big." Alex shrugged.

"Well, glad to meet you, city boy. You here for the usual, Butter?"

"Yes, ma'am, except double on both."

I pulled out my lizard-hunting money and paid for two Kit-Kats and two Dr Peppers, both a better price than my great-uncle Henry charged down the road. Just a few pennies made all the difference if you knew how to scrimp and save. Once I got my

Daisy and my Hellcat, I always asked for money on birthdays and at Christmas. Add in lizard money, chore money, tooth fairy, and Easter Bunny, and I had a decent savings account at First Palmetto. Top Secret Escape Plan A, I called it, though I didn't dare let on that I plotted to bolt this backwater when the right time came. Maybe I'd move to Aiken, go to the USC branch they had up there, even though Alex scoffed at the school and said he was aiming for Duke.

We drove home in silence, watching storm clouds scud along the horizon. Alex almost sobbed with relief when I pulled that tractor into its shed, and then we scrambled out into the thunder-charged air.

When the storm broke, we ducked under the porch of Mr. Rufus Brock's run-down toolshed. We sat on the stoop eating our KitKats while staring out at the rain. And then I caught a whiff of molten tar—the smell of flat-roof exploration, new roads winding off into the green distance, amusement-park blacktop gone soft in July sun. I jumped up.

"Smell that?"

"Stinks," said Alex.

"I love the smell of pitch."

We went into the shed, where a half-barrel of molten tar stood cooling, and I dipped a finger in.

"Still warm." I scooped up a glob and lobbed it at Alex, plopping his left cheek. At first, he stood stunned, but then he flashed a grin, grabbed a fistful of black mash, and pressed it against my throat. I felt his heart thudding as I smeared thick grime over his bony chest. And then we went at it, shoveling filth with our hands and smirching each other's bodies. We tussled on the concrete floor of the shed, wrestled and kicked our way out into the drizzle.

Like puppies, we rolled and nipped in the wet grass.

We both spotted her at the exact same time: Miss Edna, her wash-and-set hairdo ruined by rain, her bulldog face scrunched with wrath.

"Got a phone call from Mr. Rufus," she hissed. "Said y'all'd gotten into his tar. This about takes the cake."

She snatched our skinny arms, marched us to her carport, and ordered us to strip down to our underwear. We waited with bowed heads, avoiding each other's eyes as Miss Edna fetched her gas can, a bucket of rags, and a scouring brush.

As the drizzle waned and sunlight gushed, lighting every inch of our bare flesh, Miss Edna rubbed us down with gasoline, pulling a thousand hairs from their follicles as she brushed bits of clotted tar from our skin. I felt dizzy from gas fumes, flayed raw, streaked with chemical burns.

"Hellions," she hissed, and kept on scrubbing long after she needed to. Then she hosed us down, lathered us up with Octagon soap, and rinsed us off again. At last, she left us, goose-bumped and hunched in shame, our underwear transparent. We each faked interest in opposite corners of the carport—Alex absorbed with a dead geranium, me lost in a spider's web.

"Your meemaw's a bitch," I finally said, straining to break the silence.

When I turned to meet his gaze, hands cupped over my no-count titties, Alex stared at my wet underwear, and I wondered if he could see the puckered slit between my legs. I made out the shape of his thing, curled like a beetle grub in his sodden briefs.

When Miss Edna returned with a pile of towels, we turned away from each other again.

"I called your mama," she told me. "Said for you to get home this minute."

Though I pretended to run home, I slipped behind her azaleas to spy.

"Pick your switch," she said to Alex.

"What do you mean by that, Meemaw?"

Miss Edna pointed at a hickory sapling, instructed him to tear off a flexible young branch, stood behind him as he chose his torture rod, and then ordered him to strip it of leaves. She made

Alex lean face-down against the brick wall. And then his granny lashed at his poor, skinny legs, stinging those tender zones on the backs of his knees and thighs.

I closed my eyes, couldn't bear to watch Alex—green to switching—scream and flinch and jump. Running home, I looked back once, saw the poor boy hugging his knees, sniveling as his grandmother swept the carport in fury.

"Get home, hellion!" Miss Edna hollered after me, lifting her broom in the air.

I slipped into the house, which was cold and dark as a tomb, and got dressed. I hoped my mother had gone back to bed, but there she waited on the couch, vampire-pale and smelling of hospital disinfectant. My father sat in his La-Z-Boy, in the non-recline setting, so I knew I was in for some shit.

"Butterbean." Daddy moaned my baby name, the name they'd called me when I was born six pounds with jaundice. I pictured myself the size of a lima, curled in the warm wet dark of my mother, dreaming myself into being.

"Why'd you want to get into that tar?" Daddy said, his eyes red from drinking, and it not hardly noon. "Put your cousin up to mischief too, him on the honor roll and all."

"It was a dumb thing to do, but we did it," I said. "Go ahead and whip me."

"Reckon I'll have to," Daddy said sadly, but I knew he couldn't bear to beat me.

"She's too old to whip," said Mama. "How about you take her go-cart or her gun?"

"But Mama," I said. "Can't survive without a ride and a weapon, not with these hellion boys."

"Stay inside, then. Read one those books Miss Edna lent you."

I pictured myself shut up in the air-conditioning, sealed off from summer in this twilight house of whispers, and swallowed words.

"Go ahead and take my Daisy," I said.

Mama's eyes went wide.

"What's that on your hand?" she said.

I looked down, saw that my Band-Aid hadn't survived Miss Edna's scouring, that my wound was puckered purple, but at least the Neosporin had kept off the pus.

"Tore it on a catbrier thorn," I said. "But I cleaned it and put on antibiotic. It's not oozing nothing."

"Elizabeth Ann." Mama shot across the room, picked up my hand, turned it in the lamplight. "It's not infected, but it could've been. You ought've got stitches and an oral antibiotic. Tell me right now how you got this thing."

"Dragon nipped me."

I couldn't think of a reasonable fib. If I said dog bite, they might make me get twenty-one rabies shots in the belly, like Kenny Dennis suffered when that field rat bit him.

"It was an accident. I had my hand too close to his dinner."

Mama gnawed her lip, doing math in her head. She'd forgotten all about Dragon, and now she imagined how much he'd grown.

"Goddamn it," she hissed.

I bowed my head, waiting for the tornado of her fury to bluster over me.

"I slave all day at the hospital, and you drown your worthlessness in drink," she screamed at Daddy. "The least you could do is keep an eye on things around here. How the hell you let that gator get so big?"

"What do you know?" squalled Daddy. "You're never here. When you are, you're like a vampire sleeping, with us on pins and needles."

And then they went at it, screeching accusations, excuses, and insults, dragging up ancient shit from the deep latrine of their marriage, circling the room like professional wrestlers who'd never take the leap to strangle each other.

I sat on the couch and let their words lapse into noise, until Daddy went stone-cold silent. He stomped to his gun case, unlocked it, and grabbed his .22. I thought for sure he'd shoot Mama, that I'd be haunted for life by the sight of her spattered brains. But then, crook-backed and grabbing at the waistline of his pitiful too-big shorts, Daddy stomped out the back door.

"Don't you worry, Miss Dracula!" he yelled. "I'll take care of it."

I followed him out into the afternoon glare, where hellions filled the air with thunder, go-carts and dirt bikes kicking up dust. When the boys saw Daddy, mad-eyed with his gun, they idled after him. Trying to catch up, I sprinted under the high summer sun, my nose running with the snot of grief.

"Don't do it!" I cried, but nobody heard me. A half dozen engines revved.

Daddy stooped over Dragon's cage, unclamped the chicken wire, and flung the cover away. The hellions cut their motors and inched up for a better look. As cicadas chanted in the mystic heat, Dragon crawled out onto the grass and stretched to his full length, nearly three feet long, his spiked back slicked with water. The glorious prehistoric reptile opened his mouth in a fanged grin.

"Please, Daddy," I said. "Just let him run off. He'll smell swamp and head right for it."

"He might come back for food and bite somebody. Never should've let you keep him in the first place."

Still, my father seemed to consider my wish. Sat there thinking and cradling his gun.

"Shoot him!" yelled Dinky Watts. "He looks big enough to eat a baby."

Daddy shook his head as though rousing from a dream, took aim and fired, catching Dragon in the flank. The gator let out a gurgling hiss and rolled onto his side. The boys cheered. Daddy fired again at closer range, kicked the poor thing onto his back, and blasted another bullet into his pale belly.

Daddy picked up the limp reptile by the tail, swung his gory trophy in the air, and staggered around the shed toward Mama.

"You happy now?" he shrieked.

Mama stood on the back stoop, fists clenched, her skin so white she glowed.

"Idiots all," I hissed, and ran off into the woods.

It was almost dusk, light tipping toward pink. I was in the swamp, bawling my miseries to the throb of frogs—my baby gator dead, Alex switched on my account, my house a tomb of silent wrath, vampire and ogre cramming it roof to cellar with what Miss Ruby called *bad vibes*. I was a hellion, for sure, who deserved to slip back into the swamp from which the first land species crawled—those fish with legs, skink-like, primitive pining things. I had four hundred and thirty-six dollars in my savings account. Weren't enough lizards in Davis Station to shoot for college tuition. Plus, Miss Edna had banished me from her porch. Hellions like me never got scholarships, so why bother striving in school?

I was lost, doomed to attend Central Carolina Tech, master some bleak medical procedure, and turn into a vampire like my mother. I'd prick human bodies a hundred times a day at Clarendon Memorial, fill those little bags with sugar water, or worse—wash diseased feet, rub salve on bedsores, drain abscesses as big as tennis balls.

I saw myself, pale and moving in a dream through a hive of the sick and dying, a one-week vacation the only thing to look forward to. Alex had said he wanted to build rockets, and I pictured him zipping off into the twinkling black mystery of space, leaving the likes of me to rot on our ruined planet.

When I finally stopped crying, the bellowing went on, as though the spirit of my grief had haunted the forest. But it was the Swamp Ape roaring along with me. Now he, too, stilled his song. We'd twined our grief together, which had drained the poison from me. I was grateful to the man-beast for that.

Exhausted, I leaned against a cypress, watching lightning bugs sway out from whatever holes they slept in during the day.

I noticed a circle of light spotting the trees—the plat-eye, I thought, sniffing my weakness, come out of his demonic dimension to hound me until I lost my marbles. But it was only a flashlight, my father probably come to fetch me.

"Butter," said a voice high and boyish, not yet croaky from change.

Alex sat down beside me.

"Where you been?"

"Meemaw kept me locked in all day. But as soon as she dozed off, I put a fake person in my bed, towels and blankets, and slipped out the window to find you."

"You're not mad at me about the switching?"

"Not your fault. Got a will of my own and so do you."

"I guess we all do," I said, thinking it over. "Though some people got more room to move than others."

"Sorry about Dragon," he whispered, slipping his hand into mine. "Butch told me all about it."

"Daddy might've been right," I said. "That gator would've probably come back for food and bit somebody."

We sat there, sweaty hands fastened in a funny position.

"Little Matthew's coming home next week," said Alex.

They'd cut the oxygen in his brother's tank. Though the baby had struggled, he'd gotten the hang of breathing. I tried to think of something to say. I was happy for Alex but also sad. Summer would suck when he was gone, the dog days coming on, me left with nobody to play with but hellion boys.

"Good," I said. "When do they come get you?"

"A week. We could be pen pals, though."

I pictured myself trying to write a decent letter, struggling to impress. I pictured Alex sniggering every time I misspelled something or got carried away with Miss Edna's thesaurus. And what would I have to tell him? About my vampire mother and drunken father? About go-cart races and BB gun fights? About the King Arthur novels Miss Edna lent me? Or the Swamp Ape's preference for Slim Jims over beef jerky?

"Maybe," I said. "I've never been one to write letters."

We sat in silence for a spell, listening to night music—insect, amphibian, and bird. The Swamp Ape started up again, gentle and wistful, more soft-grunted song than howl. When Alex flicked on his flashlight to catch him in action, the creature lurched off into deeper swamp.

"What the hell?" said Alex.

Now big-eyed mammals glided into his circle of light—two, three, four—their limbs splayed, furry membranes stretched wide.

"Fairies," I whispered, though I knew they were only flying squirrels, come to feed on pawpaw fruit.

They landed on a branch and shimmied down to the heavy clusters.

"Fairies," Alex repeated, as though to hypnotize himself into believing, and I strained to believe too, pictured the squirrels twittering real language and working magic spells.

I could see the future of summer. Ravaged cornfields and soybean chaff. Cicadas buzzing like broken toys in parched grass. Muscadines past ripeness, fermenting on the ground, the woods smelling like wine. School would be here in a blink, and then I'd be in prison for a solid nine months.

But now, summer was at its height, offering its sweetest fruits, full of furry fairies and gleaming bugs. Alex leaned against me, humming with warm blood, his brain like a different universe.

Erl King

I'd seen the so-called Wild Professor stalking the halls of the humanities building, a haughty middle-aged man with a face going to ruin from booze and passion. He taught the poetry workshop and the Romanticism seminar. He spat curses at the coffee machine in the English department lounge. He liked young girls, everyone whispered. He ate psychedelic mushrooms, kept up with cool music, and lived in a woodland cabin all summer long, typing masterpieces on an electric typewriter powered by a generator. He gave me his famous look-over my first winter at college, in the humming submarine glow of the library. I peered up from a translation of *Venerabilis Agnetis Blannbekin* and saw him stomping toward me in muddy hiking boots. I feared he'd trample me. But he stopped and drilled me with his legendary eyes: pale green organs that floated in the darkness of his sockets like fireflies. He looked ghoulish in the fluorescent light, his scalp visible in sick pink patches, and I didn't get his appeal. I stared down at my book, reading the same line over and over: *And behold, soon she felt with the greatest sweetness on her tongue a little piece of skin alike the skin of an egg, which she swallowed.*

At last, the Wild Professor shuffled away.

In May I moved out of the dorms to live in a dilapidated antebellum mansion that had been divided into a duplex—we had three bedrooms and an upstairs sunporch that jutted out over a junk-filled carport. Punk Amy, hippie Kim, and preppy Paige got the good rooms, while I suffered the hot sunporch, which swayed in thunderstorm winds. Star jasmine snaked through busted windows. Brilliant green anoles sunned themselves on the flaking sills. But my rent was eighty dollars a month, and the downstairs living room was vast—grand with frieze molding, a marble-mantel fireplace, and a yellowed chandelier. We all worked shitty jobs, but at night we lolled on a thrift-store sixties sectional, drank jug wine, listened to *Loveless*, and watched grainy VHS recordings of *Twin Peaks*.

One night our mutual longing filled the room like a swarm of moths.

"Let's go out," said punk Amy.

"Where?" said hippie Kim.

"Rockafellas," said preppy Paige, who was trying her damnedest to be less preppy.

"The place will be crammed cheek by jowl with decrepit metal cretins," I said.

"Decrepit metal cretins!" Punk Amy hacked with laughter. "You have a way with words."

"There's this party," said hippie Kim. "A professor's. In the woods."

In Amy's white Volkswagen Rabbit, we sped down Highway 321 to some boondock hole past Swansea. The party was just breaking up, professors and graduate students with crusty casserole dishes climbing into cars. We found the Wild Professor beside a waning bonfire, smoking a joint with the theory guru Dr. Glott. I could make out a dark cabin on the hill behind them, a fairy-tale dwelling composed of logs and stone.

"The sex/gender binary is always already hermeneutically destabilized and epistemologically overdetermined," said Dr. Glott.

"The world will be undone by the flick of a young girl's tongue," said the Wild Professor, his long hair uplifted by a gust of wind.

"He looks like Bob," said hippie Kim.

"Bob who?" asked preppy Paige.

"*Bob*," Kim hissed.

"Oh gross," we whispered. "*Twin Peaks* Bob."

"Bob's not totally gross." Kim licked her lips. "I like his flowing hair."

"Flowing?" said punk Amy. "You mean stringy?"

The Wild Professor released an odd doggish yip when he saw us.

"Speaking of girls." He sniffed the air. "Be ye sylphs or things of flesh?"

"Definitely flesh," said Kim.

"Right," said Paige.

"Sylphs," I mouthed.

"Robots," Amy said in a menacing mechanical voice.

We drew closer to the fire and sat down on rough-hewn chairs. We smoked weed. We drank blackberry wine from dusty mason jars. The Wild Professor slipped a Cocteau Twins cassette into a corroding boom box.

"Dance," he commanded, and for some weird reason, we did. Paige shimmied. Kim attempted some sultry moves from her belly dancing class. Amy jackhammered in place, frowning furiously, while I leapt like a doe around her.

That night I was wearing a bell-sleeved green gauze gown, Arthurian revival from the seventies, and my skirts caught on blackberry briars whenever I danced too far from the fire. The blackberries were still hard green fruit, just blushing pink, and the night grew cool. We went back to the fire.

"Where's Dr. Glott?" asked Kim.

"Taking the high road home," said the Wild Professor. "His lumpish wife awaits him, a slimy newborn pressed to her engorged breast."

"What the fuck?" said Amy. "Let's go."

But when the Wild Professor chanted in Old High German, Amy fell into her chair. Plop, plop—the other girls followed. They slumped and stared. But I remained on my feet, arms crossed.

"She looked at me as she did love and made sweet moan," said the professor.

He spoke of femme fatales and consumptive poets. He lectured me about bird migrations, planting vegetables according to the lunar phases, and suffering bouts of automatic writing when the moon went full. When, at last, I pulled my eyes from him, I noticed that my friends had fallen asleep in their chairs.

"Did you roofie my girlfriends?"

"You're not girls." He stroked my briar-scratched arm. "But women."

He was a feminist, he said, and we were full-grown mammals who shed menstrual blood. In the firelight he looked younger, fine-boned, with a gold-green Pre-Raphaelite gaze.

"I am certain of nothing but of the holiness of the heart's affections," he said.

Rolling my eyes, I followed him up the hill. His dim cabin smelled of mold and honeysuckle. Candles flickered on the ancient mantel.

"How old is this house?"

"Built by a rum trader in 1702. Want to taste some of his rum?" the professor asked.

He pulled a crystal decanter from a cabinet, plucked the stopper, and sloshed an inch into a mason jar. Perched on a filthy brocade chair, I tasted the burning sweetness.

"It's rum all right," I said. "But I seriously doubt it's three hundred years old."

The Wild Professor laughed like a teenage stoner, falling backward onto his bed and taking gulps of air between each howl. He thrashed and kicked and then went still. As he sat up, slow and stone-faced like a movie vampire, I tensed at the sight of his black hair—a wig, I thought, that he'd slipped on during his laughing fit. But his skin was smooth and pale. His enormous eyes shed gold light. And his lips looked plump and red.

He grew six inches. His jowls vanished. Elegant muscles appeared. A beautiful man moved toward me.

"How the hell?" I said.

"The willing suspension of disbelief," he whispered, his breath on my neck, hot huffs smelling of vanilla and ham. He nibbled my earlobes. He stuck his tongue down my throat and nudged me toward his fur-strewn bed. A gust blew both candles dead.

The Wild Professor loomed over me, his antlers ivoried by the moon. I stroked the soft fur on his thighs, explored coarser tangles of groin hair until I found the meat of him, a bald weasel, warm and straining as though wanting to leap from his body into my young hands.

I woke naked, half-covered in musty fur scraps, the room cold. Brutal light gushed through a window to illuminate my bedmate. Beside me wheezed an old man—crepey skin, scrotal eye bags, a few wisps of hair on a scaly scalp, a gash of mouth open in surly snarl. I couldn't help but scream. Mortified, I leapt from the bed and found my dress—soiled, gnawed, tattered, heaped on the floor, and fouled with dark fur. I pulled on my leggings, slipped on a cardigan I found on a chair, and ran out into the yard. The girls were gone, but they'd left a note on the picnic table, the paper scrap secured beneath an empty Jägermeister bottle.

Amy thinks he's a grody perv, but I sort of get it.
Call us tomorrow and we'll come pick you up.
Peace and Love,
Kim (and Amy and Paige)

"Come inside. I've built a fire," the Wild Professor growled behind me.

I jumped, bracing myself for the old man. But now he looked younger, not as young as he had the night before, but back to his usual self: worn and semi-dumpy, with thinning hair and bold eyes, his mega-brow unwrinkled, lines like parentheses framing his mouth, his jawline gone soft with proto-jowls. He wore a velour bathrobe the color of clotted blood.

"I need to call my friends," I said.

"I don't have a phone. Let me feed you breakfast, and then I'll drive you to the Family Dollar in Swansea. You can use the pay phone there."

The Wild Professor closed the velvet drapes. The cabin glimmered with cozy firelight, reminding me of storybook animals tucked into winter dens. He fed me gingerbread glazed with honey from his beehives, bacon from a wild boar he claimed to have slain. His coffee, laced with amaretto, warmed me to the bone. In the flickering dimness, he glistened with a trace of the beauty I'd seen the night before. He plucked a book from the shelf, its leather binding embossed with stags and wolves.

"A maiden wandered through dark woods, witches snickering in the brambles. The girl found a castle, once grand, now in horrid shambles. Weeping, she fell upon the cold stone floor. She woke and saw a pale dwarf, hiding beyond a door. Come in, said the dwarf, don't be afraid, for marvels you shall see. Secrets of the ancient whale and the sacred honeybee."

The Wild Professor lapsed into Old High German. I don't know how long he went on, but when, at last, he stood and whisked the drapes open, dusk was falling.

"Let's go outside," he said. "The fireflies are hatching."

We stood on the hill and watched a thousand blinking insects float out from the dark wood.

The Wild Professor spent mornings writing poems, and then he'd feed me lunch. Today, like most days, we wove through the forest in the afternoon heat.

My ignorance was as deep as a wishing well, and the Wild Professor tossed glittering coins of knowledge into it. He pointed with his gnarled stick.

Pokeweed leaves are edible when tender, but poisonous when dark and tough. Rattlesnakes lurk in long grass and amid the wild blackberries. Orange mushrooms can be edible or toxic, depending on the wood they grow on. And the gills of the deadly amanita are as white as a comatose princess's throat.

The Wild Professor identified spots where boars had rubbed their muddy flanks against pine trunks. He explained the similarities between the mayapple and Shakespeare's mandrake, which was once thought to grow from the last seminal spurts of hanged men and shriek when snatched from the soil. He identified nine tree species, twelve scrub plants, four birdcalls, and two butterflies. He listed six obscure bands from the late 1960s and then raved about three so-called rogue states to whom the US had secretly sold weapons.

His brain was a beehive on the verge of swarming. Though greedy for knowledge, I was glad when he finally slumped against a tree and napped. I cooled my feet in the creek, trying to remember the differences between hognose snakes and copperheads.

A few weeks ago, I'd called my Columbia apartment on the Family Dollar pay phone.

"I'm taking a vacation," I'd said to Amy. "To get away from it all."

"What do you have to get away from? You're nineteen years old."

I heard Siouxsie Sioux wailing in the background. I could picture the girls lounging in the living room after a long night partying. I ached for the coziness of it all. But I remembered the restless longing, the desire to crawl out of my window at night, climb onto the rotted roof, and get swept up by a gust of other-worldly wind.

Kim snatched the phone. "What's he like?" she breathed. "Does he really put girls into trances with poetry?"

"Naïve idiot," hissed Amy, snatching the phone back. "I'm coming to get you."

"Not yet."

"Your mom has called three times this week. I've been covering for you, but . . ."

I hung up. I called the library where I reshelved books and told them that my grandmother had died. I smoked three cigarettes, pinched my arms to produce pain endorphins, and then rang my mother.

"Baby," she said, her voice rich with uncanniness. She was in the Lowcountry, down near Black River Swamp. I could hear my father's weed eater whining in the background. I pictured him in goggles and work gloves, fighting off the vines that threatened to entangle our house.

"Let them grow," I'd begged him as a child. "And our house will be like Sleeping Beauty's castle."

"You have a lovely imagination," my mother would say.

She used to take me into the shallows of the woods, just where the poison oak began to riot. We had mad tea parties—banana bread, lace-fringed napkins, juice in china cups. Mom, pretending she could talk to crows, would translate their caws. When we lingered until the lightning bugs drifted out, Dad called us in his stern voice. Mom smirked. But she always packed our picnic things right after we heard the electric garage door close.

One day at dusk the Wild Professor stood at the edge of the woods, held his cupped palms together, and blew into the slit between his thumbs. Mourning doves spun out of the forest and landed on his arms. He cooed them into a stupor and slipped them into a burlap sack. He snapped their necks and gutted them. He composted the intestines and saved the purple giblets in a mason jar.

He opened a bottle of muscadine wine. We sat by the fire watching the birds roast on a hickory stick.

"For you, my dove." The professor laughed, showing his jagged yellow teeth. "A gift."

He pulled a necklace from a shoebox, a polished dove skull strung on a chain of braided grass. I slipped it on. I closed my eyes and fingered my scalp, thinking I felt knots on the top of my head—horns, I dared to hope, but probably nothing.

When I opened my eyes, the professor was groaning in his chair, stooped over to nurse a stomach cramp.

"Sometimes it hurts," he said. "Maybe you'll understand one day, if you've got what it takes to change."

He glared up at me, a thread of drool spilling from his ripening mouth. I watched bone nubbins crack through his skull and flare into antlers. I watched eye bags shrink and wrinkles melt away. Black hair sprouted from his scalp and flowed down his back like a cape. He grew six inches. He climbed out of his pants. He cast off his shirt, puffed up his chest, and scratched his furry thighs.

"It always itches at first," he said, his voice husky and garbled.

Howling, he came at me. I opened my arms to the beast. As his gamy tongue lashed at my throat, I couldn't get naked fast enough.

Summer thickened. Summer hummed. As we walked through the meadow, grasshoppers scattered with every step, their gauzy wings catching the light. Honeybees dozed in the wild asters. The milk thistle grew tall. Each night I felt small lumps form on my head, but by morning they were gone. Cautiously, I nibbled orange mushrooms, unsure about the species. I mimicked the professor's Old High German chants inside my head, inventing new words of my own, reaching a state of giddiness that felt like power.

One evening I sat in the kitchen fingering the bumps, which seemed a little harder.

"Maybe my horns will break tonight," I said, and then I uttered a fake spell.

"I doubt it. You can't tell a *Gymnopilus junonius* from a honey mushroom, nor can you conjugate the verb *wehsalon*. Are you speaking pig Latin?"

"It's actually an obscure chant from a Celtic goddess cult. Older than Scottish Gaelic, I think."

The professor harrumphed, but he looked worried. He growled and slumped off into the dog fennel.

At dusk I ate cold potatoes and venison jerky and waited for him on the porch. Pining for the beast, I brushed my long dark hair. My heart lurched every time I heard him howl. I could barely make him out, tall and horned, raging under a paltry moon.

One afternoon like all other afternoons, we pulled our chairs from the shade and drank wine in the meadow.

A hawk swooped. Buzzards circled. Crows complained in the pines. When the sky turned smoky lavender, the wispy moon looked solid again—fat and pocked and bright. Katydids chimed in with the waning cicadas.

I walked off across the meadow alone, hoping he wouldn't follow, eager to try a new spell.

"Where are you going?"

"For a stroll."

Lightning bugs blinked in the deep woods. I slipped into the delicious darkness and listened to a whippoorwill calling its own name.

"I'm changing! I'm changing!" the Wild Professor cried, but I didn't rush to him. I crouched in my hiding place, a burrow lined with leaves and moss, covered with a dome of woven muscadine vines. I ate an orange mushroom and wild berries and chanted my language over rare stones. My skull burned. I fingered the bumps on my cranium. At last, I felt damp bone pushing through. Blood seeped into my hair. Blood trickled over my brow and ran into my left eye. I scratched my thighs as mink-soft fur grew. I scrambled from my hut and unfolded myself, standing six feet tall.

Smelling me on the wind, the Wild Professor let rip a heart-stopping wail.

I'd waited a month for this night, envisioning the glory of two beasts locking horns, hurling their passion at each other, enveloped in a cloud of musk. But now, all I wanted to do was run.

Amazed by the strength in my legs, I ran east through wild blueberries and then north through ferny woods. Howling him-self hoarse, the professor bounded behind me, but I was faster. I leapt over a rusted fence, crossing into a clearing where pine trees had just been razed. The air smelled sad from a hundred weeping stumps. I spotted a rattlesnake winding through the wreckage. The professor stopped by the fence, panting hard.

"What kind of mushrooms did you eat?" he asked, eyeing my new form.

"A red fly agaric."

"Bullshit. They don't grow here."

"I found one."

"Where?" His voice broke.

"Top secret."

He studied my antlers. He took in my long furry legs and frowned.

"Aren't you tired from all that running?" he asked.

"No," I said, and dashed off into the woods.

I stood in the glare outside the Family Dollar, the black pay-phone receiver burning my hands.

"You're not sick of him yet?" Amy asked. "What the hell do you all day in the woods?"

"There are plenty of things to do in the woods!" Kim cried in the background.

The Wild Professor bristled in his Corolla, pricking his ears to catch bits of my conversation.

I hung up and called my mother.

"Honey lamb," she said. I longed for the sweet warmth of her, before her body became taboo flesh, when she was omniscient, a mystery that I spent ten years trying to solve. I remembered the two of us pretending to be foxes, crawling on all fours and eating wild blackberries. One summer afternoon when I was twelve, bikini-clad, oiled, and tanning in the back-yard, I declared our picnics stupid. Mom bit her bottom lip and walked off into the woods alone. I longed to follow her, but some new thing inside me, something hard and heavy, anchored me to my lawn chair.

"Have you paid your phone bill yet?" she asked.

"Not yet. We're still using the neighbors'. And please don't call here—it annoys them."

"When are you coming home for a visit?"

"Soon. I promise."

"We both miss you very much."

I heard my father's lawn mower droning in the background. I pictured him in his coveralls, perched on the roaring machine, looping out to mutilate a clump of goldenrod, fighting off the wildness that crept from the woods.

A whole week of storms, and we were trapped inside like two rodents in a burrow, unable to transform in the stale air. Thunder boomed. Crows cawed. Rain dripped from a hole in the fungus-infested roof and plopped into a Crock-Pot. I picked through the professor's mildewed books.

He went back to his typing with renewed ferocity.

"Where's my fucking pen?" He slapped his desk and glared. "I can't concentrate with you in here."

His eye bags had grown more voluptuous. Gray hairs matted the filthy floor.

"I'll go for a walk in the storm. Maybe I'll change and run into the woods and never come back again."

"Don't you dare." The professor stood up to block the door. "Just be quiet."

I picked up a legal pad and started a poem.

The Erl King's song spilled from a cave, deep and dark and strange.
His hair was long, soft, and dark, but blighted with spots of mange.

"What are you writing?" he asked.

"Nothing. A poem."

His jaw creaked open and released a cackle.

"What could you possibly have to write about at your age? Let me read it."

The Wild Professor chased me around the cabin, knocking over stacks of books. *Mushrooms Demystified. Thus Spoke Zarathustra. The Anatomy of Melancholy.* Clutching my scrap of poetry, I ran out into the rain.

I glanced back and saw him glowering in the doorway. He emerged, taller than the cabin. His head morphed into a skull. Fireflies flashed in his eye sockets. The end of his beard swung lower than his crotch as he waved a bony fist in the air. I'd never seen him like this before, and I felt a sick allure: I, too, might learn this trick. But I was making progress with my own transformations and wanted to explore a new spell.

"You bitch," he cried, shrinking back down to his normal size. "My heart is bleeding."

I scanned the sky, spotted the moon behind gray clouds, glimmering like a fetus in an ultrasound. I fished a mushroom from my pocket. I cajoled and chanted until my horns came. When I felt a queasy pang of pity, something I'd never felt for this man, I almost slumped back to him. But the pull of the storm was stronger. I craved atmospheric electricity and the blackness of forest soil. I craved roiling clouds and the scent of my own wet fur. I wanted to climb a rocky hill and gaze upon the raw sublime, watch lightning jag from heaven to earth, catch the silhouette of some dangerous new beast galloping toward me across the meadow.

The more often I changed, the more depressed the Wild Professor grew. His hair fell out. He moped in the cabin and said he didn't feel like transforming, even when I slid my hand up his thigh and stroked his half-soft cock.

"Where the hell did you find that willow bark?" he asked me again and again, tearing through the cabin, looking for my stash of herbs.

Each evening he stood in the drizzle at the forest's edge. He called and called, but the doves wouldn't come to him.

One day he shot a squirrel with his air rifle, skinned it, gutted it, and boiled the rodent on the woodstove. There were bloody handprints on the white minifridge, smears of gore on the last clean towel. I craved the green scent of trees. My legs itched to run.

"Eat," said the Wild Professor, offering a plate of gray meat. "Squirrel flesh will enhance your natural clairvoyance, assuming you have any."

"No thanks. I'll stick to jimsonweed."

"You have no idea what you're fucking around with."

When he sneered, I could see the contours of his secret skull, the skin loose on it, ready to slough off at any minute and reveal new marvels. But he slumped at the table and ate weird game. He sipped dark wine and brooded.

"Just wait until the solstice," he muttered. "I'll be at the top of my game again."

After a week of nonstop rain, the tomatoes turned mushy, blighted with blisters, splitting open and oozing foul juice. The cucumbers had bloated and paled on the vine. A thousand berries fermented in the soppy grass.

"Give me a ride to town," I said.

"The car is broken," said the Wild Professor.

"I need tampons. I need Midol. I need to make some calls."

He cringed at the word *calls*, as though I'd bellowed the Old Norse word *kalla*—*to summon loudly*—and some gorgeous demon would materialize in a fiery fury to whisk me away.

We were almost out of olive oil. Ants had gotten into the peanut butter. I'd found a plump black widow tucked under the dewy seat of the composting toilet. But we still had wine. We sat drinking at the kitchen table in the stale buzz of afternoon. But the wine only thickened our mutual boredom.

"All the car needs is a new timing belt, and Sarah's bringing one to the solstice party."

Sarah was an ex-girlfriend, ten years younger than the Wild Professor, but too old, now, to be his lover.

The professor scowled. He had an eye infection, to which he'd applied a chamomile poultice. He smelled of sour laundry and armpit cumin. He looked as if he had a fever, and I wondered if the squirrel meat had made him sick.

"Fuck it," I said. "I'll bike to Family Dollar."

"The chain is broken."

"I'll run," I called, halfway down the dirt drive.

The next morning, I woke before dawn, sat up in bed, and waited for sunlight to break through the kitchen window. When the light came, I saw the Wild Professor as I had my first morning there: a bald old man wheezing in the last throes of sleep, his eyes encased in crinkled pouches, his nose dripping amber snot. I'd tried to catch him like this before, but he always got up before dawn. I'd wake to find him crouched over the sink, drinking tinctures and gobbling mushrooms, popping pills from unlabeled bottles.

But this morning he slept in. The longer he slept, the older he looked. At last, he sat up, opened his toothless mouth, and hissed like a lizard.

"Who are you?" he asked, his eyes milky with cataracts.

"La Belle Dame sans Merci," I joked. But he didn't laugh. He hid his head under the covers and whimpered.

On the solstice, the Wild Professor spread a harvest feast beneath a portable canopy emblazoned with the words PALMETTO FUNERAL HOME.

"I bought it at a thrift store." He grinned. His eyes gleamed with a new electromagnetism, and I fell into his arms. I sniffed his neck and smelled a faint whiff of beast. He hadn't transformed in weeks, but his eye infection had miraculously healed. His hair looked thicker. And I craved his other form.

The sun was still high when the first car came bouncing up the potholed drive. It was Sarah, who'd lived with the Wild Professor in the forest one summer long ago. She had a handsome ruddy husband her own age. She had a fetus the size of a frog inside her swollen belly. She had a broccoli casserole and a jug of spring water.

"Well water gives me gas," she said, sending the professor a secret smile.

A philosophy professor arrived with his fourteen-year-old daughter and his twenty-eight-year-old girlfriend. An adjunct poet, new to the Wild Professor's department, walked through the meadow in a minidress and hiking boots. She eyed the funereal canopy, the cobblers and salads and bowls of weird game, the mismatched cups and unlabeled bottles of homemade wine.

"Am I in the right place?" She waved a faded flier. "I got this invitation in my department box?"

"A thrift store score." The professor pointed at the canopy. "I assure you I'm not in the funeral business, though given recent downsizing in the humanities, never say never. Anyway, welcome to Walden. You must be the lesbian adjunct poetess?"

"The what?" The poet frowned.

Another couple came, both middle-aged with bowl cuts, both wearing work shirts and cutoff acid-washed jeans—she a deconstructive gender sociologist, he a painter who specialized in grotesque cherubs.

I ran to the meadow, stood like a meerkat, and peered. At last, punk Amy's white Volkswagen Rabbit materialized, turning from Basil Road onto the Wild Professor's dirt drive. Punk Amy, hippie Kim, and preppy Paige rushed from the car. The girls gathered around me, picked at my clothes, and poked my ribs.

"You're so skinny," said Paige.

"Too damn thin," said Amy. Her Mohawk bristled with hardened gel. Her arms were tricked out with spiked bracelets. She looked ready for battle. "Has the perv been starving you?"

"Nature girl," quipped Kim, admiring the miniskirt I'd made out of gigantic collard leaves. I wore it with the professor's Roxy Music tee and plastic combat boots from the Family Dollar.

We smoked a joint. I grabbed a bottle of blackberry wine and led my friends through the woods. I felt possessed by the Wild Professor as I recited the names of plants and animals, pointing out holes and hollows where creatures hid from predators. But then I settled into my own voice.

"Tickleweed," I said, nibbling a tender leaf that the Wild Professor incorrectly called horsebane. "A mild aphrodisiac."

The landscape sparkled with beauty again because my friends were there to share it—the trees bursting with sap, birds bustling in the shimmering leaves, the air drowsy with the fume of poppies. In the meadow, butterflies hovered over waist-high wildflowers, and bees dozed in the blooms.

"I could stay here forever," said hippie Kim, lying down in a patch of *Papaver somniferum*.

"My ultimate nightmare," said Amy.

I felt an eerie chill, though there was no breeze. The philosophy professor's daughter came skipping through the meadow in a white dress.

Dusk fell. The Wild Professor's guests sat around the fire drinking wine and eating cobblers, casseroles, flatbread with pesto and cherry tomatoes. None of the guests touched the dove-liver pâté. None of them tried the squirrel salad.

"The Cree of Canada fed squirrel meat to their children," said the Wild Professor, casting his luminous gaze upon the philosophy professor's daughter. The girl, Ashley, stood basking in his attention. She gave him a sly glance and blushed. She was just coming into her beauty, testing its power, hungry for magical change.

The sociology professor harrumphed. She jotted notes into her journal while her husband sketched a rococo cloud.

Sarah chugged spring water and eyed the wine, no doubt remembering her endless evenings here. Twelve years ago Sarah had stormed out during an August drought and walked off across a dead meadow. But here she was, tugging me away from the fire for a heart-to-heart.

"I came to check on him," she whispered. "And to see how you're doing. How *y'all* are doing."

"The rains set us back, but the garden's reviving," I said. "I'd like to drive to Columbia occasionally, but . . ."

"If you did, you'd never come back."

"But you're back." I glanced up to see the Wild Professor wriggling his pointed ears. He claimed he could hear sounds from up to thirty miles away. I turned back to Sarah. When I opened my mouth to speak, I felt the professor's hot, gamy breath on the back of my neck.

I left him alone with Sarah.

Sarah's husband watched her intently. The philosophy professor kept a sharp eye on his daughter. Having wiggled out of his lap, the philosophy professor's girlfriend was now deep in conversation with the adjunct poet.

I joined the youthful throng under the high, waxing moon, wine bottle in my fist. Dancing around the fire, I remembered my first night here, my green gown torn by briars, the Wild Professor ripping it off with his claws. Little Ashley stood amid wildflowers, watching us.

"Come on," I called to her. "Don't be shy."

The girl inched closer. She took furtive sips from a mason jar.

"Oh my," said Kim. "What have we got there?"

"Something he gave me." Her eyes looked huge. Her pupils had gobbled up her hazel irises. "It's actually delicious. Like honeysuckle and chocolate and blood."

"Blood? What the fuck did that perv give you?" said Amy. "Let me take a sniff."

The girl giggled, handed the empty jar to Amy, and executed a perfect *petit jeté*.

I pulled the Wild Professor aside from his table of elders. "She's just a child."

"It was only blackberry juice," he said, watching Ashley perform elegant pirouettes in the poppy field. "And besides, I can tell she's a woman already."

"What was that?" the philosophy professor asked.

"I said, where is that woman already?"

"Wha woman?" slurred the philosophy professor, and then he passed out in his chair.

The deconstructive gender sociologist hawed. But then she teetered. She moaned. She fought and thrashed but soon lay still in the grass.

"Honey," said her husband. But in seconds, he, too, was asprawl.

"You asshole!" I cried. "You slipped them a potion."

"It's been lovely," said Sarah, nodding fiercely at her husband.

"Yep." He put down his beer.

They hustled toward their car.

"Where is the philosophy professor's girlfriend?" I asked. "Where is the adjunct poet?"

"They went for a walk." The Wild Professor winked. "A lovely night for romance. Just look at that moon."

"Listen," I said, avoiding the moon, avoiding his eyes. "I need to tell you something."

"You're leaving me?" The professor shrank an inch, but his eyes still glowed.

"Let's not think of it like that," I said. "I just need to get my shit together. I need to pay my rent, or they'll give my room to another girl. We can see each other in town."

"I'll pay your rent."

"No way."

"Stay with me until winter, at least," he whined. "I'm on sabbatical for fall semester."

"I have to go back to school," I said.

"I can teach you everything you need to know. I see lots of potential in you." The professor grinned like a wolf, and I felt myself soften a bit. "After all, I was the one who taught you how to change. You watched me eat the mushrooms. You heard me chant the chants."

"I figured that out myself. I don't eat the same ones. I don't chant the same chants."

"What you're doing is childish make-believe. Stick around this fall and I'll show you the real deal."

Little Ashley leapt into the firelight and laughed. She stood on tippy toes and whispered into the Wild Professor's ear.

"More blackberry juice, please."

The Wild Professor's eyes glittered. He grew a foot taller. Slaver trickled from his jaws.

"That's fucked-up," said Amy, appearing by my side.

"He's so beautiful," said hippie Kim, gawking at the spectacle. "Now I totally get it!"

His hair came back. His fur sprouted. His antlers filigreed toward the moon.

"Actually, don't look at him!" I cried. "Just walk the hell away."

"That's right. It's just an illusion," said Amy. "A heap of shining bullshit."

"But I don't want to go," said Kim. "Let him bite me. Gore me. I don't care."

"I want to say here forever," said Ashley, charging off. She ran toward the glorious beast.

The Wild Professor stood over the flames, splaying his legs like Atlas. Sparks shot toward his groin. I'd never seen him so huge, so strong, so alluring. But I pictured him hunched over his typewriter when the words wouldn't come, turning toward me, his eye bags aquiver with rage. I saw him mooning around in the drizzle, failing to seduce a flock of doves. I envisioned him, ancient and brittle, sulking in his sour bed.

Now Kim walked backward, watching the Wild Professor rise toward the stars. Now Ashley danced around the fire, singing an ancient lullaby. When the professor threw back his head and howled, I reached for my secret pouch, struggling to remember the sequence: amanita, mayapple root, rattlesnake tongue, reindeer moss. Luciferin, fairy dew, cicada wing, owl bonemeal. I chanted the poem I'd written for the solstice, loud enough for the Wild Professor to hear. Words spun around my head as my antlers came, forty-seven points and glistening. My thigh muscles popped out, bigger than ever. My fur sprouted bushy and thick. Bones aching, I grew three feet, towering over the other girls.

Paige shrieked as she ran toward the car. Amy hustled after her down the slope, pausing to shout. "What the hell have you gotten into?"

"Just wait for me!" I cried, my speech garbled by the chant that wouldn't stop coming, wet words unfurling like newborn bats from my throat, darting up into the sky to circle over the Wild Professor's head. Jolted out of her trance, Kim stopped smiling.

When the Wild Professor moved toward Ashley, the bat swarm descended, flurrying his hair into a knotted mess. Swatting at the bats, he uttered words that he claimed were Indo-European, curses that pricked my kidneys and made my heart boil with black blood. I screeched a word so old that hominids had uttered it, a word that made him double over and clutch his gut. And then I ran at him. I battered his back with my horns. Kicked his flanks with my hooves. When he fell moaning onto his side, Ashley ran weeping to me, hugged me, and slipped her small hand into mine.

We ran down the slope toward the car. I felt myself getting smaller, moving slower, returning to my human state.

Hand on the door handle, I dared to look back.

The Wild Professor had burst into flames. As flesh fell like ash from his body, I thought I had destroyed him.

But the cloud of ash morphed into a wolf skeleton. He crouched on all fours and barked.

"Get in! Get in!" Amy screamed through the open window.

We piled into the white Rabbit, Ashley whimpering in the back seat.

"My tummy hurts," she said, and then she passed out.

When Amy turned the key, the car sputtered, failed, and then sputtered again. We lurched off, bounded down the bumpy drive, and skidded left onto Basil Road. We swerved right to dodge a doe, left to avoid an injured raccoon.

"Jesus, step on it," I said.

The Wild Professor was galloping toward us, his snarling muzzle full of blood-glazed teeth. He hurled his body at the car, clattering bones against molded steel. His ghost tongue lashed like an electric eel as he barked.

We rolled up the windows. Paige shifted to fourth and gunned it. We left the Wild Professor whining on his haunches, his snout aimed at the moon.

We hooted in triumph.

But tears leaked from my eyes as I watched the professor shrink back down into a puny man. He stood like a hitchhiker on the side of the road, his jeans covered in home-sewn patches.

"I'll make you beds of roses. I'll teach you how to fly!" he cried, his voice breaking. And then he turned away.

As he hobbled back toward his cabin, light leaked out of him with every step.

The Maiden

Our parents said the Watts were lunatics for put-ting a trampoline in their backyard, out behind their garage full of souped-up dirt bikes, in the tiny meadow still strewn with their dead horse's droppings, out where a honey locust had just burst into bloom. We didn't believe it until we saw it: hoisted by silver tubing, its round nylon bounce mat glimmering like a black lagoon in the endless summer light. We watched from the woods the first day of its glory, the Watts boys kickboxing in the air, performing backflips, torpedoing their agile bodies off the side and landing like Olympians in the long grass.

Our parents said we'd knock out our teeth, break our necks, paralyze ourselves. Our parents said we'd suffer concussions, bashed noses, ruptured organs, broken limbs. But how could we resist the miracle of fake flight, the mockery of gravity's law? How could we resist the cool kids that gathered each day in the fragrant shade of the honey locust, jocks in jogging shorts and suntanned cheerleaders showing off their new curves? The girls bounced and laughed and danced in the air. The girls did slo-mo flips and gymnastics stunts, ballet leaps and jazz-dance moves— all except the girl we called Cujo, a stunted, breastless bitter thing—freckled, redheaded, bony as a shad. When she looked us over with her weird bulging eyes, we felt a burn in our guts, as though her gaze had lasered though skin and muscle to singe our organs, changing us from the inside out.

Cujo crept in the shade. Cujo mumbled foreign words—curses, we suspected, for she came from North Augusta, from Irish Travellers, people said. Her parents made dulcimers for a living and didn't go to church. When Troy Hutto attempted a crash dive and fractured his femur, we spotted Cujo crouched under the trampoline, scratching in the dirt with a stick. When Tammy Day dislocated her elbow on the metal rim, we saw Cujo up in the honey locust, sprinkling leaf confetti onto the mat. When Chip Watts, King of the Air, piked off the tramp and landed on a brick *that had not been there the day before*, Cujo ate a fucking acorn (three separate kids witnessed her shelling it), hexing Chip, who spent the next three weeks earthbound and hobbling on a sprained ankle.

Though we whispered of banishing Cujo from the Watts property, we got the creepy feeling she could hear us plotting. What if she went apeshit and telekinetic, tossing our helpless bodies around like dolls? Truth told, the accidents could have been much worse, leaving us mangled and tragic, as our parents feared, so we let the freak lurk, let her stare with her weird gray eyes, pace and mutter and gaze up at the sky as though communicating with aliens beyond the clouds. We scrounged up good-luck charms to protect ourselves—rabbit feet, heirloom jewels, possum penile bones—and carried on with our business, always conscious of the darkness radiating from Cujo's small spotted body.

The day Chip Watts stepped back on the trampoline, Cujo emerged from the woods with a garter snake wrapped around her left wrist. At first, we thought it was a plastic toy, but when she crept near, we saw it slithering, saw her whispering to the serpent, saw her snickering as though the reptile had hissed some irresistible joke. When Chip started with a fliffis, we held our breath, imagining him bashing his head on the T-junction, but he went right to a Randy and ended his routine with a perfect Miller Plus. Cujo be damned, he leapt from the tramp with an axe kick, falling right into the arms of Tammy Day, who rewarded him with a kiss.

As cicadas pulsed in the July heat, the kiss went on and on, making us tingle with lust-tinged shame. Though we should've slunk home, leaving the couple to their private passions, we couldn't pull our eyes away from the storied quarterback and his head-cheerleader love, young and easy under the locust boughs.

That's why nobody saw Cujo mount the tramp. That's why nobody witnessed her first few stunts.

After the lovers parted and wiped their beslobbered mouths, we turned to the trampoline just in time to catch Cujo back-flipping over a locust branch. Landing with ease, she launched an effortless quadriffi, a stunt that even Chip hadn't mastered, each somersault more elegant than the last, her body lithe as a lemur's, her face glowing with an uncanny beauty we'd never seen. When she straddle-jumped off the mat and landed in the grass, the loveliness drained from her body. She was Cujo again, speckled and smirking, her eyes too big for her head. She high-tailed it toward the woods, leaving us shaken.

"What the hell?" said Tammy Day. "Where did she learn how to do that?"

Like a rose blooming in time-lapse video, a boil sprouted on the tip of Tammy's nose. As warm wind blew through the yard, pustulous acne erupted on the head cheerleader's face.

"What?" Tammy scratched her nose.

Wendy Dyches handed her a compact. When Tammy opened the small round mirror and beheld her affliction, she wailed, crumpled, and wept. Refusing to speak to us, she shielded her face with her hands. "Maybe it's the heat," said Wendy. "Hives, scabies, or poison oak. Got to be some logical explanation."

But we knew Cujo had cursed Tammy. Fearing some contagion, we backed away from the sobbing, zitty girl. Our sense of reality forever fucked, we gazed at the sky. Beholding convoluted clouds that evoked airbrushed paintings of the apocalypse, we half expected Jesus to whizz down in a flying saucer and summon the chosen among us. A gust of strong wind blustered through, along with ethereal yellow light, but a storm didn't erupt. After Mrs. Watts called her boys in for supper, other kids drifted home, leaving just the two of us, Joe and Glen, sitting on the trampoline, discussing the day in hushed tones.

We decided we needed to see Cujo in her natural habitat, see if she had a trampoline in her backyard. We waited until dark and then set off through the woods, winding toward the place where Cujo's dank split-level perched on a ravine above boggy land. When old Miss Emily died there in 1982, her family found possums nesting in the living room, mushrooms growing in damp shag carpet, the furniture velvety with mold. The house sat empty for five years before Cujo's family moved in: her dulcimer-making parents, her three younger brothers who spoke a secret language that nobody but Cujo could understand.

When we crossed the creek, we spotted the house. The split-level, covered in wisteria, seemed to float in a bubble of light, a dwelling that existed outside of time. Clutching at exposed roots, we climbed up the eroded hill, at last reaching a chain-link fence. In the overgrown yard, Cujo's small, pale dad strummed a dulcimer, his bald head glossy in the porch light. Cujo's skinny mom emerged from the darkness, swaying in a white nightgown, standing a full head taller than Cujo's father. The couple yodeled eerie harmonies, a song that made us forget why we had come.

"Kyarn!" yelled a child, jarring us from our trance.

Wielding spiked sticks, Cujo's three brothers, none of them older than ten, rushed toward us—tiny wincing boys with dark hair, dressed in cutoff shorts.

"What's the fuss?" cried Cujo's dad.

"Sorry foons!" the boys yelled, climbing the chain-link fence.

We bolted, going the wrong way, running so far that we came out where Pocotaligo Road turned to dirt, a hundred dogs losing their shit at Country Canine Academy.

Though we never got used to Cujo's stunts, we relaxed into the wonder of it all, the mid-July heat lulling us into a stupor, a fever dream of shrieking insects and eternally grumbling thunder. We learned to watch for the moment when Cujo lapsed into beauty, high in the air, her face surging with light, her hair a streak of fire, freckles glittering like flecks of copper on her skin. Perhaps the light that filtered through the honey locust tricked us. Perhaps ecstasy transformed the girl from within. Maybe distance and movement blurred her features as she catapulted and triple-flipped and performed grand jetés and cabrioles. Still, we braced ourselves for her landings. The second she touched earth, her ugliness surged back, and she hustled away, tittering and graceless. She kept to the margins, that weird zone between woods and yard, watching—waiting for her curses to take effect.

As long as we were respectful, and Cujo got her time in the air, her curses were harmless, a mild nuisance—like Tammy Day's acne (which cleared up the next day), Marty Cope's flatulence (nothing he hadn't suffered before), and Crystal Goodings's hiccups (which lasted until sunset)—curses so mild we wondered if we were imagining them. But then, one hot, gusty afternoon, a clutch of girls sniggered as Cujo lost her footing while mounting the tramp. Cujo jerked her head around and glared at the girls. Cujo murmured strange words. Nodding, clenching her fists, she stepped to the center of the mat. Dark clouds thickened above her as she warmed up with pikes and pucks. And then she went full-on whirling dervish, spinning and flipping so fast we couldn't keep track of her tricks. As thunder boomed and lightning jagged, Cujo bounced higher than we'd ever seen her go, disappearing into the honey locust branches. And then she swan dove so quick we knew she'd break her skinny neck. But she touched down with a handstand and springboarded off the tramp, her skin flaring yellow the second she landed in the grass.

Cujo groaned and rolled her bloodshot eyes. Snot ran from her nose. Heaving, she staggered off into the woods.

As the downpour came, we made a run for the garage, relishing the dim light and the warm proximity of other bodies. Wendy Dyches sat on the chest freezer, chatting with her two best friends. But then she screeched and spat something into her hand. In her open palm, she displayed a molar with long bloody roots. Of the three girls who had laughed at Cujo, Wendy had been the boldest, releasing a cackle that had made her body shake. While Tina Platts had tittered into her fist, shy May Mood had merely snorted and smiled. Now Tina scratched her head, groaning as fistfuls of hair came loose from her scalp. We backed away from the afflicted girls, watching as bald spots appeared in Tina's dark hairdo. We thought May might escape unscathed, but soon she was whimpering. She stared at us with puffy eyes, her lids festering with multiple styes.

"We've got to do something," cried Hope Crews. "Can't let that little freak dog us."

A hush settled over us as we watched Hope, waiting for her to spit out teeth, lapse into baldness, or break out in leprous sores. Hope examined her slender arms and touched her cat-shaped face, testing for curses. When nothing happened, she strode to the center of the carport.

"Everybody has a weakness," said Hope. "We've just got to figure out Cujo's."

Glen Cook stepped forth. In a quavering voice, he told the crowd the story of our excursion, how we'd ventured through the woods to Cujo's home, finding no trampoline in her yard, only her yodeling parents and her younger brothers, who'd wielded homemade spears.

"But we didn't see Cujo," said Glen.

"You didn't look hard enough," said Hope. "She was probably floating right over you like a vampire child."

After the other kids went home for supper, Hope lingered in the yard with us—Glen, Joe, and Crystal Gooding—setting up a secret rendezvous, vowing to solve the mystery of Cujo's powers once and for all.

The muggy night smelled like boiled cabbage. The moon was a piddling thing, stars swarming above the field where the four of us—Glen, Hope, Crystal, and Joe—met up. We had flashlights and binoculars, knives and BB guns, orange pocket Bibles handed out by Gideons at Tillman Middle School. We took the shortcut through the woods, following Toadstone Creek down into the flood zone where Cujo's split-level hovered above the ravine in an eerie orb of lamplight. As we climbed the hill, we heard bewitching singing, like something from beyond the moon. And then we saw her bouncing on a mini-tramp, her hair aflame around the pale shimmer of her face, her eyes flashing silver sparks. We couldn't bring ourselves to call her Cujo in this form, the name Marty Cope had given her on the Tillman playground the time she nabbed our football—the time we cornered her behind the jungle gym. Snarling, she'd bared her crooked teeth. And Marty had forever branded her with the name of a murderous, rabid dog.

This creature that bounced slowly, performing languid stunts, was not Cujo. This being that sang in a timeless voice was not Cujo. Stunned, watching the girl hover in the rich night air, we couldn't recall her real name. Though we'd seen flickers of her beauty in the Watts backyard, she'd moved too quickly there for us to focus, to suck in her loveliness with our eyes and fill our bodies with it, charging our very marrow with light.

Who knows how long we stood there, mouths slack, lulled by her music, yoked together by the inexplicable vision before us? When the brothers came yowling out into the yard, their sister ceased to sing, but still she bounced, luminous, sustaining states of unnatural buoyancy. The brothers whirled around her, lashing at her ankles with their spears. The brothers lunged and gibbered. They pulled fistfuls of powder from pouches strapped to their belts and flung it into their sister's face, causing her to sneeze, stumble, and fall into the grass. When she stood up, her skin crinkled, and her lovely lean form became bony and crooked. Her hair turned gray and thin.

"Hag!" the brothers yowled, dancing around a tiny crone.

The crone's hair floated away like ash, leaving her bald, her scalp scaly and faintly blue. She spat out teeth. She shrank several inches. We feared she'd shrivel to skin and bones. But then, in a blink, she was Cujo again, freckled and pubescent, snarling and cursing. The brothers climbed the fence and fled to the woods, running right past us, out to a flat stump, where they began pounding objects with rocks.

We showed up the next afternoon as the others did, stood around watching Chip do warm-up jumps. Everybody seemed restless, disturbed by the absence of Wendy, Tina, and May, watching the woods for the appearance of Cujo.

Wendy, kids whispered, had been rushed to Dr. Burroughs, a dentist who assured her parents that X-rays revealed a mouthful of healthy teeth, though it was crucial that the girl be fitted with an implant to replace the missing molar. Doctor Pendarvis had informed May's parents that though her styes were unusually numerous, they fell within the range of normality and would take at least a week to heal. Tina's dermatologist, who babbled vaguely of hormonal shifts, teen stress, junk food, and trichotillomania, could not predict when her hair might grow back, though he assured the girl's parents that her follicles were not dead.

At the height of afternoon, cicadas pulsing in the muggy air, Cujo came staggering from the woods. Bent and scowling, she looked even punier than she usually did. She had gray streaks in her hair, bags under her eyes, lines around her mouth. Mumbling to herself, she lurked in the shade of the honey locust, glaring at Tammy Day, who bounced idly on the trampoline, attempting the occasional straddle-jump. When Tammy finally saw Cujo skulking in the shadows, she hurried to the edge of the mat, climbed down carefully, and slipped behind her posse of girlfriends.

Cujo climbed the tramp, muttering as she scrambled over the edge. She stood wincing in the circle of blackness, a small, scrunched creature, her eyes squinting in concentration. We didn't realize we were holding our breath until she started jumping, two-foot tucks that any four-year-old could manage, not her usual starting fare. When she pulled off a pike jump, we relaxed, waiting for her to launch a backflip and then leap into her otherworldly form. But Cujo fell flat on her bony ass—a spot drop, we thought, even though she never messed with such trifling stunts. Cujo crumpled and moaned. Grunting, she heaved herself up, tottered to the trampoline's edge, and tumbled into the long grass.

As the girl writhed and whimpered on the ground, Tammy Day sashayed forth, walking with the same hip-sway her beautician mother had perfected. With a flourish, Tammy kicked Cujo in the ribs, making the girl go limp—playing possum, we hoped.

"That's what you get for messing with Tammy Day," said Tammy. "My granny told me to tell you that, you freakish devil child." Tammy stood triumphant over the fallen girl, her glorious hairdo, shellacked with Aqua Net, glinting in the sun. We pictured Tammy's granny hunched in the back room of Delilah's Salon, her jet-black beehive sitting crooked on her skull. The old woman, who'd started Delilah's back in the fifties, now told futures by flipping through a Bible at random, pronouncing fates in hifalutin King James while Tammy's mom did hair.

We wondered if the old lady had powers, wondered if Cujo suffered from a double curse. When Tammy's friends crowded in, we feared they'd maul Cujo, but the girls just stood behind Tammy, glaring and radiating hatred.

At last, Cujo lifted her head, gazing at the long stretch between herself and the woods. At last, she rose, crooked and swaying. As she stumbled away, we stood in silence, listening to her bones creak, sighing when she disappeared into the trees.

The next day, when Cujo failed to creep from the woods at her usual time, Tammy Day stepped simpering onto the trampoline. She did a double-back somi, landing in pirouette pose. Laughing with full-throated ease, she twirled and swished, her limbs golden, her feathered hair shining with blond highlights. Chip Watts scrambled onto the mat, slipped his arm around her waist, and gracefully lowered her into a dip. For hours the couple cavorted, pawing at each other as they leapt and flipped, leaning in for kisses, showing off their perfect bods. They were King and Queen of Summer again, showing off in the air, leaving the rest of us earthbound. The fools among us cheered them on, leering slavishly in the heat, charged with vicarious glory.

Enveloped smugly within a bubble of secret knowledge, the four of us—Glen, Hope, Crystal, and Joe—slunk off to the shade. We were the only ones who'd glimpsed the heights of Cujo's beauty and the depths of her hideousness, her vulnerability to the people who knew her best, her abrupt morphing into miniature hagdom. Speaking in low tones, we wondered what powers she possessed. Her rapid balding, tooth loss, and bodily shrinkage embodied the horrors of annihilation. When her freckled teen form surged back, it had seemed extra juicy and potent, almost pretty by comparison—the very essence of human life.

When we finally got our turns on the trampoline, we felt strangely deflated, as though our stunts had no meaning without Cujo there. Soon it started drizzling, as though the sun had eyes only for Tammy and Chip, and the Watts boys' mom declared the trampoline too wet for jumping. The four of us drifted toward the woods again. We found the footpath Cujo took through the forest, a trail so light it might've been made by bobcats. We wove deeper into the trees than we'd ever gone, finding a dim swampy floodplain loud with frogs. Vines swaddled the trees. In a clearing, cabbage-like plants clustered around a pool of water. We stood around the tiny pond, watching weeds waver from obscure currents. Speaking again of Cujo, we wondered if we could help her somehow, wondered if we could find her brothers and take their magic pouches away. We all admitted we hated Chip and Tammy, that we wanted to see them curse-stricken and staggering in the July heat, bereft of beauty, unable to escape gravity's grip.

A mourning dove called. A tree frog barked.

And then we saw her—the girl, pale as a sand bass, sunk in the pool's depths.

"Drowned," Glen rasped.

As though awakened, the girl whooshed up through the water in a rage, clawing at air, screaming words we didn't understand. Her eyes looked filmy, and she didn't seem to see us as she staggered down a forest path, bumping into trees. Though we tailed her through the woods, we couldn't keep up. Soon her house appeared, perched above the gulley, and we climbed up the eroded terrain. But when we reached the top, the fence was gone. We found no split-level house—only a bald hill littered with broken bricks.

"Cujo," we called, ashamed we didn't know the girl's true name, something lovely and old-fashioned, we guessed, like Guinevere or Christabel.

"The Maiden," whispered Glen, and the name stuck.

The four of us—Glen, Hope, Crystal, and Joe—stopped hanging out by the trampoline. We spent our afternoons searching for the Maiden, vowing we'd vanquish her brothers and release her from their spell. We mused as always on the riddle of her address—level when approached from the front, perched on a hill when glimpsed from the deepest part of the swamp. When climbing from the south side of the woods, we always found a scraggly hill. When climbing from the north side, we sometimes found her house, blocked off by a chain-link fence, though we never saw a single soul in the yard.

One long hot Saturday, we walked down Wisteria Way, the crumbling asphalt road that led to the vine-smothered split-level where Miss Emily had died in 1982. We found no cars in the driveway, no action in the overgrown yard. Though we banged the brass knocker and pounded the peeling front door with our fists, nobody answered. Nobody stirred inside the house. When we slipped into the yard from the side, we found ourselves in the woods again, winding down toward swampy land, no house in sight.

"Lost," mused Hope, as we walked in circles, the soles of our sneakers caked with black mud. That's when Glen and Crystal found the pool again, concealed by a scrim of dead leaves that we brushed away with our hands, marveling at the coldness of the water. Hunkering around the tiny pond, we gazed into its dark depths, detecting wavering weeds and tiny silver minnows. The forest breathed around us, frogs and insects throbbing.

We gasped when we spotted her—the Maiden sleeping at the bottom of the pool, pale as a ghost salamander, her skin translucent and faintly aglow. She had not been there two seconds before—the girl we'd seen bouncing on the mini-tramp, the girl whose singing made us stare too long at the moon. Perhaps she'd floated up from deeper depths. Perhaps she glowed sometimes, and other times stayed dark. Maybe she flickered in and out of our plane of existence, surging in from another dimension, the fourth or the fifth—we could never remember the differences between the two. We discussed these theories later that night. But in the woods, we stayed quiet, focusing on the wonder of her face. We didn't want to wake her again, send her blind and reeling through the swamp.

When the woods went dark and chuck-will's-widows called, a light flashed on at the top of the hill. We again saw Cujo's split-level, which seemed to float in the trees. Returning our gaze to the pool, we found only darkness—no gleaming Maiden sleeping in the silt. We took a long foot trail up the other side of the hill, catching glimpses of the old brick house, but we couldn't access it from the woods, no matter how many paths we tried. Exhausted, we found ourselves on Pocotaligo Road again, farther away than before, out near the Pentecostal Holiness Church.

July was almost over, and we stalked the woods with desperate ferocity, sweating in the muggy heat, longing for the feel of cool water, pining for the sight of the celestial Maiden submerged in the depths of an uncanny pool. Doubting our vision, we compared notes, bickering about trivial details—the length of her hair, the shape of her lips, the intensity of her luminescence.

"Maybe it's all just tricks," said Glen. "Her family a bunch of shifty travelers."

Disgusted by this thought, we took the shortest path up the hill, discovering, once more, eroded terrain and scattered bricks.

"Sick and tired of this," hissed Crystal, kicking a brick.

We were sick and tired of our shit town. Sick and tired of Chip and Tammy lording it over everybody. Sick and tired of the endless summer day breathing down our necks like a panting dog. The Maiden had given us a glimpse of otherworldly possibilities, and now we couldn't find her.

"I say we sneak in," said Crystal.

"You mean break in," said Hope.

"Semantics," said Crystal, a vocabulary word the rest of us didn't know. We didn't ask what *semantics* meant. We followed Crystal down the path to Wisteria Way. Finding no cars in the driveway, we climbed the familiar front stoop with its lichen-covered brick and rusted screen door. We knocked and waited, listening for the rustle of humans inside. And then Crystal tried the knob.

"Unlocked," she whispered.

We crept into a shadowy living room decorated with orange shag carpet and lime brocade drapes. A white baby grand piano stood in a far corner, surrounded by piles of books. The house smelled of mold and rat piss, the windows sealed with electrical tape. On the wall was an oil painting of Miss Emily's only son, immortalized in his pug-nosed, towheaded toddler form, the boy who'd grown up to become a playboy podiatrist in Atlanta. We found boxes of dishes in the kitchen, a naked mattress in the master bedroom, a plastic stool in a stained pink bathtub. We tested the switches for electricity, the faucets for running water, finding neither.

"She doesn't live here," said Glen, his voice hoarse with despair.

We exited by the sliding-glass door, finding ourselves in the overgrown backyard we'd viewed from the other side of the chain-link fence. On a rusted iron garden table, we found a dulcimer, rain-warped and lacking strings.

"Miss Emily," Crystal reminded us, "was a music teacher."

"Right," said Hope. "But Cujo's parents make dulcimers. We saw them singing that night."

This dulcimer had been rotting for at least a decade—its wood splintery, furred with yellow fungus.

"Wishful thinking," said Crystal, striding off toward the gate that led to the road. "I'm done."

The rest of us climbed the fence and descended into forest gloom. We stumbled around the woods looking for the pool, knowing we wouldn't find it.

Over the next few weeks, the Maiden became a hazy memory, and we wondered if we'd been fooled by an illusion, a mannequin or doll immersed in water, Cujo concealed in a pile of leaves, rising so fast she tricked us. We wondered if her trampoline stunts seemed spectacular only because we didn't expect much from the strange, ugly girl. Every time Glen uttered the words *the Maiden*, his voice all whiny and wistful, Crystal sneered: "You mean Cujo?"

The last Saturday before school started, we went to the Watts place for their annual catfish stew party, keeping our distance from the drunken adults, who gabbed about their boring lives as tall, potbellied Mr. Watts manned his propane cooker, scarlet-faced, stirring an eighty-quart aluminum pot that bubbled with his pungent specialty: catfish nibbles and potatoes simmered in tomato sauce and Campbell's Cream of Mushroom, spiced with generous splashes of Worcestershire and Texas Pete, flavored with fried hog jowl and served over rice. Mr. Watts had spent the summer catching enormous bottom-feeding catfish, stashing them in his chest freezer, and now the big day was upon us, a scorcher to beat all scorchers. The air smelled of pond funk and burnt Crisco. The birds sounded hoarse, and dying cicadas buzzed in the parched yellow grass.

The four of us joined the teens that thronged around the trampoline, watching the lesser jocks and cheerleaders perform the prelude to Chip and Tammy's new routine, a number they'd been practicing for weeks. Kids whispered that they'd perform a strip tease in the air. Kids whispered that they'd consulted the *Kama Sutra*, that they'd mime intricate sex acts from heights of twenty feet.

Heshers and skags who'd already graduated rolled up to the spectacle in Firebird Trans Ams and Camaro V8s—long-haired dudes who blew their cash on cars, bad boys accompanied by underage girls in acid-washed miniskirts. This crowd pulled Millers from mini-coolers and smoked Marlboro Reds right out in the open, getting glares from Mrs. Watts, who was up to her elbows in hush-puppy dough.

Teens sipped beer from Solo cups. Teens slipped behind the shed to smoke and make out. Heat-stunned and tipsy, teens ate fishy slop from paper plates that soon turned grease-soaked and floppy. We all watched Chip and Tammy hold court under a beach umbrella, at ease with the world, as though they'd never tasted Cujo's curses, as though they'd never been bested and never would be. Summer's royals lolling in lounge chairs, stretching their sun-bronzed limbs, they'd reign at Swamp Fox High just as they had at Tillman Middle.

It was half past two o'clock, and Chip and Tammy lingered over their dessert, feeding each other banana pudding, toying with our expectations, chilling as though they hadn't been dreaming of the glory of this day. By the time they approached the trampoline, there was a dangerous charge in the air, too many kids crowding in, older heshers mingling with teens, drunk adults screeching cheers from the patio. The sky looked green-tinged, the clouds jaundiced. Weed smoke wafted from obscure sources. Somewhere in the distance, a chain saw started up.

That's when Cujo skittered out from the woods, so fast she blurred, so fast that nobody saw her except us—Glen, Hope, Crystal, and Joe. Everybody else had their eyes on Chip and Tammy, who stood frozen in the middle of the trampoline as the opening keyboard riff from Europe's "The Final Countdown" blared from a boom box. Cujo scurried behind the azalea hedge. When the drums kicked in, Chip and Tammy popped into action with a triffis for each of them, performed simultaneously, landing with doggy drops. When they rebounded with Axl Rose snake-dance moves, Cujo came screaming from the shrubs—freaky teeth bared, fists clenched, thin red hair streaming. From a distance of six feet, she leapt onto the tramp, popped Chip in the neck with a front kick and Tammy in the face with a side, knocking them both off the mat, sending them rolling into the overgrown grass.

The collective murmur of the entranced crowd resembled a distant rumble of thunder. Cujo stood still, psyching herself up for her first jump—her eyes closed, her goblin face scrunched in concentration. For a second her homeliness seemed to condense, as though to fuel the marvelous stunts to come. And then she was airborne, her body curled in the turns of a perfect quadriffi, soaring higher with each flip. By the time she reached her fourth salto, she'd shaken off her earthly form, morphing into a being of movement and light.

She was *the Maiden*, lunar-skinned and silver-eyed, her hair a flurry of flames. The adults went stiff and silent on the patio, frozen with beer cans in their hands, their mouths open mid-sentence. Chip and Tammy sat up in the grass, dull-eyed, their faces slack. The other kids, who'd never really seen the Maiden, stood stunned and panting in the heat. The heshers lost their cool-dude vibes as wonder overtook them.

The Maiden touched down and sprang into a double quadriffi, spiraling past the highest branches of the honey locust. And then she swan dove, a fiery streak plummeting. Just when we thought she'd crash, she veered upward and hovered above the trampoline, three sets of dragonfly wings fluttering on her back. Except for the two glossy orbs that spun in her eye sockets, her face was blank—no mouth, no nose. But then a fang-fringed orifice opened near her chin. The sounds of flutes and chimes floated out, high and sharp in the bright air.

That's when Chip and Tammy stood up and started twitching. At first, we thought the Maiden had cursed them with run-of-the mill seizures. But then we noticed they jerked in sync, contracting into terrifying rigidity and then going limp, their faces slack and expressionless. With each move, Chip and Tammy lapsed into intensifying ugliness—gargoyle-faced and scaly-skinned, bat-eared and dog-snouted. Their hair was greasy and matted. Their eyes glistered a sick snot green. Long gray tongues flopped from their mouths. Though we'd never been able to see it before, this repulsiveness had always been inside them.

The other teens stood spellbound, unable to speak. The adults remained frozen on the patio, all except Mr. Watts, who, hexed by Cujo, sprang into action, amping the heat on his propane cooker and whistling an intricate tune beyond his normal capabilities. As Chip and Tammy danced spastically around the yard, Mr. Watts added items to his stew, throwing in whatever was at hand—beer cans, Solo cups, flip-flops, and sunglasses—filling the air with the apocalyptic stench of molten plastic.

We four—Glen, Hope, Crystal, and Joe—were the only ones the Maiden hadn't hexed, the only people who served as true witnesses to whatever the hell was going on. The Maiden was an angel of death, we hoped, there to reveal dark truths and announce the day of reckoning—insect plagues, blood rain, meteor showers, and wormwood-tainted water. We scanned the clouds for swarms of angels, pop-eyed with fury, shrieking at decibels that would bust our eardrums. We hoped the Maiden would sweep us up into some frenzy, whisk us away to an otherworldly locale where she, reverted to her comely form, would crown us as chosen. After all, we were the ones who understood her true beauty, the ones who'd searched for her in the forest, the ones who'd found her sleeping in the bottom of the pool. We were the ones who'd plotted to thwart her brothers, who seemed hell-bent on destroying her.

But the sky didn't erupt into apocalyptic havoc. Mr. Watts sat down in his lawn chair, by all appearances a normal man exhausted from outdoor cooking. He dozed off, his head slumped forward. Chip and Tammy fell to their knees, ecstatic looks on their hideous faces. The other teens turned away from the Maiden. Only the four of us—Glen, Hope, Crystal, and Joe—kept our eyes locked on the terrifying but eerily beautiful image of her true form—wings, whirling eyes, and glittering, exquisite teeth. We secretly longed to be devoured, chewed up, and incorporated into the body of the Maiden—anything to escape the future that awaited us in this shit town. How could we return to our paltry lives after witnessing her glory? How could we face the indignities that awaited us at Swamp Fox High, where monsters like Chip and Tammy reigned?

When a hundred smoke-blue songbirds stirred in the honey locust and started twittering, we four reached for the Maiden, extending our arms like toddlers. But the Maiden didn't pick us up. She whirred in circles, up past the highest branches, and darted off into infinite space. Sighing, we hoped she'd return to gravity's clutch, touching down upon the bounce mat as she always did, springing into the grass, lapsing back into flesh and blood. But the Maiden shrank to a fleck and passed into distant clouds, twinkling with pink light as she vanished from our world.

Flying

At first you think the monster is old, all skin and bones and rancid rags, crinkled hands resembling bird claws, talons that snatch babies up by the scruffs of their necks. She whisks the plump squallers to her woodland hut and slits them throat to groin, savoring the steam they give off. She siphons their blood, sorts organs, pickles some, pounds others into porridge, grinds delicate skeletons into bonemeal. She boils and ferments and stocks her rough-hewn shelves. Though her bottles are old, chipped, and marked with scabby fingerprints, the wine she makes gives off a pomegranate glow. It looks delicious. When you gaze through her sooty windows, you forget about killing her: you want to drink the wine and see where it takes you.

Her hut—ringed round with bones, buzzards dozing in the fungus-blasted trees—is never in the same place twice. Every time you find it, you fall asleep, wake up freezing in the middle of nowhere, a fox nosing your rucksack. You go back to your cottage at the edge of the village, back to the hearth, the wife, the plow, the children who eat you out of house and home. When the cows' hooves turn to jelly, when the green wheat spikes go pale, when well water comes up muddy and your wife laughs at your soft cock, you go back into the woods to kill the witch.

This time you wander through a sun-dappled forest, butterflies thick in the late summer haze. Crickets chirr in the brush, a sleepy silver sound that makes you wonder if you're dreaming. You eat wild fruit so ripe it gives you a buzz. By the time you find her in an afternoon glade, you're stumbling and muttering, starved and thirsty, dumbfounded by the opalescent pallor of her skin. Her hair is the brown of wrens, braided and coiled—fake, you think, for you have seen the Lady of the Manor cavorting in a flame-colored wig. When the Lady laughs, her teeth are black and jagged. She hides them behind a silk fan.

But the monster's teeth are white, her lips a shame to roses. Her eyes, grape green, look you over. She smirks. A beautiful sweet evil flickers between you. Perhaps she's not a monster after all, you think, fingers loosening around the haft of your knife. She takes you deeper into the woods, where the path thins and strange birds call. When she pulls a bottle of glowing wine from her willow basket, you know it's the same stuff the hag makes. Same stained cork. Same dark fingerprints on the glass.

Pushing this knowledge down into the cellar of your mind, you lick your lips.

You've dreamed of this wine, dreamed that the hag landed on your thatched roof, that you slipped out a window, lifted your wooden cup, and begged for a taste of it. You screamed when she flew away, waking your youngest, who blubbered until the sun came up. That's when you found the blighted wheat. That's when you found the blasted cows. Mud in the well. The whole land kissed with curses.

But everything is different now. The woman speaks an old language, a tongue your grandmother mumbled in bits and bobs, words children sometimes babbled around secret fires when you were small and the world still amazed you. Some of it comes back to you now.

"Eat," she says.

Braided barley cakes glazed with honey. Six roasted birds on a stick. Mushroom tarts. A salad of herbs and flower petals. You've never tasted food like this, food that makes your eyes water, food that makes you stare too long at the moon. How did it get to be night so fast?

The glow of the woman's skin ought to scare you. The coppery taste of the wine ought to give you pause. But you pass the bottle, quaff and laugh and hang on to her every word, the guttural dips of her voice that make you wonder if she's a wolf in disguise.

She goes on about stars and planets, solstices and equinoxes, the sun and moon. You sigh as you slide a hand up her smooth thigh. She takes a long pull from the bottle, sets it aside, and leaps upon you. Crouching, she husks your pants, slides a long tongue up your throat, and huffs hot breath into your face. She's astride you before you can say *jackrabbit*, her hair wind-whisked, wild and lovely. Her bony rump chafes your skin as she rides you. Everything changes except her eyes, shining like twin moons in the wreckage of her face.

As she screeches with pleasure, a cold wind whips through the forest, carrying her hair away like pale dandelion seeds, leaving her mouth toothless, her scalp pocked and bald. Whooping, the hag hops off you, scampers away in the moonlight, her fox's tail bobbing as she goes.

Drained, dreading the curse she's left upon you, you hobble back to your village. You bathe in the creek, sleep for two days, and then: back to grueling work and scant crops, back to shrill children and scolding wife. You bury another cow. Your oldest child collapses in the turnip field and suffers a lavish fit. Sniffing some taint upon you, your wife eyes you with suspicion, stiffens when you stroke her wrist. She whispers with the village holy man, rifles through your rucksack, scrutinizes the moist, plump mole that recently sprouted on your inner thigh. *It looks like a baby toad*, she says, *or the kind of mushroom that grows from dung.* She claims you smell peculiar—like sour whey, like tripe and barley soup, like a nest of newborn mice.

When autumn comes, the village granary is half-full, your lard supply low, your cupboards stocked with misshapen gourds, bags of feed-grade peas and moldy grain. You remember the feast the beautiful monster fed you—tarts and cakes, mushrooms and flowers, tender songbirds with edible skeletons. You remember the crunch of crispy skulls, the sweet pasty meat within. When you tasted it, you heard nightingales and felt a delicious terror.

Against all reason, you want to see her again: fuck her, kill her—you don't know. You imagine yourself kissing her, lapping at the nectar of her mouth. The second you taste bile, you'll whip out your knife, stab her in the heart. Death, you think, will show what she really is—leathery crone or luscious girl, harpy or siren, some diabolical hodgepodge of human and animal parts. You'll hack off her goat-horned head, carry the fanged and snake-tongued trophy home, toss it at the feet of the pompous priest, the man who has his clammy hands all over the hot, quaking soul of your wife.

Stomach aflutter, you leave before daybreak, stale bread in your rucksack, your leather bottle full of murky water, your knife fresh-sharpened. You're already a mile in when sunlight floods the forest—red and gold leaves, butterflies to match, the last of the season. You spot a russet fox, plumped for winter, memories of the last frost faint in its mind. Or maybe the fox can already smell the misery of January, chilled bones and pinched stomach. You know nothing of the minds of foxes. You've never really thought about their lives, though you've trapped them, cut their throats, made slits in their fur, and peeled off their stunning hides.

Another mile in, you realize you're following the fox. You understand that deep inside yourself—the self with name and deeds, wife and children—there's a secret self that has known this all along. Each time the fox loses you, it scampers back, catches your eye, coaxes you down another trail—trails tramped by boar and deer, faint footpaths etched by wildcats and hares. You think of all the bustling animals, hunting and foraging, prepping winter burrows. You imagine the smell of their lairs—musk and milk and earth. You hear strange birds again, the ones that moan and titter in turns, birds you've never heard in your village or in the shallows of the woods. The fox leads you to a cluster of gnarled oaks, sits to rest, and then slips off into the forest.

The woman emerges in a plum velvet gown, her skin pale as poison mushrooms. Her hair is loose, her eyes luminous, her belly blown and high, impossibly huge. She moves toward you, so light on her feet you think her belly is a trick, a feat of sorcerous swelling—something stuffed under her dress, a balloon made from the inflated bladder of a prize sow.

She takes your hand, plants your palm on her stomach, holds it there until you feel the kick and squirm of life within her. When you pull your hand away, it tingles with pins and needles.

"My time has come," she says.

"This has nothing to do with me," you say, but you remember the day in the woods, the lovely girl astride you, howling and withering and spitting out teeth. You remember how her laughter rang in the air after her body had shifted away. You fear you've cooked up something diabolical, a hellion that will reveal the vilest depths of yourself.

Trembling, you let her pull you deeper into the woods, into a forest of stunted trees, moss-covered boulders, mist so thick you can barely see her. But when she shucks her gown, her skin gives off a sickly green light. She drops to her knees and wails, a sound you recognize, a howl you once, as a boy, mistook for a wolf.

The monster hunkers. Arches her back. Squats and pants. Her thigh muscles bulge.

Glimmering with blue veins, her great belly pulses.

Grunting and panting, heaving and grimacing, she pushes a warm steaming creature out into the world. A limp, cloven-hooved thing, slicked with blood curd—dead, you think. But the monster scoops it up, licks it clean, sets it prancing onto the ground. A perfect little goat kid, frisky and curious, it nibbles your sleeve and trots off into the woods.

Next, the monster births a shoat, wobbly and matted with gore. But soon it's clean and prancing, snuffling and snorting, a tawny striped creature so soft and fluffy you want to pet it. But you know better. Fingering the handle of your knife, you kick the piglet away, imagining poison in its mouth, spit that will strip off a man's skin.

The monster births a fawn, a bear cub, a wildcat that paws at your shoes.

The monster births a badger, a dormouse, a mink—blind, half-bald things that squeak for milk. But soon they are on their feet, sniffing and sporting.

The monster births rabbits and voles, shrews and mice.

The monster births bats that unfold new wings and flit around your head.

The monster births birds—sparrows and hawks, crows that shake dampness from their feathers and flutter up into the trees.

By the time a litter of newts slithers from her, the hullaballoo of beasts is so loud you can no longer hear the monster keening. The air is heavy with the smell of new animal bodies. You doze off, drop your knife, startle awake to bees and flies thick in the air, the clatter of beetles on the forest floor, worms writhing on mossy stone. You fear they'll close in on you, press their tingling damp lives against you, and smother you to death.

By now the monster's flaccid belly droops like an apron past her knees. Still, she squats, grits her teeth, rocks on her haunches, pants in a rhythm that seems to pulse through your bloodstream, driving your own life.

The last creature comes out with a sputtering of frog spawn, a gush of brine and minnows, soft fleshy blobs that look like oysters. A human infant, mottled and pink, frog-eyed and puffy—a boy. The monster catches it before it slips onto the rocks. She flips it over, gnaws through the cord that yokes it to her, and ties the boy's belly knot. Holding the baby by the feet, she shakes it until it gasps. The boy has her eyes, green and alert, a thatch of hair as black as your own. The monster smacks the child to her left breast, sighs as it suckles.

Night falls. A sickle moon rises. All the little animals hide in the forest, watching with shiny eyes. As the baby sucks, the monster withers, shrinking from maiden into crone—baggy-eyed, sinewy. She places the sleeping infant between two rocks. Hooting, she shrivels down to skin and clacking bones, dissolves into dust, whisks away on a gust of wind.

The fog clears. The moon sits high.

You poke the baby with a twig, expecting it to lapse into mist or shrink to a bundle of tiny bones.

But the naked infant screams and pants, eyes bulging—a being of splotchy flesh, pissing itself and writhing.

"Come back," you scream, "and get your baby."

You hear wind and laughter, trilling nightingales.

You pace around the infant with your hand on your knife, ready to slay the monster once and for all. You're an idiot, you think. You should have stabbed her in the heart while she was stunned by pain and spurting rodents.

"I'm leaving now!" you yell, marching off into thorny brush, westward, you think, judging by the constellations. You find a creek, follow its winding path until the baby's cries grow faint and your heart stops pounding. You reach a clearing, hunker in the wild fennel to study the stars. Now you hear whimpering again. You smell piss and sour milk. Look down to find the infant right under your nose, squirming in a willow basket, white froth oozing from its mouth. Though it looks like a normal baby, you imagine misshapen organs inside it, eyes that shoot infectious curses, snake fangs nestled in soft, pink gums. You flee, splash through the creek, run into an oak trunk and bash your nose. There, hanging from a bough, is the willow basket, rocking in the breeze. No matter which way you run, you find the baby, spitting up hag milk.

You think of the village holy man, who claims that a woman's first milk is poison, who advises new mothers to drain their breasts by suckling puppies. You picture him, constipated with piety, placing the host on your wife's pink tongue.

When a wolf howls in the forest, the baby quiets.

You creep closer, peer at his face, revel in the infant's beauty, a flattering mirror that reflects your own features: arched eyebrows, large forehead, pointy chin. The baby smells of peaches and sun-dried flaxen cloth. The baby gurgles and coos. Smacks his perfect pink lips. You suffer a vision, a fantasy, perhaps—the child as a young man, shapely and strong, waving a sickle in the air. You lift the boy from his basket, cradle him, sniff his fragrant neck.

You carry the baby back to the village, tell your wife you found him in the woods—a poor infant abandoned by a hapless girl or, worse, snatched by a witch intent on butchering him.

"We can barely feed the children we have," your wife says, eyeing the baby's features.

"Should I take him back to the forest," you say, "leave him to starve, be devoured, perish from frost?"

Your wife grunts and sucks her teeth.

"It has weird eyes," she says.

"Think of Moses, mewling in the rushes."

"I don't want it."

Your wife walks back to the hearth, back to pickling turnips and stirring cabbage soup. In the cramped cottage, your four-year-old feeds your two-year-old boiled groats. Your eight-year-old gives your shrieking six-year-old a wedgie. Your ten-year-old tromps off to harvest goblin fingers, the last of the pale, puny carrots that grow in the northern field.

You rummage through old linens, strap the baby to your back with the skirt of a ruined dress, rat-gnawed with a singed hem. After filling a leather pouch with goat milk, you stuff your rucksack with bread and rags. You go out to the woods to check your traps.

As the baby coos and smacks, you find yourself whistling. You sing as you change his diaper, a ditty your mother sang to you.

Here was an owl liv'd in an oak,
The more he heard, the less he spoke,
The less he spoke, the more he heard—
O, if men were all like that wise bird!

The baby grins as you swaddle him in a blanket you find hanging from a branch, cloth of fine-spun wool, stitched by the witch, you suspect, embroidered with silver stars.

A fox barks. A hawk swoops.

You find your traps stuffed and bustling: a rabbit, two pheasants, four partridges, three ducks. You stuff as many as you can into one trap, carry them home, and secure them in pens.

When your wife beholds this bounty, the pink drains from her cheeks.

"Where did you get all this?"

"How would you like a roast rabbit?" you ask. Your wife backs away, but the children gather round and cheer.

"We're starved for meat!" they cry. "We're skin and bones."

The children dance like skeletons, rubbing their bellies and smacking their blanched lips.

You gut and clean the rabbit, a duck, a fine fat partridge. You build a fire and roast the game whole on spits.

With your two-year-old perched on her hip, your wife goes back to the cottage. She calls the children in for cabbage soup.

Ignoring her, the children dance around the fire, screaming for meat. When the moon creeps up, when the stars pop out, when owls bicker in the trees, the children feast. The baby licks grease from your fingers, slurps goat milk from your pouch.

"Bedtime," your wife calls, but the children hide in the forest. They nest like thrushes on the ground.

You sleep in the barn, the baby cradled in the crook of your arm.

Your nanny goat, afflicted with some distemper, bleats throughout the night.

By morning she's dead, dazzled with flies.

"There's evil in the forest," says the village priest, stomping around the barn in spotless boots. He strokes your wife's arm. His skin is white and soft, imbued with weird moisture like the belly of a frog. A garnet ring glimmers like a blood drop on his pale right hand. He lives on a hillock surrounded by blooming shrubs. You have heard that his bed is draped with crimson curtains, his mattress stuffed with gosling down, that he visits the Lady of the Manor late at night, entering by a secret door.

"Where did you find this baby?" he demands.

When he leans in to have a look, you smell frankincense and rotting teeth.

The priest nibbles fine cakes with the Lady of the Manor, greases her up with holy oil, blesses the bathwater in which she bathes.

"Beside the stream," you say, avoiding the word *forest*.

"Child of a whore," pronounces the priest. "It must be baptized."

As the holy man strides around inspecting things, your wife can't take her eyes off him—his twinkling ring, his silky cape. She follows him out into the yard, leaving you with the dead goat.

The goat is too foul to eat. You bury it beyond the turnip field. Reclining in the willow basket, the baby watches you with green eyes—eyes of the hag, the monster, the beautiful girl. When you have finished your work and washed your hands in the stream, you feed the infant the last of the goat milk. And then you walk over to Old Man Sprott's place, knock on the door, ask him if he can spare a splash of milk.

"Not for an unbaptized child," he whispers, as though afraid the priest can hear him. "Sorry. Come back when the heathen has been touched by the Lord."

Old Lady Harrow hisses the same, slamming the door in your face. Though the Bonnets are not the pious sort, they have no drop to spare, with thirteen children devouring every morsel they produce.

By noon, the baby is fussy. At sunset, he starts to squall, furious that your finger yields no milk. You take him to the wood edge to avoid the wrath of your wife. Sitting on a stump, you jog the infant on your knee, singing a song your mother sang to you:

Lily, Lily, please be gone.

Don't come near my baby's bones.

The moon gleams like a polished skull. A chill wind blows right through you. Wolves are on the hunt, making a racket, circling closer—sniffing the baby, you fear. When a wolf leaps right on top of you, you reach for your knife. But the beast licks your hand and whimpers—a bitch, you see, with swollen dugs. She offers a teat to your young one, scampers on her haunches to slide a nipple into the baby's mouth.

As the child sucks a bellyful, the wolf pants gamy breath into your face. You keep stone-still, fearing the bitch will rip out your throat when she's done with her mothering. But she wheedles like a dog, nuzzles the baby, and then scampers away.

In the brush you find a fresh-slain shoat, neatly killed with a clean bite to the neck. You take it home to your clamoring children. They have built a fire at the edge of the turnip field, set up the spit, devoured all the game in your pens. But they are still hungry.

"Meat! Meat!" they cry, their mouths smeared with grease, blood on their tunics, feathers stuck in their grime-tufted hair.

Your ten-year-old seizes the shoat, skins and guts it, sets it on the spit before you can say *porcupine*.

The piglet crackles as fat drips into the flames.

Your wife steps out into the yard and sniffs.

"Come in, you wild ones," she cries, "and eat your cabbage stew."

But the children won't heed her. They dance around the fire with bones in their fists.

Gnawing a shoat haunch, you sneak off to the barn, bed down with the baby in the crook of your arm, covering the both of you with the witch's blanket. You dream of the monster, fresh-faced and smiling while chewing a tart. When she picks up the baby, her hands turn to chicken claws. She pokes him on the belly and whisks him into the sky. You run outside and scream at the stars.

When you startle awake, the baby is still there, familiar and weird, his breath warm against the palm of your hand.

The next morning, he smiles at you, gurgles, and kicks his little legs.

When you go out to check your traps, you find the wolf bitch waiting, dewy drops quivering on the tips of her pink nipples. You set the child down to suckle, keep your hand on your knife just in case. When the baby dozes off, the wolf slips away. Birds forage for late autumn berries. A cold wind blows the last of the leaves from the trees. But your traps are packed: three rabbits, two geese, an otter, a red grouse, four wood pigeons.

You fill your pens again. Cook up two fowl and a rabbit for lunch. Call your children, lazy bones still dozing in forest brush. Just when the game starts to crisp and smoke, just when the hungry children gather, just when the baby wakes up smiling, wriggling in the warmth of the fire, your wife comes storming down the hill with the priest, three knights from the manor tromping behind them, waving metal pikes.

"The baby is wicked," says your wife. "My children have run wild, possessed by the evil among us."

"The child must be cleansed with holy water," says the priest.

Two knights seize your arms, force you marching to the chapel, the baby squirming on your back. At the church door, the priest seizes the child and stuffs a lump of salt into his mouth.

"I banish the demons that cavort within you," the holy man pronounces, wafting frankincense and mildew as he lifts a robed arm. You feel sick, dizzy, as though the spirits that sustain you are leaking from your body. The child cries. When you attempt to snatch him from the priest's hands, two knights pinion you, pushing you against the church wall. You try to catch your wife's eye, but she's kneeling before the priest in blasphemous supplication, kissing the toes of his calfskin boots.

Before you can say *nanny goat*, the wolves are upon you, a pack one hundred strong, great dark beasts that shroud the church in mist and musk. You find yourself astride a wolf, clutching soft neck scruff, bounding off into the woods. Spears whizz past your ears. The wolf crawls through thickets and leaps over shrubs. The wolf splashes through creeks and clambers over boulders. At last, the animal stops, hunkering to let you slide off its back. Curled in a sun-dappled glade is the wolf bitch, the baby nestled against her flank.

You take the child into your arms, check his diaper, relish the apricot scent of his neck. In the distance, knights shout and bellow, clacking their pikes together. You fear they'll find you, drag you back to the village, hang you as a heretic. You can't build a fire, lest they track your smoke.

Darkness falls, damp and thick, making you shiver. You try to keep still, for the baby has fallen asleep in your lap. A nightingale sings, out of season. You sense the bustle of wolves around you, a sound that makes you feel safe. Slumped against an oak, you fall asleep.

The next morning, you strap the baby to your back and set off early, the trees white with frost. You feel eyes upon you. You turn to look, expecting a wolf, a fox, a maiden, a hag. You see nothing. When you find a crowberry bush fruiting out of season, you eat the ripe black berries as fast as you can pick them. You clutch your gut as you stagger onward, discovering tiny apples that taste like cake. As you move deeper in, the forest feeds you: wild carrots, sow thistle, clams from the creek.

In the blaze of noon, just when the baby starts to get cranky, the wolf bitch slinks out. After she settles, you place the baby against her flank. The boy roots for a teat, finds it, suckles and smacks. You hear the clattering of knights again, voices carried by wind. You picture them picking you apart with their spears, impaling the baby, wagging it in the air as they tromp in triumph to the smug priest.

You have no idea where you're going, but you know you must keep running, start a new life somehow. Perhaps you'll live in the woods with the wolves, bring the boy up wild and strong. Maybe you'll find a new village, tell them your old home burned to the ground, that you don't wish to talk about it—let them take you in and make you one of their own.

Walking for hours with the sun at your back, you hear something shuffling behind you—wolf, rodent, witch. You turn repeatedly, see nothing. When dusk comes, you dip into a hollow filled with fog, sensing a presence behind you, bolder than before, blooming into flesh and blood. Steeling yourself for the witch, you turn, find your ten-year-old standing defiantly, the one who fell in the turnip field and trembled on the ground—bewitched, your wife said.

"Dad," says your daughter, the girl who wears breeches, the girl who cuts her hair with a knife and knows her way around fields and woods, your strongest child, the stubborn one, the firstborn, who came out screaming, two teeth in her mouth.

"What are you doing here?" you ask.

"I'm coming with you."

"I don't know where I'm going."

"I can't go back."

When she falls into step with you, you feel a surge of love you didn't know you possessed—a shock to your heart and lungs. The baby who came before her died of measles at age one. The baby who came after perished of smallpox at six months. As a new father, you learned to temper your feelings until a child turned two. By then, the distance was ingrained.

When the baby starts to fuss for food, you feel relieved to have something to focus on.

Your daughter plucks the infant from his sling and bounces him up and down. When the wolf creeps out, the girl doesn't flinch. She sets the baby down to suckle.

Your daughter hums a quiet tune in the voice of a girl who has learned to keep things to herself, a melody that makes you think of tiny flowers growing between stepping stones. You long for a fire, for warmth and light, for meat crackling on a spit.

After the wolf is gone, you spend a cold damp night tossing on the ground, falling in and out of shallow sleep, dreaming of pike tips pressed against your throat, of knights leering above you, of the priest slipping the baby into the sleeve of his robe and billowing off into the darkness.

You wake to the smell of smoke, to knights singing raucous songs. You coax the dozing baby into his sling, gently wake your daughter, shush her before she says a word. You hurry down a fox trail that meanders through difficult thickets, a path that takes you into denser woods, a humming place where birds warble and titter in turns. There you find bones on the ground, a cottage built into the treetops, a rickety ladder ascending toward a trapdoor.

The baby wails.

Knights shout—closer, now, rustling in the brush.

Your daughter climbs the ladder first, urging you up into the trees.

When you are halfway up, the world starts to spin, birds flitting around your ears. You spot a dozing owl. You spot chickens roosting high in the boughs, squirrels leaping from branch to branch. You see snakes curled in hollows, beetles scurrying, a haze of gauzy flies floating in a slant of afternoon sun.

You pause. The ladder sways in cold wind. Whimpering, the baby squirms in his sling. You worry he'll slip out, plummet to the ground, but you can't move.

Knights storm the clearing, bickering about who will climb up the ladder after you.

"Hurry, Dad!" your daughter cries.

Slowly, you rise, one step and then another. Your daughter reaches for you. With a flood of shame, you take her hand, let her pull you into the hut. When the first knight is halfway up, your daughter kicks the ladder away and closes the trapdoor.

You look around, flinch at the sight of bones—bones sorted and arranged into piles, bones brimming from wooden buckets, some polished, others gristly—human or animal, you cannot say. Shutters closed, the hut is dim, a small fire burning in the hearth, heating a cauldron as black as the devil's beard. Bottles and bowls gleam on shelves. Skinned beasts dangle from hooks. Herb bundles hang to dry. You hear chickens clucking, a person humming in a deep, low voice.

Now you see her—the woman tending the cauldron, the monster, hunched in a cloak. You walk to a window to observe the knights. When you pull the shutters open, thick mist flows into the room.

"Clouds," says your daughter.

You look down, see treetops. In the clearing below, ant-sized knights move in agitation.

"We're flying," your daughter explains, patting your arm as though you're a mooncalf.

Dizzy, sick, you slump against her. How did you come to be here, whisked skyward in a hut full of bones? What if the monster chucks you out, keeps your children for herself, turns them into beasts, or gobbles them up?

Your daughter guides you to the table, coaxes you into a spindle chair, and sets a bowl of stew before you—a rich concoction flecked with shreds of meat. It smells of mushrooms and nuts, roots and giblets.

You pull the baby from his sling into your lap.

"Come here," says the monster, her voice gruff, "and let me hold my baby."

Though you fear she'll bash his pretty skull, you have no choice.

"Don't worry," she coaxes, her voice fluting, high and musical.

You dare to look, see a maiden face shining from the hood of the cloak, a beauty that burns, slender white hands reaching for the baby. But when she takes it, her fingers twist into claws. She's bald and crinkled, droopy-lipped, two teeth left in her mouth. When she sniffs the baby's neck, she turns young again.

"Are you hungry?" she asks.

The baby smiles—kicks his little legs.

The hag speaks the old language—half-grunt, half-song. She mews and trills, barks and caws.

She tells you to eat, and you do, growing used to the strangeness of the stew.

Your daughter adds another log to the fire.

The baby kicks and whimpers.

When the monster presses the child to her breast, she changes again. Her hands look strong, chapped from work. Her sparrow-colored hair is streaked with gray. She smells of broth and earth and onions. The kind of woman who could chop down a tree with a baby strapped to her back. The kind of woman who could dig a well with a hand shovel or make a stew in February with pickings from a frosty wood.

A fawn totters from a dark corner of the hut. A shoat skitters out from under the table. Small, silky creatures—ermines and minks and weasels—creep around your feet, pressing their softness against your ankles. Birds appear as though hatched from knots in the rafter timber. Your daughter laughs, pulling a badger onto her lap.

The hut pitches like a ship, and the shutters fly open. The air that blows in from the night is strange, thin and cold, tinged with the smell of turpentine. You rush to a window, see the moon ahead, vast and craterous, bumpy with mountain ranges.

You stagger toward a cot heaped with small, slippery furs. You collapse into the bed and sink into prickly softness, tiny claws tickling your skin. You want to leap from the bed, jump from a window before it's too late, but you can't move. Your daughter stomps around the hut, sweeping and tidying as though she has lived here forever.

Beside the fire slumps the obscure shape of the monster, singing to the baby in a husky voice, a song your mother once sang to you: *Hey, diddle, diddle, the Cat and the Fiddle, the Cow jumped over the Moon.*

Arcadia Lakes

Fern was nine when the great rains came, bust-ing the levee and swelling the lake into a terrifying choppy sea. She remembered standing on the porch, watching the water rush in to flood the lower realm of their split-level, her parents shrieking when liquid oozed up through the floor planks. She imagined wondrous creatures out in the tempestuous depths— anglerfish and wobbegongs, ghost octopi and bioluminescent squid. She pictured a sea monster—clammy-eyed, old as the moon—the kind of leviathan that swallowed people whole, imprisoning them in its gigantic belly. Fern half hoped the flood would obliterate her house, that she and her parents would sail off in their green rowboat and explore the world.

When the rains stopped and the water retreated, their small manmade lake shrank to a pond, leaving their dock jutting out over a muddy slope. Blue-green algae bloomed in the stagnant water, creating a dead zone. After their home value plummeted, her parents turned against each other, bickering and boozing, sometimes flaring into rages deep in the night, filling her dreams with growls and thumps. When they woke one morning to the stench of a thousand dead fish floating in the remnants of the lake, their passion for arguing dried up, leaving them sullen and reticent. They moved to separate bedrooms, where they each lapsed into middle age. Her father grew soft and listless, her mother tense and wiry, and Fern descended to the lower level of the house, a dank space that smelled of mold and Lysol.

During her adolescence, she thought of herself as a solitary subterranean creature pupating in a burrow. She pictured herself unfurling new wings and flying off into a warm summer night, escaping the human drama and social anxiety that gave her panic attacks, a thousand shining words flitting inside her head, disconnected, somehow, from her tongue, making speaking to others her age almost impossible. She grunted and grumbled and abruptly turned away. But in the depths of her room, she wrote gut-wrenching poems and delivered soliloquies of astonishing eloquence. She played her keyboard, singing and chanting like a crazed nun. She covered her walls with murals depicting the bizarre jungles of Hathor, an imaginary planet with clean purple oceans and untainted creeks. She painted writhing scaly trees that bore spiked fruits, gorgeous flesh-eating flowers, transparent water fauna with visible organs. On Hathor, the violet mist swarmed with flying creatures—tiny reptiles with delicate patagia, alien-engineered drones composed of otherworldly metals, green simians with moth wings and giant, glossy intelligent eyes. Fern shrouded herself in a cocoon of art, a compressed emotive existence that pined for infinite expansion.

Now Fern was sixteen and stuck—stuck in a neighborhood that bustled with snickering teens whizzing around in golf carts, stuck at a brutal high school where she struggled to escape detection, stuck in a house that her mother claimed was cursed—for not all the small manmade lakes in the subdivision had drained and died; not all the houses had flooded. Her mother's ex–best friend's property value had doubled, for their deck still overlooked a respectable expanse of water. Even if it teemed with fecal coliform and E. coli that prevented swimming, they had a *fucking view* (her mom's words)—not a dismal gulch where countless dead fish had festered and sunk, a watery grave filled with tiny skeletons.

When the blooming algae was at the height of its toxicity, Fern could detect a fishy smell. She liked to stand on their rotting dock and gaze out at the pond, screaming at ducks and herons when they glided down to sip poison. But she, too, was drawn to the sickening swamp. On fragrant spring nights, when moonlight shone on the chartreuse water, she longed to dive in and explore the murky depths. Sometimes, when she stayed up too late, listening to owls calling from the meagre patch of forest abutting their doomed property, she thought she heard the bellow of an animal coming from the pond, a mournful complaint that lapsed into higher frequencies, silvery sounds that drew her to the edge of the dock.

At sunset, Fern rode her bike through the subdivision until she found a wood-fringed road winding along a golf course. Here the air was cooler, the streets lined with large houses tucked into lush landscaping. Some of the houses were nestled so deep they vanished into cultivated woods, but she knew the houses on the right side of the road had a view of big water, a vast glimmering lake that put the ponds of her neighborhood to shame. There was a special house she burned to see up close, a house with stone turrets that peeped over the woods, its driveway a winding gravel road, its forest wild and dense. She fantasized that she'd find a mansion from another century, some vestige of the time before the gridded subdivision. She'd find a kind, intriguing hermit with a house full of ancient books. And then an adventure would unfurl like a magician's cape embroidered with suns and moons.

When night fell and lightning bugs swayed out from the damp lower zones, Fern switched off her bike light. She pedaled slowly up a gravel driveway lit with old-fashioned lanterns. At last, she spotted the house, smaller than she'd imagined, despite its turrets and portico. Light brimmed from a walled courtyard. Laughter echoed in the balmy spring air. But when she drew closer, she could tell the castle was fake, a cheap architectural facsimile of a medieval manse. The driveway was choked with cars. Teenagers swaggered on the porch, beers in hand.

She was about to flee when she heard someone calling her name, a cajoling female voice, tinged with a familiar, menacing sweetness. It was Campbell Patterson, a simpering, ferret-faced girl with long platinum hair. Campbell leaned against a column, dressed in a bikini and sarong, coolly sipping from a wine flute.

"Oh my God!" she cried. "Look, y'all. It's Fern Hobbins. I can't believe my eyes. Did you bring a swimsuit, Fern? Would you like a glass of prosecco? Brice, please fetch Fern a glass of prosecco."

"I didn't know," Fern blurted.

"Didn't know what?" Campbell strode over.

"About the festivity."

"Festivity?" Campbell laughed.

"I meant gala, of course," said Fern. "Duh."

"That's even better. Fucking *gala*."

Somehow the normal word, *party*, floated just out of Fern's thought range, though she could sense it there, bobbing like a helium balloon stuck in a tree. She felt the familiar stirring of panic, a knotting in her gut.

"Uh, revels," she blurted.

When Campbell moved closer to Fern—tittering, cocking her head—other teenagers shifted with her. They were a pack of wolves sensing her floundering, sniffing the air for fear pheromones. After Campbell, the alpha, lunged for Fern's throat, she'd rip through her viscera, devouring her heart. And then the betas would swoop in for her liver, kidneys, and spleen. After that, the mid-rank wolves would gnaw flesh from her bones. Finally, the lesser canines, the omegas who slunk in the shadows, would creep out to snap up scraps: bits of intestine, shreds of tough muscle, slender gristly bones.

"Gotta go," said Fern.

"No," barked Campbell, clutching Fern's arm. "Stay with us."

Though Campbell smiled her creepy show-biz smile, she dug into Fern's arm with her manicured claws.

"Can't." Fern jerked away, felt a tingling pain. Blood trickled down her arm as she dashed for her bike.

"What the hell." Campbell laughed. "I'm not going to bite you."

Pedaling furiously, Fern imagined Campbell as an inverse werewolf. Her scratch would turn Fern into a plastic girl, mean and sneering, sexy and taunting. Fern's dark hair would fall from her scalp as blond curls pushed through. Long red nails stinking of polish would pop from her fingertips. Her teeth would blanch, lunar and shiny, her incisors glossy with spit. She'd lick her painted lips and sniff the air for the delicious smell of vulnerability.

Fern found her father in the dark kitchen, gazing mournfully through the window of the microwave, watching a pork chop sizzle and spin. Her mother was in the living room, climbing imaginary mountains on a NordicTrack, huffing and grunting as though her effort would transport her to some enchanted alpine tundra. Fern remembered her mom and dad whisking her across the lake in a small green rowboat, both parents fast and energetic, brimming with witty banter and tall tales. Now the rowboat rotted in the mud. Now her father, slumped and balding, seldom spoke, while her mother delivered bitter monologues, neck tendons taut.

Fern grabbed a banana and retreated to her room, which was once a carpeted den where they all hung out and watched movies together. Though her space boasted a private bath and a door leading to a small patio, it had damp concrete floors and a mildew-speckled ceiling. Her parents seldom descended into Fern's habitat. When they did, they eyed her murals with worried looks and sniffed the air as though detecting toxic chemicals in the atmosphere of Hathor.

After the horrifying encounter with Campbell and her retinue, Fern needed validation, so she opened her laptop and clicked onto her secret Instagram account, where she posted drawings of fantastic flora and fauna from Hathor. Her recent creation—a humanoid-jellyfish hybrid floating above a stand of transparent cacti—had received over fifty likes and encouraging comments from artists and art lovers around the world. Fern scrolled down the list, feeling the neurochemical perk of elation when she saw notifications for new comments.

Hail thee Fern Hobbins, Queen of Hathor, Empress of the Dorks.

Fern Hobbins is a psycho, TBH.

As Fern deleted comments, they kept popping up, so she disabled them.

The puerile insults, the stock fare of basic teens, did not hurt her, but she felt violated, like some lustrous mammal curled in a burrow, waking to eye-stinging sunlight and the roar of bulldozers. Though she went by a pseudonym and followed no one from her high school, the normies had sniffed out her secret life. The only person in town she followed was a homeschooled girl she'd met at an art camp two years before. Phoenix had pink hair and a nervous smile. Her favorite color was mauve. She blushed incessantly, which made her seem like a cartoon character whose shame was so intense it surged through her hair and clothes. Could Phoenix have betrayed her, perhaps unintentionally?

Fern closed her laptop and walked out into the throbbing night, crickets and frogs going full throttle. Stars shimmered over the paltry tainted lake, and Fern could not see the moon. Through the thatch of night sounds came a familiar moaning—she could hear it distinctly now—a bellow that veered into high-pitched squalls. She walked down to the dock and sat on its edge, listening. Some animals had secret calls they seldom unleashed. Herons could make jarring noises, as could cows and donkeys. Even rabbits, when terrified, emitted shrill screams. Perhaps someone in the neighborhood had a menagerie of exotic pets.

Fern sucked in a deep breath and forced out a passable howl. Though the beast responded with a wail, Fern knew it was just a coincidence. Fern's next howl was better, more rhythmic, with a spooky soaring coda thrilling to release. The beast cried back, a suspended squall followed by high staccato barks. When Fern mimicked this sound, the animal released a series of agitated twitters and then went silent. Fern pricked up her ears. Though the calls seemed to emanate from the pond, Fern knew acoustics could be deceiving—especially since the gulch below their house functioned like a giant satellite dish.

She stood up, cleared her throat, and crooned an eerie lullaby that made her think of changelings rocked in rustic bassinets. Next, she shifted to a chant that intensified into a guttural incantation. By the time she veered into a soaring soprano, she was enmeshed in her music, forgetting her surroundings, forgetting that her parents had asked her not to sing outside. When she paused to take a breath, metallic cries whirled around her ears, and then a high-frequency keening that reminded her of echolocating whales. Something splashed in the dark waters below. Fern climbed down the embankment and stood barefooted in mud.

"Fern?" her mother called from the house. "Where are you?"

Fern woke with a shrill tone in her head—tinnitus, she thought, an affliction her father suffered. She walked outside to get a breath of fresh night air. The green water glowed so intensely she wondered if the algal blooms had become bioluminescent, a new evolutionary quirk. Fern heard ripples and bells, a rhythmic moaning. Out in the water a dim shape flickered beneath the surface.

She walked down to the dock and again sat on the edge, feet dangling. As the creature whizzed toward her, Fern struggled to make sense of it—a giant catfish, she thought, immune to the toxicity of the pond. But down in her secret psyche, the intuitive depths of what scientists call the reptilian brain, the place where dreams and fears and instincts muddle, Fern understood that the being defied logic.

A large organism shimmered in the water, silver-scaled—all flickering fins and billowing membranes. The crickets went quiet for a spell. The creature seemed to mirror the starry sky, and Fern imagined it floating in the black endlessness of space.

A security light flared on the hill, so bright that Fern shielded her eyes. When her elderly neighbor, Miss Pauline, appeared on her deck, the pond went dim, and Fern could no longer make out the undulating shape of the animal.

"Well, Leonard ain't gone be happy 'til everybody's miserable," said Miss Pauline, who held a chunky cordless phone. The old woman lit a cigarette.

Fern waited for Pauline to finish her smoke and return to the air-locked chill of her house, a carpeted cave filled with the incessant chatter of multiple televisions. When Fern was small, Pauline would invite her in for cookies and forbidden Cokes. Now, every time Pauline spotted Fern, she turned away and pretended to tend her overgrown azaleas. But Pauline couldn't see Fern sitting on the dock down by the dark water.

"Ain't that the truth!" Miss Pauline hacked with laughter.

Fern wondered if the creature could hear Miss Pauline. She imagined the beast brooding down in the silty depths of the pond, its scales scummy, its eyes dull.

After her first sighting, Fern waited on the dock every night after sundown, envisioning the creature rising from its subaquatic den, filling the pond with uncanny light. Fern crooned and warbled, twittered and moaned, attempting to communicate with the water animal, but it never appeared. When two weeks had passed, she feared it had died. She worried it had swum through some obscure channel to another lake, in search of an open expanse of water where it could feed on fish and frogs. Perhaps it could move on land, wallowing like a seal or creeping on tentacles like an octopus. Maybe it moved back and forth between woods and lakes or burrowed underground like a caecilian. Or maybe it didn't exist, and Fern was a psycho after all, just as her Instagram bullies claimed.

Fern hadn't looked at her Instagram since that night. Now it was June, school was out, and she hadn't been able to paint for almost a month. Each time she picked up a paintbrush, she imagined a thousand eyes on her, ridiculing her every stroke. She no longer rode her bike or walked in the woods or went to the grocery store with her mom. Her mother, normally a whirlwind of neurotic activity, had retreated to her room, where she brooded and scoured the internet for stories of doom—natural disasters wrought by climate change, new strains of viruses and bacteria flourishing, refugees fleeing catastrophes and war. This happened every summer, when temperatures spiked and the air thickened and mosquitoes swarmed in strange, ghostly clouds. Her parents resembled desert species that kept to their cool, dark holes.

Sometimes Fern stumbled on them at night, standing in refrigerator light, feeding from a tub or carton, their eyes distant, and she felt an ache in her gut, a longing for the family they used to be—her mother a bastion of oddball facts and a genius of ad hoc word play, her father a patient and gentle soul who taught her how to swim, how to bait a hook and pull gleaming, healthy fish from their beautiful little lake. It amazed her that these were the same people who once splashed each other in the water, laughing as though summer would never end, her father floating in an inner tube, her mother swimming endless laps around him as little Fern descended into the aquatic hush, holding her breath for as long as she could, observing the underwater terrain through goggles that made her resemble a cartoon frog.

One evening Fern woke to the swelling of light in her windows, to a metallic sound like a sustained chime. When she walked out into the glow, she felt she was moving through water, the warm night loud with katydids. Air-conditioning units hummed on and off. Fern suspected she was the only human out in the degraded yet wondrous ecosystem that had fostered a new and shining species—some mutant evolved in tainted slime. Maybe an alien had slipped from the waste pipe of a UFO or teleported on purpose, brimming with sentience and curiosity, ready to abduct the first misfit girl it encountered.

Perhaps, perhaps.

Whatever it was, Fern felt no fear as she scrambled down the cracked concrete steps that led to the dock. This time, she went straight to the edge of the pond and waded out into the water. She stood knee-deep, sounds and light bouncing off her. The beast moved toward her, billowing, larger than she recalled. Fern remembered a picture book she'd read as a child, a fish fed too much, growing so big that the girl who owned it moved it to a bathtub, which quickly became too snug. Somehow the girl transported the fish to a pool. Somehow, she released it into the sea. Fern recalled an illustration of a whale-sized goldfish vanishing into the deep.

Fern jumped when she felt a slick membrane brushing against her leg. The beast expanded, sending out tendrils and tentacles, the scales on its back surging with greenish light. *What if it pulls me into the water?* she thought. *What if it eats me?* Instead of moving away, Fern extended her hand. A fleshy tendril slithered from the water and twirled like a vine around her wrist. Hundreds of lustrous cilia pulsed on its underside, palpating Fern's skin, producing a pleasant tingling. Relaxed, Fern sat down in the sludge and looked up at the sky, searching for the invisible moon. *A new moon*, she thought, *a new friendship*. A glistening tentacle slipped up her left leg, pulsing with suckers. Stunned and floating, she gazed at swarms of stars, remembering that for several prehistoric eras, the whole region had been underwater. She imagined primeval sea creatures bobbing in the air around her—plesiosauri and frilled sharks, squid as long as buses, sea worms with spine-fringed jaws.

Fern woke up on the floor of her room—mud-smeared, feverish, itchy. In the shower she discovered bumpy purplish tracks on the undersides of her arms and the pale skin of her inner thighs. She recalled the summer she got stung by a jellyfish at Pawleys Island, her mom treating the inflammation with cortisone and calamine lotion. Her father had used the last of the cortisone on his mosquito bites, and their old bottle of calamine had dried up.

Dressed in long sleeves and jeans, Fern rode her bike to the CVS on Forest Drive.

By the time she got there, she was sweat-drenched and dizzy, stumbling around in the garish fluorescent light. Just after she found the first-aid section and selected her ointments, she heard the bright chatter of a girl pack rifling through the makeup section. Fern glanced over, saw Campbell and three minions making eyes at their phones.

"Only Campbell could pull off frosty eye shadow," said Brooke Lane.

"Maybe," Campbell puckered.

"Just do it," said Alexis Wolf.

"You've twisted my arm," said Campbell, spinning around just in time to catch Fern hurrying to checkout.

"Oh my God," she squawked. "It's Fern Hobbins, dressed for winter in ninety-degree heat. Sounds about right."

"It all makes sense," said Alexis, "because she's from another planet."

"I almost forgot." Sneering, Campbell followed Fern to the register. "We hail thee, Queen of Hathor, great Empress of the Dorks."

Fern quickly scanned her purchases and dropped them into her backpack.

"Cortisone," Campbell snarked. "Good for leprosy, monkey-pox, and scabies."

Cheeks burning, Fern fled the store. She ran to the stunted crape myrtle where she'd chained her bike, fumbled with her lock, and sped off toward the scant shade of an apartment complex—her shortcut back to the neighborhood. She pedaled in a frenzy, taking a wrong left turn onto Laurel Road, which led to a broken bridge, another casualty of the great flood of 2015, now overtaken by vines and saplings. Fern stared down at the sludge of yet another ruined lake, wondering if it, too, contained a beautiful monster.

The bumps on Fern's arms and legs hardened into dusky nodules that would not shrink away, no matter how much calamine lotion she applied. Though they ceased to itch, they tingled when she pressed them. Fern scoured the internet, examining rashes and eruptions, pustules and buboes, sores and bumps and barnacles. She found nothing that resembled her affliction, which she hid under winter pajamas. Her parents, who both worked online, had now lapsed into deep estivation mode, lowering the AC to seventy-six degrees, dimming the lights, and keeping the blackout blinds closed. They left the house only to check the mail.

Only Fern left the house at night, her dry skin soothed by the balmy air. She went down to the shore and gazed out at the dark water, scanning every moonlit ripple for signs of the animal. She trilled and crooned and whistled, hoping the creature would answer, imagining it rising from the silty bottom, flexing its luminous limbs.

The creature did not surface until the next new moon, filling the black night with self-made light, moaning and billowing down in the murky water. Fern waded in up to her waist this time, relaxing as she felt tentacles entwining her thighs. When she held out her arms, purplish tendrils swirled around them, cilia quivering against her skin. This time she experienced a prickly sensation as the organism affixed itself to her, startling her with the firmness of its grasp. She was about to pull away when a green head surfaced, large protuberant eyes shining like opals. When the creature warbled, an orifice opened in the flat, gelatinous expanse of its face, releasing a sweet and sorrowful song. Fern leaned closer, catching a flicker of teeth, pale in the moonlight, elegant as rose thorns. She could smell the animal's breath, fishy with a tinge of ammonia, an odor that made her dizzy.

She sank into the water. Lifted by soft, slippery membranes, she floated on her back.

Searching for her house, Fern scanned her surroundings, spotting the familiar brick structure high on a hill, half-obliterated by vines. She imagined her parents sleepwalking inside. She imagined vines slithering fast as snakes until the house disappeared, her parents buried, fused to their laptops. A swelling of love ambushed Fern. *My parents will die in this house*, she thought. *Dad first, Mom hanging on until the bitter end.* She pictured her mother as a skinny crone, fierce and cursing, refusing to leave the crumbling house—floors caving in, ceilings and walls collapsing.

Fern jumped to her feet, feeling the tension of the creature affixed to her. When she struggled to escape its grip, it slowly released its hold. With a great moan, it heaved off toward the middle of the pond, where it went dark and descended.

In glaring bathroom light, Fern plucked wispy spines from her arms and thighs, barbed stingers that left blooms of blood, which she swabbed with alcohol-drenched cotton balls. She covered the wounds with circle Band-Aids.

Everything will be fine, she whispered. She tried not to remember the unsettling meld of fear and sadness that had swelled inside her when the organism whisked away through the dark water. She pictured it sulking down in the muck, bottom-feeding, nursing a grudge.

She had the irrational urge to run to her parents' room and jump into their bed, eliciting the reassuring tickles of her childhood, soothed by the collective mammalian musk of parental intimacy. But she knew she'd find her mother alone and startled, closing her laptop abruptly, hiding an article about brain-eating amoebas or polar bears dying in puddles of icy sludge.

Fern ascended to the upper level of the house, where she glimpsed her father scurrying from the kitchen, muttering like the neurotic rabbit from Wonderland, late for something, behind on something, terrified of something. *Off with his head!*

"Dad," Fern said, but he pretended not to hear her, slipping into her old room, which he'd inhabited for five years now, getting back to playing Tetris or working his tedious medical transcription gig, copying audio into endless text. Suffering from asthma, her father ran a humidifier, and his room smelled of luncheon meat and eucalyptus. Fern felt uneasy in there, as though she'd invaded the terrarium of a rare and fragile species that would suffer from her alien breath. So she went to her mother's room and knocked on the door.

On the queen-size, formerly connubial, bed, her mother sat nested in a tangle of sheets, typing.

"I'm working!" she cried, as though to reassure her daughter that she was still employed, doing graphic design for a local hospital chain.

"I know." Fern longed to hug her mom, but her mother seemed too tense. Fern recalled the time she'd picked up a fluffy rabbit—how bony it had felt underneath the fur, how violently it had squirmed, how it had left a nasty scratch on her arm.

"Fern." Her mother removed her reading glasses and squinted. "Are you okay? Why are you wearing long-sleeved pajamas? Are you cold? Are you sick?"

"It's cooler down in my room."

"Something's different about you."

"I'm older?" Fern tried to joke. "We grow up so fast. Anyway, I just popped in to say hi."

"Hello!" Her mom waved enthusiastically as Fern backed out of the room.

One morning, Fern woke to discover that the nodules on her arms and thighs had sprouted pink fleshy tissue that resembled the ethereal caps of delicate fungi. The tender growths prickled when she touched them. Though she should have been horrified, she felt a dreamy fascination as she stroked the secret accretions that connected her to a magical creature, making her special. Perhaps the growths would give her powers—levitation or telekinesis, the ability to make things burst into flames. Soon she'd be flying through the treetops, creeping invisibly through people's houses, or breathing underwater.

Now Fern understood that the creature only surfaced during moonless nights. According to Google, the next new moon occurred on August 15. She imagined herself in a white gown, walking neck-deep into dark water. This time, when the organism twined itself around her, she'd gaze into its eyes without fear.

With steely resolve, Fern endured summer days indoors, envisioning the animal, lit from within, filling the night with its radiance. She spent her afternoons lying in bed, inspecting her fleshy appendages. Arranged like a row of suckers, the growths contracted when she touched them. But then they opened like flowers and secreted a viscous pink fluid that smelled of honeysuckle and some sharp aerosol. The scent gave Fern the stomach-churning adrenaline of quick descent, a terror that left her giddy.

She consulted online lunar calendars. She scoured the internet for information on water monsters—sirens and krakens, merfolk and selkies, aquatic panthers that swam up from the underworld to seduce lonely maidens. She attempted to sketch the creature with colored pencils and metallic pens.

On the evening of the new moon, Fern bathed in an herbal infusion she'd bought from CVS and then slipped into a white linen gown she'd scored at T.J. Maxx. She put on a garland of bog sage and milkweed flowers, picked from the feral garden her mother once fastidiously maintained. Fern peeked out the window, sighed when she saw the sun still ablaze, albeit sinking, swirling the sky with pink and purple. She imagined the creature hunkered down in the silt, eyeing the surface, waiting for the air above it to go dark—a species that shrank even from moonbeams.

When the night thickened into a darkness marred only by the feeble rays of distant human lamps, Fern walked down to the water and waded in up to her waist. The night was windless and muggy. An owl called from the remnants of a forest that once stretched from the mountains to the sea.

Fern felt the currents of the creature as it roused, the pond rippling when there was no wind. As the beast zipped toward her, the water surged with light. Quick and urgent, filaments and tentacles twined, probing with cilia and suckers as the organism attached itself to Fern, aligning its anatomy with hers. A green face popped up from the water—protuberant opal eyes, a mouth opening to reveal circles of teeth that spiraled down into the depths of the animal's throat—menacing and beautiful. Choppy waves rocked her as the face drew near.

When the beast latched onto her neck, Fern panicked, kicking and flailing. Tendrils slipped into her mouth and nostrils. She held her breath, suffered a stinging pressure in her head as the creature pulled her under. Fern gasped, but water did not fill her lungs.

The animal tugged her deeper, down into glistering silt, its heartbeat pulsing through her.

Fern woke, sprawled in muddy shallows, her dress wet and torn, crows complaining in the pines. The pond was thick and cloudy, clots of algae floating in olive-drab water. Fern sat up, head spinning. Nauseated, she hurried up the concrete steps to her room. She made it to the bathroom, where she vomited a thin green gruel just before her mother knocked.

"Breakfast," her mom said.

"Not hungry," said Fern.

"Let me in." Her mother rattled the knob.

Had Fern remembered to lock it? Yes.

"I'll check back in ten," her mom said.

Fern inspected her face in the mirror, gasping when she saw a circle of bite marks on her throat, neat black incisions, pink and puffy around the edges. She swabbed them with alcohol, daubed on Neosporin, and taped on an antibacterial adhesive pad.

"Let me in." Her mom was back at her door, hovering, badgering.

"Not now. Got to take a shower."

But Fern felt too weak to shower, so she peeled off her dress and crawled into bed. She figured she was sick from the algae—nausea, burning eyes and throat. Shivering, she fell into a dream, swimming down through endless layers of silt, searching for the creature, which moaned in the fathomless depths.

School started, and soon September swept in, blustery with unseasonable wind, hot and dry and relentless, setting record temperature highs. Two weeks before the next new moon, the air-conditioning system malfunctioned, sending warm fishy air into the classrooms, air tinged with ammonia and the odor of burning plastic. So the school switched to online mode, leaving Fern to do as she pleased after finishing her assignments.

Each day, the pond shrank, leaving a muddy margin that Fern obsessively measured—four inches, nine inches, twelve, eighteen. To stave off panic, she jotted records in a notebook, checked the weather every few hours, and studied the color of the pond, which darkened into a chocolate-colored sludge as the days went by. When she couldn't sleep, she studied online drought monitors, wildfire maps, and water-table depth measurements.

Though the wounds on her neck had scabbed over, leaving purple scars, Fern was still anemic—pale and dotted with yellow bruises. She suffered dizziness and shortness of breath. She had hazy memories of the last new moon, the journey under the water, which jumbled with lucid dreams—flashes of the organism's teeth, ribbons of blood trailing, filaments probing her nostrils and throat, allowing her to breathe underwater.

She craved the creature—membranes cocooning her, opal eyes staring into hers, teeth so sharp she could barely feel them. She longed for the cool depths of the pond, the stunning quiet, the soft glow that pulsed in time with the animal's heartbeat. She lay in her bed summoning images, stroking the swellings on her arms and thighs. But the growths had chafed from the dry weather. They itched and cracked and shed scaly skin. Touching them no longer filled her with wistful wonder. Instead, she felt the weight of dread—a leaden heaviness in her gut and limbs.

On the day of the new moon, Fern slept late, exploring endless underwater channels in her dreams. She woke in a giddy mood, only to discover that her nodules had shrunk to pale knotty bumps that resembled warts. When she walked outside, the patio concrete burned her feet, and she gazed down at the cracked mud of the pond with a feeling of resignation. Over the last week, the pond had thickened into black mud that now resembled igneous rock. The leaves of the dogwoods and crape myrtles had shriveled, and her parents had started bickering again, an endless lazy altercation that reminded Fern of the passionless chants of aged monks.

She longed to escape the house, to ride her bike for hours until she came upon lush terrain—fertile meadows and dewy forests trickling with cool streams—but meteorologists had presaged a scorcher. Though she couldn't bear another day in front of her laptop, Fern returned to her room and opened her online assignments, a list of pointless busywork punctuated by teachers chattering on Microsoft Teams, berating sluggish students who could no longer concentrate. Everybody looked ghoulish and disheveled, even Campbell Patterson, bags swelling under her made-up eyes. Fern tried to focus on algebra, to lose herself in the cold elegance of an equation, but she found herself brooding over the creature again. She imagined rainstorms—wild and pounding—lashing against the packed dry earth. She pictured the lakebed filling up with clean water, saw herself swan diving from the dock, breaking the crystalline surface, and darting to the bottom, where fish flickered in the gloom.

The sunset seemed to go on and on, an obnoxious orange glare. Fern recalled the evenings of her childhood when the lake mirrored the sky and she floated between two magical worlds in the little green rowboat, her parents sipping wine from plastic cups. She pictured the creature, tucked like a ghost crab in a moist hole, waiting for darkness to fall. She recalled a video in which an octopus had escaped a tank in a lab, climbing over rocks, pulling itself across the sand with its tentacles, and then plunging into the sea.

When, at last, the sun slipped below the tree line, Fern walked out into the night, the air dry and cool. She took the concrete steps down to the pond bed, where dried silt crumbled beneath her feet. Moving toward the deeper part of the bed, she scanned the ground with her phone flashlight—looking, she realized, for a corpse—a mass of shriveled membranes, desiccated fins, and wispy bones. In the alluvial soil she detected a multitude of glittering flecks—quartz or some other sparkling mineral, reflecting the faint porch light. She kneeled to collect a specimen, plucking a speck of light from the soil, thin and flexible like a sequin—a scale. Thousands sparkled around her, the skin of the creature, she realized, scattered in the soil.

Had the beast molted, she wondered, morphing into another form? She pictured a giant frog hopping off toward the scent of water. She imagined a winged reptile, pteranodon-like, circling above a primordial forest. Or had the animal died and, boneless like a cephalopod, rotted away in the slime, leaving nothing behind but its shiny scales?

Fern heard a chime so faint she thought it was a memory of the creature's call. The sound came from the deepest part of the pond bed, where a single shimmering puddle remained. Fern walked over and kneeled before the scant body of water, gasping when she saw a silver blob surface, veiny and translucent, a clot of red tissue at its core. Though she had no idea what it was, the organism glistened with life, bobbing and glowing in the tiny pool. She ran to the shed for her old plastic bucket, the one in which she'd trapped frogs, lizards, and fish, taking them inside to nurture in a tank. Some of them had died, leaving her with a queasy meld of guilt and grief. But others had lived, growing larger, and Fern had released them back to nature, cheering them on as they swam or hopped away.

In the shed, she rummaged behind her father's old fishing gear, found the blue-striped tin bucket on a shelf between a cricket basket and a tackle box. She swiped spiderwebs from it and ran back toward the puddle, fearing the blob would be gone, the puddle dark or drained.

But the organism was still there, floating and luminous, alive. She dipped her bucket, scooped it up, and carried it back to her room.

She planned to retrieve her old aquarium from the garage, equip it with pumps and filters, keep the water at optimal temperature. But she sat for a spell, watching the organism spin in the water, listening for the high ring of its song.

The Mothers

Kate can see the children from the window of her cabin, eight wearing papier-mâché animal masks—six dancing in the meadow, two standing off to the side (a fox and some snub-snouted weasel). Kate recognizes the fox's brown hair— her daughter, Ivy, slouching, cocking her head as she listens to the other child.

Kate pictures the pack streaking down to the creek—Darwin, Zoe, Benj, Elijah, Ivy, and Rikki, the small girl with huge eyes. *Are there actually eight children?* Kate wonders before returning to her horror screenplay about the demonic dog, the part where the portal to hell opens behind the growling Boston terrier. After struggling all morning to make the scene ominous, not comic, Kate replaces *portal to hell* with *hellhole*, but that sounds even more ridiculous. She needs a walk, fresh air. She grabs her bag, rushes out into the shimmering day.

She lights a joint as soon as she gets to the abandoned shack, a rust-roofed raw-timber building hemmed in with feral bamboo. Smoking, she contemplates the situation of her heroine—alone during the pandemic, living in a basement apartment, discovering that her Boston terrier is a creature of the underworld. *Ridiculous.* Once again, Kate doubts her vision.

Glittering damselflies dart beyond the window. Cicadas drone, the sound of high summer. Breathing in rich forest smells, Kate relaxes, remembering that the art colony board chose her proposal among many applications.

"Here it is," says a child's voice.

Kate stubs out her joint.

Two children rush in—Ivy and the kid in the weasel mask.

"Who's your friend, Ivy?" Kate asks.

"I'm not Ivy," says her daughter.

"Is this your famous mother?" asks the other child, a girl, Kate thinks, with a raspy voice and wispy pale hair—Rikki? But Rikki's hair is darker.

"No," says Ivy.

The children dart back out into the summer day, leaving an unnerving bluster in their wake—some obscure atomic disturbance, the disruption of invisible particles. Kate thinks of birds veering off from a V-shaped flock, ants spewing from a crushed nest, moths fluttering out from the musty darkness of a closet that has not been opened for fifty years.

The women drink wine on the porch of the Victorian house, glancing out at the meadow where masked children frolic, straying toward the darkening woods. Pepper, the Montessori teacher who minds the kids from eight until three, drove back to Asheville at four, so the women can't fully relax, even though the oldest child is twelve.

"How many children are there?" Kate asks.

"Six," says Lily. "Right?"

"That's what I thought," says Kate. "But there are eight out there."

They count the children. Yes, there are eight romping in the meadow. Absurdly, the mothers inventory their own children.

"Ivy is mine," says Kate.

"Right," says Misha, her hazel eyes looking larger than usual, as though inflated by her vigilance. "Elijah and Zoe are mine."

"Darwin and Rikki belong to me," says Jae. "I mean, I bore them. I don't *own* them."

"I can vouch for Benj." Lily rakes her fingers through her shaggy bob.

The women laugh.

"Who are the others?" asks Jae.

The mothers call the children in, even though the chef has not rung the dinner bell.

The stubborn children dally amid the wildflowers, making the women rise from their chairs and scream. Six children spiral in, while two remain in the meadow—hazy figures in the blotchy darkness. The mothers demand that the children remove their masks, sighing with relief when they recognize their offspring.

"Who are those extra children?" asks Jae.

"Extra," says Zoe, the eldest, willowy and swaying in combat boots. "That's funny."

"We mean business," says Misha. "Tell us who they are right now."

"Siblings," says Ivy. "Brock is twelve, Elva nine. They don't have anybody to play with."

"Except each other," says little Rikki, her eyes wide and mournful, rimmed with lush lashes.

"They come from the mountains," says Darwin, kicking off his checkerboard Vans.

Kate squints at the meadow, noting white tendrils of fog flowing from the forest, encapsulating the unfamiliar children in what appear to be glowing cocoons. The cocoons ooze into the trees. The dinner bell rings.

Kate types, describing her heroine's cramped apartment, brightly decorated, the colors pulsating, relentlessly psychedelic.

Standing before the portal to hell, the terrier's ears look extra pointy, elegant and diabolical. The portal leaks smoke that smells of grilled pork. When the heroine inches closer to peer down into the hellhole, she sees a bewitching vista of well-appointed interior spaces, all of them more inviting than her apartment.

Kate pauses to ponder the heroine's descent into hell. Is it too soon? If she waits until another scene, will it be too late?

Just after Kate types a new scene heading, Ivy slips into the cabin. The blond child in the weasel mask creeps behind her. The girl, who wears a purple polyester dress, smells of artificial grape—candy, Kate suspects, a substance the mothers dispense sparingly.

"We must be quiet," says Ivy, "because Mom is writing."

"Your mother, the genius," says the child.

"Genius is a relative category," says Ivy, "a political category. Who gets to say who's a genius and who's not a genius?"

"The word *genius* goes back to classical Latin," says Kate. "It originally referred to a kind of attendant spirit, something innate that everybody has. You have to learn to access it."

"Hello, Mother," Ivy says in a fake British accent.

"Who's your friend?" Kate asks, trying not to sound suspicious.

"Elva," says Ivy. "From the mountains."

"Nice to meet you, Elva," says Kate.

Elva tiptoes around the cabin, inspecting things. When she picks up Kate's good-luck charm (the clay amulet Ivy made when she was five), Kate cringes. She's about to tactfully shoo the children from her space when Pepper summons them to the barn with a flute motif. It's time for the kids to work on their projects. As the colony's manifesto explains, they will contribute to the August exhibition: "Though your children will have ample time to recreate during your fellowship, the childcare provider, a certified Montessori teacher, will mentor them as they produce pieces for the exhibition, which will open to the public on the first of August. The Sophia Art Colony takes the work of children very seriously. 'Art must *be* life—it must belong to everybody.'—Marina Abramović."

On Sunday, the mothers chill. Stoned, day drinking, they do lo-fi karaoke in the Sound and Light Studio, a cork-lined windowless garret space decorated like a seventies den. In the mellow light of vintage mushroom lamps, the women sprawl on velvet sofas, sipping whiskey, crooning pitch-corrected songs through condenser microphones.

Though Pepper does not come on weekends, Miss Audine, a retired schoolteacher from town, watches the children from one o'clock until four. That's why the women toked up immediately after lunch, to take advantage of three solid hours of child-free time, singing in the cozy studio, a ritual during which the women rethink their projects, jotting notes and making voice memos.

"A communal sensory deprivation tank," says Lily, dressed in silk pajamas, propping her bare feet on the burlwood coffee table.

"With nostalgic music," says Misha, who wears a gauzy white tunic.

"And whiskey and weed," adds Kate.

The mothers laugh, for they have hit their groove, one hour in, hunkering together in the air-conditioned half darkness, recharging for the workweek. As Jae sings Portishead, Kate relaxes, for Jae (a composer) has a lovely voice, what she calls a "passable contralto and a half-assed fake soprano."

Defiling the vibe, the kids burst in, masked and shouting, sending zigzags of restless energy through the room. Misha hides the micro-bong. Jae sits blinking, as though coming out of a trance. Lily stands up, hands on hips. "Where's Miss Audine?" she cries.

"We're doing a scavenger hunt," says Darwin.

"Authorized by Miss Audine," says Zoe.

Brock stands between them, shirtless, barefooted, a dark-haired boy with alert eyes.

Kate spots Ivy and Elva at the dim end of the long garret space, rifling through cardboard boxes. She walks over. While Ivy is maskless, Elva wears her weasel mask.

"What are you looking for?" Kate asks.

"Something that moves on its own," says Ivy, opening a box. "It could be a Slinky, windup toy, music box, Weeble Wobble, whatever."

"But it can't be an animal," says Elva.

"Dolls!" cries Ivy. "A shit-ton of them."

The girls crouch over an open box.

"Language," says Kate, noting a weird smell in the air—corroded plastic, moldy cloth, some sharp petrochemical scent.

The mothers find Miss Audine pacing the porch, smoking a cigarette, her sticky hairdo askew.

"Sorry," says Miss Audine. "Thought a quickie would be okay."

Miss Audine winks. Kate wonders if she knows about the whiskey, the weed.

"They're not supposed to come into the main house without supervision," says Kate, feeling guilty for chiding Miss Audine.

"I'm sorry," says Miss Audine. "I'm not used to eight."

"I get it," says Misha, "but Heather's compensating you for the extra responsibility."

"But these new children." Miss Audine sighs. "They're not bad children—just peculiar."

"What do you mean?" asks Lily.

"I'm not one to talk." Miss Audine takes a long pull from her Winston and stares off at the blue mountains.

Kate finds Ivy and Elva on the porch of her cabin, sorting through the box of dolls—dolls of china and wood, dolls of cloth and plaster, dolls of rubber and celluloid and polyvinyl chloride, baby dolls that pee and cry, racist dolls donning aprons and kerchiefs, sexy dolls with fetishy feet in tippy-toe mode, their breasts sticking out like missiles, Barbies that seem to shriek, *Fuck me now*, their voices both quiet and piercing, ultrasonic and faux ecstatic, echoing in the summer air.

"We don't know who these dolls belong to," says Kate.

"Heather says we can have them," says Ivy. "Pepper texted her. Heather's the director, after all."

"Where did the dolls come from?" asks Kate.

"The house," says Ivy.

Kate pictures ghostly children from ages past, playing with dolls, mimicking nurturing mothers. She recalls pulling the legs off her baby dolls, filling their torsos with bathwater, switching the heads of her Barbie and Ken, and making them have sex. Once, when she found a black widow's nest in the belly of a doll she'd left in the yard, her father burned the toy, filling the air with toxic smoke.

"Thought you hated dolls," says Kate, recalling how she used to pick up dolls at Target and chase Ivy through the store, crying, *Take me home, I need a mommy.*

"I do, per se, but we're going to use these for the installation."

"Thought you were working on a series of paintings?"

"Change of plans," says Elva, her mask askew, revealing a pointy chin, a small, pursed mouth.

In the abandoned shack, Kate contemplates her heroine's descent into hell—a vista of tantalizing interiors, lovely in the distance. But the second the heroine inhabits one, she notices flaws in the finishes and furniture, strong chemical smells squiggling up from the vents. People bicker in distant rooms, filling the heroine with dread.

Hell is other people, Kate thinks, imagining herself on stage, reading from her screenplay, her audience bored, restless—or worse, tittering, amused by her heroine's relationship with the demonic Boston terrier. Kate longs to fill her audience with novel terror, the kind of fear that will jolt them awake, reminding them that they are animals, alive.

Idly following a wisp of weed smoke, Kate gazes up at the ceiling, starting upon noticing what looks like a giant pupa dangling from a raw-timber beam. The pale, ridged pupal form hangs just out of reach, twined to the beam with jute—a foot-long papery art object. She wonders if Misha, a sculptor and stop-motion animator, created it (though Misha usually works with cloth and clay). Maybe one of the children made it, for it is mid-July and the kids have thrown themselves into their artwork, spending long hours in the barn.

With the public exhibition looming, the infinite promise of June has retracted, revealing summer's limits. They're in the dog days, cicadas throbbing in the mugginess—delicious depths that Kate should sink into—but her mind has already zoomed forward to August.

"You sure it won't hurt her?" asks Ivy.

"She'll say she had the most amazing nap," says Elva.

"Why couldn't we wait until she's gone?"

"We have to do it within the next hour."

Kate floats over the sofa. No, she lies *on* the sofa. The air around her swirls with dark flecks, like leaves whisked into the air on an autumn evening. The girls move in an orb of light, maskless. But Kate can't bring Elva's face into focus. She makes out a pale flurry of hair, a triangular face, smudges where the child's mouth and eyes should be.

"Here's the website," says Ivy.

The girls hunch over Kate's laptop, scrolling.

"Stop there," says Elva.

"I've brought the bugs," says Ivy.

"You need to crumble them to powder while I say the incantation."

"I want to say the incantation too," whines Ivy.

"You don't know the language."

A brown haze thickens in the air as Elva chants in a deep, mannish voice. *Old High German*, thinks Kate, *or Norse—something from the Viking age.*

"Dramatic, much?" says Ivy.

"Hush and focus. Don't mess it up."

When Kate awakens from troubling dreams, she finds the girls on the cabin porch, eating cheap fruity candy and doing papier-mâché, swaddling dolls with strips of gluey tissue paper. At last, Kate can see Elva's heart-shaped face, her lips thin, pale, and shiny like an old scar. The girl's eyes are a startling silver-blue.

Elva's father left when she was a baby, just like mine, Ivy said. *Elva is homeschooled. Her mother raises rabbits for fur and food.*

"Strange," says Kate, sitting on the porch swing. "I took a nap. I never nap."

The girls exchange looks.

"Do you feel refreshed?" asks Ivy.

"Not really. My thoughts aren't right. Synapses, neurons—whatever. Anyway, what are y'all making?"

"You'll see at the exhibition," says Ivy. "We're going to win."

"It's not a contest," says Kate.

"Not officially," says Ivy, "but everything is always a contest. You mothers don't take our work seriously."

"Of course we do," says Kate. "We're deeply respectful of children's artwork."

"*Children's artwork.*" Ivy sneers. "Just as dismissive as *women's artwork*. Is that how you define your art, as *women's art*?"

Ivy's mouth is stained, her teeth red from some confection, as though she has savagely fed from a candy carcass. Her eyes shine. Her chin twitches.

"You need to cool it with the sugar," says Kate.

"What sugar?" Ivy smirks. Elva laughs, a low phlegmy gurgle.

The girls turn their backs on Kate. Elva chooses a doll from the box, a potbellied Kewpie made of celluloid.

"Nice," says Ivy, dipping a strip of tissue paper into a bucket of goo.

Howling, the kids perch in the trees. The mothers run through the dark forest, frantic, casting iPhone flashlight beams into the boughs. As they call their children's names, the words seem strange, like dangerous chants.

Kate scans the sky, expecting a full moon, but the moon is *gibbous, hunched, bent.* The children, cautious climbers, have never climbed this high. The children, obedient and empathetic, have never lingered this long in the forest after the mothers called them in. They hoot and bray and mock the mothers.

"We need to calm down," says Misha. "They're feeding off our panic."

"It's the new kids," whispers Kate. "They seem a little wild."

"Undisciplined," says Jae.

"Disciplined in a different way," says Lily. "Different boundaries. This is a dangerous situation only because our children are unaccustomed to that kind of climbing."

"Right," says Kate. "They could get hurt."

"Mama!" cries Rikki from above. "I can't get down. I climbed too high."

"Sweetie!" cries Jae. "We'll talk you through it."

The mothers cast their collective beams into the treetops, gasping when they spot little Rikki straddling a pine bough, legs dangling.

"Fuck," hisses Jae.

"See that branch below you?" shouts Misha. "The big one. Step down on it while holding on tight to the one above."

The other kids keep silent as the mothers direct Rikki down, from branch to branch, until, at last, the child weeps on the ground, hugging Jae's legs.

"Gravity," she cries. "I love you now. But not while I was in the sky."

The other children linger in the trees, shrouded in glowing fog, yodeling intricate harmonies that stun the mothers. The mothers sit on the ground and stare at the moon. Humming softly, Rikki crawls into Jae's lap. When the singing stops, the mothers jump to their feet, anxious and ashamed.

The children choose this moment to float down from their heights, each child enveloped in a luminous pod of mist.

Shadowy, laughing, Elva and Brock scamper off into the woods.

That night in the cabin, Kate and Ivy argue—Kate exhausted, sprawled on the couch; Ivy amped up, pacing around her mother.

"Tell me right now," demands Kate. "How did you float down like that?"

"Float down like what?"

"Enough with the BS."

"Climbing equipment, hooks, and retractable ropes. It's not rocket science. Brock and Elva do it all the time. Their grandfather worked for a lumber company."

"It was dangerous. You don't know how to climb."

"I do now."

"I forbid it."

"Whatever."

"And the singing. What were you singing?"

"Folk songs."

"What language?"

"I don't know—Gaelic?"

Their argument becomes a labyrinth of words entrapping them. They traverse the same twisted passageways over and over. Kate jumps from the couch and yells. Furious, Ivy bugs her eyes and puffs her cheeks. She stomps off to her room and slams the door.

Dizzy, Kate falls into bed. The night thickens outside the cabin. Kate can feel the wildness of the woods pressing in on them—owls swooping, the coyote pack sniffing the air for prey, crickets and katydids calling, a loud red pulse.

"Mama," Ivy says, hovering in the darkness.

The child wriggles in beside Kate, warm and fidgety.

"I'm sorry," says Ivy. "I love you."

Pepper, dressed in paint-spattered overalls and work boots, a flute in her pocket, keeps glancing at the barn, where the children work on their projects. Pepper has a purple-streaked pageboy. Pepper has a tattoo of Lowly Worm on her slender bicep.

"The new children aren't dangerous," she assures the mothers. "The kids are collaborating, doing amazing work."

"What about the tree-climbing incident?" asks Kate.

"Try accustoming yourselves to shifting boundaries," says Pepper, "as the children learn new skills."

"Like climbing into the troposphere," says Misha.

"They were pretty high up?" says Pepper.

"Literally in the clouds," says Lily.

"The children mocked us from the trees," says Kate.

"Which means they're comfortable around you," says Pepper. "Would you rather they fear you?"

"Of course not," the mothers call as Pepper walks away.

"She thinks we're insane," says Kate.

"Maybe Pepper knows we were stoned," says Jae.

"Maybe it was a fogbank rising up from the creek," says Misha, "and the children weren't so high up."

Kate feels disenchanted with her screenplay, as though she's trapped in hell with the heroine and her Boston terrier, walking through endless elegant apartments that smell faintly of scorched hair. Kate longs to write about children in the treetops, yodeling in the mist, but she's stuck with her project. The other mothers complain of a similar feeling. Jae wants to compose a score for a film set in some otherworldly setting infused with haunting folk songs. Misha, sick of her bright palette, longs for muted moody hues—puce and gray and ochre—colors that evoke the strangeness of dusk. Lily complains that she can no longer inhabit her choreography, that she feels like a wooden puppet tromping through movements that once made her want to transform into a lynx.

When the women hear a child bawling, they are relieved by the distraction. They rush out to the meadow, where Rikki sits weeping.

"What's wrong?" asks Jae, kneeling.

"Nobody will let me work with them. They say I'm weak and stupid, a baby, because I climbed down from the tree instead of using the equipment."

"The word *stupid* is not allowed," says Lily.

"You mothers are naïve." Rikki rolls her eyes.

The burned-out mothers need a break, so they microdose while sipping light spritzy drinks made of moonshine and mineral water. Giddy, the mothers wind through the woods. The forest throbs, deep and strange. A flock of grackle whirs up from a live oak. A fox slinks off into blooming brush. The mothers spot a large pupa, high in a pine, dangling starkly from a dead branch. The women blink, noting numerous pupae in the treetops. They stand for a spell, marveling, wondering what species of lepidoptera will hatch from the large chrysalises.

"Perhaps they're not as big as they look," says Misha. "Our eyes getting wonky with age."

"Maybe they're not so high up," says Lily, "our depth perception affected by the shrooms."

"Look." Jae points at a pupa hanging from the branch of a small poplar.

In the slanted light, the women detect a dark shape inside the translucent shell—a bony, crumpled creature, wriggling, scheming to break free.

Recalling the pupal object she found in the shack, recalling the girls doing papier-mâché on the porch, Kate feels dizzy.

"I think the children made them," she says.

The other mothers shake their heads.

Kate leads them to the shack, points at the pupa dangling from the rafter, which looks cruder than the others, thick and opaque, its ridges less elegant.

"An early attempt," she says.

Lily stands on an overturned bucket and tears the object from the rafter.

Squatting, the mothers poke at the pupa. They pick up rusted nails from the floor and tear the object open, discovering a misshapen doll, its plastic melted but not charred, as though disintegrated by acid.

Unsettled, the mothers sit on the porch, downing fizzy cocktails, dreading the moment when Pepper will emerge from the barn and play a high, sharp note on her flute, signifying her departure. When the afternoon sun glares onto the porch, the mothers take refuge in the fragrant shade of the pergola. They regard the old Victorian house, meandering and gray in the stark light, its porch fringed with rhododendrons. They admire the pitched roof, the Gothic turrets, the ornate woodwork.

"Fuck, look." Jae points.

Pupae dangle from the eaves and turrets. Pupae dangle from the branches of the dogwood trees. In the skewed light of late afternoon, the mothers can see dark bent creatures inside the chrysalises, intricate and spiny. As though to punctuate the mothers' unease, Pepper blasts a loud F-sharp on her flute, sustained and pulsing.

The children gambol in the meadow, leaping higher than they usually do. The dinner bell rings. Voices strained, the mothers call the children in. When the children linger in the meadow, the women feel relieved. They go in for dinner, enjoying the quiet of the dining room, with its brutalist chandelier and modernist paintings, its amoeba-shaped tables and Arne Jacobsen chairs. The women sit in silence as college kids from Asheville serve them arugula salad with locally foraged chanterelles.

Sighing, the mothers pick at their salads. Kate cannot taste the mushrooms, wood-smoked and doused in sorghum vinaigrette. When the waiters present a bottle of prosecco, the mothers hold out their glasses. Their afternoon buzz is wearing thin. They have no appetite. There is nothing left to do with the evening but drink.

Just as the waiters bring in grilled trout, just as the windows go dark, just as the coyote pack makes a ruckus in the forest, the children rush in, chattery and kinetic, smeared with paint and dirt, tainting the room with their excessive energy. They jostle over seats at the table by the window. Perching in their chairs, they eat with their hands, smearing their faces with grease. The mothers, too tired to scold them, slump before half-eaten fillets, wishing the waiters would bring more wine.

"Rikki!" Jae calls, scanning the room. "Darwin, where's your sister?"

"I'm not my sister's keeper," says Darwin, tossing his long bangs.

The other children titter and snort. Their eyes shine. Their teeth look larger than usual. They speak in a secret language, something akin to pig Latin, and make loud gulping noises as they drink.

"I mean it, kids," says Kate. "Where's Rikki?"

"Chill out, Mom." Ivy rolls her eyes. "There she is."

Rikki limps into the room, her face stoical, her arms and neck covered in yellow pustules.

"What the hell?" Jae cries.

"Looks like poison oak," says Misha.

The mothers meet in Jae's cabin, where little Rikki lies in bed with a fever, her body smeared with calamine lotion. Her blisters ooze amber liquid. Asleep, she twitches and groans.

"Darwin says she got mad and ran off into the woods," Jae whispers. "Darwin says she brought this affliction on herself, his words."

"They won't let her work on the pupae," says Kate, "or whatever the hell they are."

"Zoe insists the pupae are no big deal," says Misha. "She claims they're combining folk magic with artificial intelligence and basic robotics."

The women laugh nervously.

"They've been wrapping old dolls in papier-mâché," says Kate.

"And using the 3-D printer in the barn," says Misha.

"Mumbling nonsense spells," says Jae.

"What about Pepper?" asks Kate. "Does she know what's going on?"

"Benj says Pepper is fully aware of what they're doing," says Lily.

"At least Pepper thinks she is," says Jae. "I talked to her on the phone. She insists that rebellion always accompanies true creativity, says she'll talk to the kids about including Rikki when she comes back on Monday."

Sipping whiskey from paper cups, the mothers hover over Rikki, who seems remote, like a fairy-tale child sleeping in the bottom of a well. The women drift out to the front porch, where the air is cool, fragrant from obscure summer blooms. Silvered by moonlight, pupae gleam in the trees. In the darkness of the woods, the children hoot and growl, playing arcane games. The mothers should call them in to bed, but they feel too weak to negotiate, their brains foggy, their tongues heavy in their mouths.

Gathered in the Sound and Light Studio, the mothers circle the coffee table, where they have deposited unsettling contraband: cheap candy, cigarettes, pocketknives, retractable ropes with sharp hooks, and smooth blue stones marked with rune-like symbols painted in glittery nail polish. Though the mothers have scoured the internet, they cannot decipher the runes.

After drinking too much whiskey the previous evening, each mother returned to her cabin to find her offspring sitting on the sofa, eating candy, defiantly throwing garish wrappers on the floor. The exhausted mothers smelled artificial cherry and a hint of cigarette smoke. The exhausted mothers ranted and raged, forcing their children to empty their pockets, discovering the contraband now arranged like forensic evidence awaiting further analysis. The children smirked as they pulled knives and crumpled packs of Marlboro Reds from their pockets. When the mothers wailed in outrage, the children urged them to "stop acting hysterical."

"Little provocateurs," says Jae, "pulling our strings."

"It's Elva and Brock," says Misha. "I don't want to say *bad influence*. But there, I said it: *bad influence*."

"We don't know for certain that the stuff came from them," says Lily.

"Where else would it come from?" asks Kate.

"Miss Audine smokes," says Jae.

"Winstons," says Kate.

"We ought to talk to their mother first," says Lily. "Set some fucking boundaries."

The women vote on who will serve as diplomats, selecting Kate and Misha.

Kate and Misha use GPS to find the address Miss Audine scrawled on an index card, a half-hour drive through the valley and then another fifteen minutes winding up Goat Mountain Road. Dizzy, they step out into the muggy air and peer down a driveway overgrown with saplings.

"We'll have to walk it," says Misha.

"Hope they don't shoot us," says Kate.

"Can't believe they don't have a phone."

They walk for ten minutes before the dwelling appears, a three-story shotgun house smothered in Virginia creeper. Intricate hives hang from the eaves, and the humming air smells of honey.

"Hello!" Misha calls, startling a flock of barn swallows.

Brock steps out onto the porch, husky and shirtless. Elva creeps behind him, wearing a rose polyester dress.

"We came to talk to your mother," says Kate.

"About what?" asks Elva.

"Some dangerous things our children had. Stuff we don't allow."

Smiling, the children pull cigarettes from their pockets.

"Got a light?" Brock asks Elva.

"Yep." Elva flicks a purple BIC and lights their smokes. The children take insouciant puffs, exhale perfect smoke rings.

"Our mama's not here," says Brock. "Gone to town to sell rabbit meat and honey."

"Sorry about the mess." Elva points at six skinned rabbits hanging among the beehives, their sinewy red bodies glistening in the sun. "Been pretty busy today—dressing rabbits, gathering from the hives, foraging for greens and blackberries."

"Plus, our well pump broke," says Brock, "but it didn't take too long to fix."

"Don't fear the bees," says Elva. "They don't sting. Come on in and have some cider."

The children guide them into a den decorated with painted skulls, hundreds of tiny crania forming an intricate mosaic in yellows and reds—a sun hovering over a dark sofa.

"Those are from animals we ate," says Brock.

"Animals that give us life," says Elva.

The room smells of kerosene and burnt wood, fruity candy and cigarette smoke, rancid lard. Dizzy from the thick air, the women sit down on the sofa, a rickety camelback covered in a patchwork of animal skins. Elva brings them plastic cups of cider, thick home brew made with fermented juice and honey.

As Kate sips, the room surges with light, suncatchers spinning before windowpanes, dangling on invisible strings.

Now she can make out paintings on the wall, intricate and surreal: a flying house with upright beasts dancing on the roof, an elaborate cloud city bustling with birds.

"The artwork," says Misha, sinking deeper into the sofa, "is stunning."

"Can you tell which ones are mine and which are Brock's?" asks Elva.

"I don't know," says Misha.

"Because we collaborate," says Brock.

"Who taught you to paint?" asks Kate.

"Mama did."

"Where *is* your mother again?" Kate asks, rubbing her eyes.

"She's in town—hawking honey, buying lard and nails, getting a tooth pulled," says Brock.

"Buying a goat, selling her toes, dancing with his highness," says Elva.

An animal—long, dark, musky—brushes against the women's legs. When they lean down to pet it, it slips under the sofa.

"Dog," Misha mutters uncertainly.

"Bugbear," says Elva.

Kate notes library books on a low table: *A Brief History of Time*, *Gulliver's Travels*, *Tubes: A Journey to the Center of the Internet*. Kate notes a toy box overflowing in a dim corner, stacks of preserves on rusted metal shelves, a twilit forest outside the windows.

Whispering, the children leave the room. The animal slinks off to the kitchen. When the children return, they light kerosene lanterns and hover in the glow. Strumming mandolins, they sing impossibly ethereal harmonies, muddling the women's thoughts.

"It's late," says Misha, making a half-hearted effort to stand up.

"Your mother," says Kate. "Shouldn't she be back by now?"

The room fills with rhythmic clicking noises—toys skittering across the floor: a Mr. Potato Head with a beetle's body, a plastic wiener dog with numerous twitching legs, a scaly metal train with a serpent's flicking tongue.

Speechless, the women sip cider as the moon rises.

Misha and Kate wake up in the car, the forest whistling with morning birds. They have trouble remembering what happened the night before.

"Music," says Kate. "And moving toys."

"The cider," says Misha, "much stronger than we realized."

"Shouldn't we go back and talk to their mother?" says Kate.

Though the women use GPS, though the women drive up and down Goat Mountain Road, though they get out of the Subaru and walk a familiar bend of dirt road, the one Miss Audine described in her directions, they cannot find the driveway.

When Brock and Elva do not appear at the colony that afternoon, the mothers feel deeply relieved, even though their children mope and whine—all except Rikki, who sits smiling on the porch of Jae's cabin. Weaving randomly through the meadow, Zoe and Darwin bicker. Elijah sulks amid the milkweed. Ivy broods in the branches of a mulberry tree. Shouting forbidden words, Benj hurls rocks at empty Perrier bottles.

Though Pepper summons them with her flute, the children do not heed her. Pepper stares at the mountains, their peaks wreathed in mist. Pepper performs the tree pose, standing on her right leg. After releasing a final note, long and shrill and wavering, Pepper walks briskly back to the barn.

The mothers drink coffee on the Victorian porch. For the second time, Misha and Kate attempt to explain what happened, describing the strange house with its vines and bees and skinned rabbits, the sun made of skulls burning inside it. They admit they drank too much cider.

"The slinking beast was just a dog," says Misha.

"The plastic creatures were probably windup hodgepodges made of old toys," says Kate.

"The children were not floating per se," says Misha.

"Though they played beautifully," says Kate. "Sang beautifully."

"Hauntingly," adds Misha, shivering.

"And no mother there?" says Jae. "What if they have no mother?"

"Miss Audine knows their mother," says Kate, "but she hasn't seen her since the pandemic."

"I would hate to call DSS," says Jae.

The mothers gasp, as though Jae has sputtered a slur.

"The children could be a danger to themselves and others," says Kate, recalling Brock and Elva's nonchalant blowing of smoke rings.

The mothers gaze out at the trees, the pupae more numerous, opaque in the morning light.

When Brock and Elva stay away the whole week, the last full week of the fellowship, the mothers feel a weight lift. They hope that someone has made a call—Miss Audine or one of them, even though they did not reach a unanimous decision. Maybe Heather, the director, who drove up from Asheville on Wednesday, got wind of the situation, even though the mothers have been hush-hush, even though the children sulk and pine, speaking little, refusing to work with Pepper, lolling on their beds and exhaling long melodramatic sighs—all except Rikki. Rikki frolics with renewed vigor, her blisters healed. Basking in the sunlight of Pepper's full attention, Rikki sings and chatters and somersaults in the meadow.

Heather, busy prepping for the exhibition, sometimes pops in to watch the mothers work. While the children normally throng around Heather, attempting to charm her with their talents, they keep their distance, refusing to speak about the pupae dangling from eaves and trees. The mothers reveal only that the objects are made of papier-mâché. The mothers suspect that Heather—a scattered multitasker, always bustling, phone in hand—has not really looked at the pupae. Heather has not stood in the slanted light of late afternoon and seen spiny things twitching inside their shells.

On the afternoon of the exhibition, various donors drift in, receiving cocktails and hors d'oeuvres on the porch. A wealthy old couple appears first—the man a pharmaceutical mogul, the woman a theater actor who played Tamora with exquisite cruelty in a 1970s production of *Titus Andronicus*. A famous politician and her goth niece arrive in an Uber. An NEA bureaucrat and a television producer drive up in a sixties Lamborghini. An architect, a philharmonic director, and a venture capitalist stroll up to the bar. A digital artist whose grandfather was a Guggenheim flutters across the meadow in vintage Versace.

Drinking light cocktails, the mothers hide out in the Sound and Light Studio, ignoring "friendly reminders" from Heather. *The donors expect to interact with the fellows and their children*, texts Heather. *Excited by the colony's feminist mission, the donors have been extraordinarily generous this year.*

This morning, all the kids except Rikki refused to get out of bed. The children faked fevers and nausea, congestion and migraines, vertigo and blurry vision. The children claimed they felt depressed, overwhelmed by existential dread. The children said they suffered diarrhea and earaches, toe cramps and itchy eyes.

"They're trying to sabotage our day," says Misha.

"The best thing to do is ignore them," says Jae.

By the time the mothers make their appearance among the donors, art lovers from Asheville and other nearby towns have arrived, milling around in the meadow where a pop-up brewery sells beer and wine. A food truck releases enticing aromas of roasting meat, reminding Kate of her screenplay, from which she must read an excerpt on the open-air stage. She will go on in twenty minutes, followed by Jae, Lily, and finally Misha, whose short film will hit the screen just as dusk thickens into night. And then the fellows will chat with the crowd and attend the donors dinner.

"Where are the mysterious children?" the actor who once played Tamora asks Kate. "I heard there would be children, young and fresh and delicious." The woman titters. "Ah, there they are."

Seven children romp beyond the food truck, wearing papier-mâché animal masks. *Elva and Brock have not returned*, Kate assures herself, *for that would make eight—not seven*. But then she sees little Rikki weeping in Jae's lap, her arms covered in blisters.

"I haven't been anywhere near the woods," wails Rikki, "and the rash is back. *They* did this to me."

Kate suffers a spell of vertigo. Her stomach drops as Heather steps onstage and welcomes the crowd, reciting the Sophia Art Colony's mission—its devotion to the creative work of mothers and children, to gynocentric wisdom and the radical female gaze. As Heather reads Kate's bio, art lovers file into the roped-off seating area.

Dizzy, Kate moves toward the stage. She trips on the steps, bumps her knee, stumbles to the lectern. She has lost her screenplay, but thoughtful Heather has left a fresh-printed copy for her, right beside the microphone. Kate forgets to greet the audience. Kate forgets to speak of the American obsession with dogs, of pandemic dogs acquired and neglected. She forgets to emphasize that though horror has long demonized children to produce terror, it has not fully probed the uncanny relationship between humans and domesticated canines.

Kate stares at her opening scene, takes a deep breath, and begins. When she flips to page two, she dares to glance out at the audience, relieved to see thoughtful expressions. Beyond the audience, out under the dogwood trees, seven masked children dance in sync, their movements fierce and jerky. The air around them surges with golden light, making the pupae in the trees look darker.

Kate returns to her manuscript, to her heroine standing stunned as the portal to hell opens behind her Boston terrier. Kate pauses after the scene, scanning faces for smirks, but the audience stares intently, curious to learn what happens next. Confident, Kate continues, her voice clear and steady as she guides her audience into hellish depths, revealing the vista of deceptively beautiful apartments. Shadows flicker over the audience as birds fly past. Focused on her reading, Kate does not glance up. When she reaches the most chilling part of her story, the part where the Boston terrier transforms into a jackal-headed demon of the underworld—Anubis, snarling and holding a small dripping dog heart in his human hands—the audience gasps.

Birds circle above—buzzards, Kate thinks. A theatrical gust of wind ruffles her hair. Delighted that scavengers have descended just as she delivers her coup de grâce, Kate deploys a pregnant pause, hoping the audience will marvel at these harbingers of death and doom, birds that purge and purify.

As the audience lifts their faces toward the sky, Kate hears the clickety-clack of tiny, motorized plastic parts. When she looks up, she does not see majestic carrion birds swirling in the late afternoon light, but a swarm of synthetic creatures soaring on glistening cellophane wings. The other mothers, seated in the front row, stand up, glancing frantically between the flying things and the chrysalises from which they crawled—flimsy paper shells fluttering in the wind.

Kate rushes toward the other mothers, women who have become her sisters over the past two months.

"Where's Rikki?" cries Jae.

"With Pepper," Misha assures her.

"Oh my God," says Lily.

Out in the meadow, Rikki screams. When the swarm veers toward Rikki, the mothers run after it. The mothers huddle over the weeping child, checking for wounds and broken bones. Uttering soothing words, the mothers shield Ricki with their bodies. The audience gathers around them, snapping photos with their phones. The audience murmurs in awe as the clicking swarm descends, hundreds of whirring creatures that smell of superglue and spray paint. Their acrylic eyes flash. Their sheer wings glimmer as the day goes dim.

Out near the edge of the woods, where the wildflowers grow thick and tall, seven masked children walk calmly, holding toy remote controls.

Moon Witch, Moon Witch

The moon was a hairless hag, seeded by the sun, who swelled up pregnant once a month.

"Slith, Slith!" We cried her name, running through grasslands lit by her.

I leapt over a spotted snake. I leapt over a sharp rock. I leapt over a maggot-blown antelope fawn. We chased a mega-rodent, big as a hippo, that trailed a pungent scent. I passed Vrog and elbowed him in the gut. I passed Zlegtha and kicked dirt into her eyes. I passed Gronid and Krothor and Slonz. I darted out alone and pounced on the beast, all musk and sinew and squirm. I sank my flint knife into its neck. I leapt back from a flailing foot, dodging razor claws. I kicked the animal over and hacked at its heart area. Messy in my work, I yanked out a punctured dribbling thing. Gagging at the pulp of it, I sank my teeth, chewed gristle, spat blood. The rodent was mine. I lifted its heart to Slith and howled. I was the Moon Witch, anointed by rat blood, and the others ran circles around me, chanting, *Slith, Slith, Slith.*

Krothor and Gronid got busy summoning fire. Slonz and Zlegtha gathered sacred herbs.

"That gut punch," said Vrog, easing up too close behind me. "Impressive."

"Too bad it had to be a giant rat," I said.

"Slith works in mysterious ways."

Vrog and I skinned and gutted the game, quartered limbs, and shaved off muscle tissue. We loaded up a spit with a shoulder and loin. We roasted and feasted and recited ancient poems. Brewed psychoactive bark. Sipped holy juice from mud-glazed pinch pots. When Slith reached her pinnacle, I cast off my elk-skin skirt.

"Moon Witch, Moon Witch," my clan chanted, their faces slack with rapture.

I reached for Slith. She scooped me up and cradled me in her bosom of light.

～

I sat at my Lucite desk at Hone, clicking my way through a 3-D model of a minor hoarder's interior, tagging RFID microchipped objects for the truck that would arrive at the bewildered client's house to haul off his extraneous crap. Every now and then, I'd mark an object for the Curate Collection—a talking Darth Vader mask, for example, that would be chicly displayed above a sleek hearth of blackened metal.

Hone *cuts clutter and distills your style.*

Hone *lets YOU BE YOU more mindfully.*

Minimalist. Feng shui. Zen. Lagom.

Client 67A's curated objects would be shipped to the refurbishment center in the hinterlands of Atlanta. A masked crew would gut his rancid ranch in Buckhead, raise the ceilings, tear down walls, salvage all precious wood and brick, and then resurface every square inch with fresh polymers, oils, paint, tile, stainless steel or modernist brass, sustainable wood and eternal stone. The client would return to his home to discover his impeccably renovated and deodorized objects tastefully distributed throughout the spartan interior of his dreams, not one smudge on his gleaming floor-to-ceiling windows.

A speech bubble popped onto the screen.

—*Please don't take my Star Wars figurines. They're worth a lot of money, you know.*

—*I know, and we'll get market value for you. How about you pick three of them for emphatic display?*

—*But they're a collection. That's the point. Can't we arrange them on a wide wall shelf, something glossy and black, minimalist?*

—*Take a deep breath. Close your eyes and visualize your temple. Your Star Wars phase will be more, not less, memorable when rarified. And don't forget that we'll store your belongings for one year. If you can't live without an object, you may retrieve it after a month of living in your new space.*

—*But . . .*

—*A house is a machine for living in. If one's life is simple, contentment has to come.*

—*Right. OK. Yoda, Jabba, Chewie.*

—*Excellent curating.*

—*Thanks.*

~

I donned the rat skull. I wore a cloak made from its reeking fur. I saw the future in its bones.

On the night of the new moon, I stood outside my cave, sipping bark juice, watching Slith be reborn in a cocoon of glittering stars. I saw sacred stories blinking in their patterns, among them a woman slaying a giant rat. An owl hooted. Glowing bugs floated up from swampy lowlands. Some sly night beast watched me from the forest's edge.

"Moon Witch, Moon Witch," a voice chanted from woods. "Tell me what's in my bones."

"Come here, you," I said.

Out slunk Vrog into my firelight, looking a little sheepish.

I arranged the bones of sacred kill. I beseeched the blooming moon.

I saw Vrog wrestling a giant boar. I saw Vrog putting a move on Gronid and felt a flint prick of jealousy.

"Uh, well. You'll kill that pig that roots through the lowlands, eating all the choice roots. You'll get busy with Gronid."

"Gronid? No way."

"We'll see."

"Can I have some of that bark juice?"

"Why not?"

We sipped bark juice. The night pulsed with infinite mystery as the moon goddess incubated new life amid a shimmer of stars. We wondered if it was true that Krothor could see as a wolf on the night of the first frost. We wondered if Zlegtha had been visited by Old Ones, for her belly had blown up with a child.

I felt a pining in my loins and placed my hand on Vrog's fuzzy thigh. He groaned and leaned toward me. We licked each other's lips. When he opened his mouth, I slurped hungrily, tasting daikon root and rat jerky. I lifted my elk skirt and squirmed atop him. He grabbed my hips to guide me.

~

I sat in the post-lunch malaise at Hone, the air heavy with take-out fumes and the sighs of two dozen Simplicity Consultants anxious to escape their desks. People squirmed in Aeron chairs and dicked around on Instagram. People slipped on light sweaters as the office chill amped up. Some people sneaked out to enjoy taboo cigarettes in the subtropical funk, despite a recent spike in hazardous air-quality-index warnings. I minimized my Hone screen, logged into Time Travel Dating, and clicked on my message box. Of course, there was a message from Vrog. I was elated but racked with guilt—I was the asshole who'd kept quiet since our hot night in the Moon Witch cave.

—*That was really something. Looking forward to seeing you in the forest again.*

I remembered his scent, pungent as ham but sweet like grass.

—*You can bet I'll be skulking by the fire tonight.*

Did I sound too eager? Did I sound too blasé? Did the word *skulking* make me seem like an old schoolmarm or a chic intellectual? Such was the chatter of my cyborg-monkey mind, my overthinking/nonthinking loop. I needed to go to the Meditation Room and tap into the Eternal for twenty minutes, wallow in the ocean of my deepest self and lower my cortisol levels. But I had too much work to do.

I hit *send* and got back to Honing. I was in the basement of the minor hoarder's house, deep into boxes so old that the objects inside weren't chipped. Each box was electronically labeled by client 67A—*Stray Artifacts from My Hellish Marriage (incinerate immediately), Pictures of My Kids (would like these preserved in old-school photo albums), Actual Letters (these can be scanned and digitalized, but not saved to the cloud).* The material in the boxes was what Hone called dark matter, electronically invisible, stuff that could never be replaced by an insurance company if destroyed by water, fire, or tempestuous air.

I made a note that six choice kid pics should be displayed in identical round walnut frames, that the preservationists should make sure each child was equally represented, and that no shadows of the ex-wife should darken any shot, however obscurely. *Photos containing mirrors should be scrutinized,* I advised. *Look for subtle things, like a lipstick stain on a dirty glass or women's shoes strewn amongst background clutter.*

I thought of a former client who, after joyously running from room to room of her new house, broke down upon scrutinizing an enlarged photo of her children frolicking in uncut grass. Behind them, glinting in a distant shaft of sunlight, was her ex-husband's push mower, his young brown hand on the handle, his lithe arm cropped off at the elbow.

〜

I longed for a 401(k) and decent health insurance. I longed for a mod Scandinavian cabin overlooking a windswept lake—ostensibly classless but reeking of privilege and hygge. I longed for slate stepping stones that led into an evergreen forest, a soulmate to walk with in the cool dark wood, down to the Zen gurgle of a stream. We'd wear handknit alpaca and rustic boots. We'd gather woodland mushrooms to fry in home-churned butter. We would not photograph our fare and post it on Facebook between links to subtle think pieces on identity politics and climate change. We'd eat by the fire as nineties shoegaze flowed from wireless speakers designed to look like vintage radios.

The west-facing windows of my studio apartment blazed with light, illuminating smears of grub and challenging my air-conditioning unit. My furnishings, mindfully curated knockoffs of high-design fetish objects, succumbed to entropy: peeling walnut veneer, molded plastic coming unglued from tarnished hairpin legs, a chunky-knit poly-wool rug shedding like a sick sheep. Accent pillows hid stains on the cushions of my prize "piece"—a thrifted space-age sofa I couldn't afford to have reupholstered. I needed at least twenty minutes of yoga to unblock my chi, but how could I concentrate in this seven-hundred-square-foot cube, where I often imagined myself dying alone? Every object bore testament to my clumsy American aspiration, to bouts of feverish internet shopping that interrupted endless scanning through cat pictures, stage-managed social events, and an increasingly alarming array of disasters. I often imagined Ila, my decade-younger supervisor at Hone, chuckling as she clicked through a virtual re-creation of my subpar nest, her minimally padded skeleton draped in three-ply silk.

Instead of throwing myself into a nervous fit of tidying, I sat down at my desk and held my Time Travel Dating helmet like a ceremonial bowl. The outside was covered in some thin shiny metal mined from the mantle of the moon. The inside contained a dynamic combo of circuitry and wetware. The bioengineered interior, stippled with moist, throbbing squid-like suckers, pulsed electrical signals into my brain. I took a deep yogic breath. I smeared AquaSonic gel on my head and slicked my hair to my scalp. I logged into the program, plugged in my helmet, and slipped it onto my head. The familiar map of Forest Primeval gave my heart a jolt. With a trembling hand, I clicked on the Great Tree.

～

Gnarled and knotted and evergreen, wreathed with hairy vines, bearing fruit and flowers simultaneously, the Great Tree was so tall that its canopy disappeared into clouds. On clear days we could see it, zooming up into the heavens, dark fruit gleaming in clusters, inviting numbskulls to climb and climb. Krothor had tried it once, got stuck when darkness came, and spent a miserable night branch-perching as small chattering marsupials crawled all over him. He came down speechless, spent hours sitting in a stream, picking glitzy rocks from the sand. He never got his hands on the strange fruit.

"Moon Witch, Moon Witch." I heard a voice chanting.

I circled the tree and found Zlegtha squatting, eating snake, rocking on her haunches. Snake meat would give her baby wisdom, but only if the Moon Witch blessed the feast, which I did pronto, reaching into my pouch of owl bonemeal and sprinkling a few grains onto her tongue.

I cajoled Slith, the clouds parted, and moonlight shone upon Zlegtha's gigantic, blood-smeared belly.

"Thanks," said Zlegtha. "The Ancestral Spirits are pleased with our offering."

"What about Slonz?"

"Slonz has nothing to do with this."

"I don't know," I said. "What if Ancestral Spirits entered his body first and flowed from his man-root into your belly?"

"What a heap of mammoth dung." Zlegtha snorted, waddling sway. "Thanks again for blessing the snake. I've got to go wash my belly in the stream."

"Moon Witch, Moon Witch." The voice was deep, flirtatious, the voice of Vrog. "Let's get hammered on bark juice and chant until the scum clears from our mind-ponds. Then we can see the deep things flickering."

Vrog smirked by the Great Tree, a game sack slung over his back. He was big and broad-shouldered. His hairline tangled with his exuberant eyebrows, and auburn tufts flowed down his back. His legs were encased in a nimbus of reddish frizz. I admired his sinewy thighs, the frank bulge of his loincloth, the glint of mischief in his hazel eyes.

The Moon Witch controlled the harvesting of bark, and I couldn't take too much from the Great Tree. But I had a decent store in my cave.

"Missed you at the hunt today," he said.

"I was tied up."

"Nothing exciting. Gronid and I caught a bunch of trifling mammals with a net—mostly squirrels and voles."

"Where was Krothor?"

"I don't know. Navel-gazing. You know Krothor. Look, I wanted to hunt with you. I had to have somebody work the net with me, and it was all business. I looked for you at the cave."

"I know. I'm late."

"Anyway, let's roast these poor suckers."

When we'd tossed back a few cups of bark juice, when the low sun lit the fluffy tips of seeding grasses, when the smell of roasting meat enveloped us, we came together with a clacking of teeth. We laughed and wiped our mouths and went at it again, thrusting and squirming and untying the sinew strings of our elk-skin clothes. Vrog climbed upon me with his great musky bulk, howled and wallowed and chafed me with his belly hair. When I felt Vrog slacken, I flipped him over, milked what I could from his softening man-root: a small spasm wrung from tense toiling. Vrog pushed me off him and turned to the game, blackened now—dry but still edible. We sorted the dainty bones between us, for necklaces and needles, and spoke of clan matters—whether the ancestors would give Zlegtha a girl or a boy, whether Krothor and Gronid had been beasts together, whether Krothor really knew what was up with the herds. Lately he'd been wearing horns, following the elk, charting their movements with the stars.

"Krothor is a numbskull," said Vrog.

"I don't know about that," I said, thinking of the time Krothor and I had watched a male elk mount a female. Krothor claimed that the female would birth a calf in nine moon cycles. That made me wonder if ancestral elk spirits flowed from the male elk's man-root into the female elk's belly. I marked the female elk's ear with beet juice. I kept track of her growing belly. Nine months later, she pushed out her fawn.

"You can learn things from animals," I said.

Vrog harrumphed, slipped under my bear-fur coverlet, and fell asleep.

Client 67A lurked in his basement amid boxes of dark matter, scattering un-trackable objects into the abyss. An emotional meltdown could lead to his canceling our service. If I lost a client, I'd be called in for a humiliating interface with Ila, during which she'd tweak her geometric earrings and suck in her cheeks until her shapely malar bones twitched. I thought about messaging our mental health officer, but he was tapped out lately, and I didn't want to cry wolf. So I downed a latte, rolled up my rayon sleeves, and clicked on the speech bubble.

—*Hi there. Everything OK?*

It took him five minutes and thirty-two seconds to respond.

—*I don't know. I'm having second thoughts about some of my souvenirs de matrimony.*

I pictured him drunk and unshaven, dressed in stained sweats, wallowing walrus-like in the detritus of his failed marriage.

—*Try not to sabotage your own intentions.*
—*I have to admit that she expanded my capacity for joy, but then our blissful universe contracted into a black hole. The deeper the love, the more toxic its turning.*
—*The root of suffering is attachment. Don't forget that any untagged objects, unless boxed and marked in bulk, cannot be part of the curating process.*
—*Fuck your curating process. I have feelings. I have a past.*

I took a mindful breath. I mustered a modicum of sympathy.

—We want to help you manage your past, your chaotic feelings.
Decay is inherent in all compounded things.
—You must have chaos within you to give birth to a dancing star.

I pictured him dancing in his basement, a furious jig of anguish, the pits of his sweatshirt dark with sweat. I pictured him in track shoes, rocking on his haunches, throwing his head back to howl. I thought of Krothor watching the alpha wolves mate, slinking around their frenzy, finally joining the ruckus, running in circles with the betas, yipping with vicarious pleasure.

—Hone recommends that you choose three objects to represent this painful period from your past. You will keep them in a black metal box with a thumbprint lock. Only you can open this box.

∿

Naked, full-bellied, Zlegtha reclined on the sacred knoll. Decked out in my rat cloak and painted skull crown, I chanted over a bowl of mud and snake blood. I'd found them at dusk, at least a dozen fresh-hatched green snakes, dangling from a vine that coiled around the Great Tree. I'd plucked six, hacked off their heads, and pinched the blood out of them. I'd added kaolin from the creek bank, a sprinkling of skullcap. I rubbed this gory porridge around the plump knot of Zlegtha's navel.

"Slith, Slith," I chanted, and the round goddess beamed down her silver. I praised the moon, who blessed the sacred bellies of women. I beseeched the Ancestral Spirits to shape a healthy child.

"A boy!" yelled Slonz, drunk off tree bark and squirrelly in the shadows.

"Or a girl," I said, "to carry the flame of life."

Slonz and Vrog whispered and stumbled toward us.

"May she receive a man-root and be plied with ancestral light," said Vrog, stepping into the moonlight with his cup. Sniggering, Slonz crouched behind him.

"Great Slith," I said, mustering my most solemn priestess voice. "Forgive these mortal men their foolishness. Having not the miracle of life within them, they disrespect your power."

"Women are empty vessels," Slonz spat. "And men pump them up with light."

"Bullshit." Zlegtha sat up. "I can feel the Old Ones swarming inside me. They have nothing to do with you, Slonz."

Zlegtha waddled off toward her hut.

"A bad case of gas!" Slonz shouted after her.

"Don't follow me, Slonz." Zlegtha waved her hatchet in the air.

I circled the Great Tree, noting diseased bare spots where someone (not me) had stripped too much bark away.

"Slonz," I hissed. "And Vrog."

"At your service." Vrog slunk around the tree.

"Have you been stealing bark?" I asked.

"Stealing? Does the Great Tree belong to you?"

"I'm the damn Moon Witch. I'm the one who controls the harvesting of bark."

"Who says?"

"It is known."

"Cool down. I won't take any more, promise."

Vrog pressed his hot body against my back, slipped his arms around me. One hand found a thigh, another a breast. Grunting, he thrust his man-root against my spine.

"Come on," he said. "Let's drink more bark juice and chant until the scum clears from our mind-ponds."

"You've already used that line."

"Only because I meant it."

Vrog felt too hot. He smelled like he'd been grappling with a half-dead dingo.

"Not tonight."

I tugged away from him, grabbed my herb pouch, and ran into the forest. I heard Vrog panting behind me, but he was wasted on bark juice and not the best woodsman. I splashed through the creek, darted up a thin path, and walked along a ridge.

"Moon Witch, Moon Witch," Vrog pleaded. He soon lost my scent and scrambled south through thick brush.

Heading down toward the stream, I came upon a glen I'd never seen—edged between two rows of poplars, lush with tall grass, warm with the breath of sleeping elk.

Antlered, Krothor popped up from the grass and beckoned me.

"Their den," he whispered. "First night I've followed them here."

"Where's Gronid?" I sat down.

"Not one to stray too far from her hut."

I offered my bladder of bark juice. Krothor, odd and small with mismatched eyes (one brown, one green), took a smooth swig. We whispered about elk migrations. We spoke of what might lie beyond the mountains we'd never crossed. We discussed Slith and the recent blasphemies of Vrog and Slonz. We opined that Ancestral Spirits entered the bodies of both men and women to make a baby whole.

"How did Vrog and Slonz get wind of this?" I asked him.

"It's probably my fault," he said. "I tend to babble when I'm in a trance."

"Or it could be mine. I mentioned the idea to Zlegtha once. Maybe they overheard."

We listened to the crickets. We watched bats cut their jagged way through the moonlight. A mutual mood wove around us like spider silk, cocooning us together. We reached for each other. Krothor's mouth tasted of fermented plums, and his hands were soft and deft. We slipped off our elk skins. Our bodies glowed, filled bone to skin with fluttering spirits. We rolled in the lush grass. We tried not to wake the elk.

Afterward, we spoke of the ancient spirits who inhabited every leaf and stone, every ant egg and dot of dust. They rippled through the waters and pushed the fish to spawn. They coaxed dead stalks into purple blooming and guided the herds toward greener hills.

We talked until our whispers turned to rasps, until pink light rimmed the mountains and the elk stirred.

～

I usually enjoyed a voyeuristic thrill the first time the cameras popped on in a client's empty house. Though there were no personal objects to gawk at, there were always telltale signs: black blight deep in toilet bowls, pubic hairs thatching shower drains, dark shapes on sun-bleached carpet. But today, the sight of Client 67A's warped linoleum made me sad. I examined a moisture-damaged corner where a sickly cat had eked out its last days. I assessed navy-and-wine-striped wallpaper and flaky popcorn ceilings. I descended into the basement and noted mildew-spotted cinder-block walls. I stared into the pores of a rusted floor drain and wondered what lurked below.

I pulled myself away from the computer screen. Autumn weather had finally come to Atlanta, deep in November, and I decided to grab something greasy from a food truck and sit in the park across the highway. It took me five minutes to cross a road whizzing with self-driving cars. It took me twenty minutes to get my hands on a chimichanga. It took me another ten to find an empty bench.

The park was crammed cheek by jowl with humans, and every human had a dog. Large loping hounds and spastic terriers and floppy-eared spaniels. Slavish retrievers and puffy collies and chihuahuas so small and frail-looking that they probably needed a climatically controlled terrarium to stay alive. Dogs converged into tangles of barking and flew apart again. Dogs fetched sticks and leapt for treats and rode stoically in pet slings. They strained against leashes and clambered up human legs. They licked and snarled and yipped and drooled. In every direction I looked, at least one dog crouched and quivered as it deposited dung into the grass—pellets and loaves and thick coils of crap. Dog wranglers stood in line to snag plastic waste bags from the park's dispenser. Dog lovers swooped and squatted to pluck turds from yellow-splotched turf. One dog owner knelt as though in prayer before her hound's hind, a plastic bag spread across her supplicating palms, awaiting a gold nugget.

The park reeked of dog feces and pungent fur. The air was marshy with the rancid Milk-Bone breath of canines, a species that had first wheedled around human fires about thirty thousand years ago. I looked down at my chimichanga and noted that several dog hairs had stuck to the guacamole topping. I fled the hell of dogs.

Back at my Hone desk, feeding from a monkish bowl of arugula and beets, I logged into Time Travel Dating and found two messages, one from Vrog and one from Krothor. I clicked on Vrog first, saving the presumably more interesting words of Krothor for later.

> —*What gives? Thought we had a connection, girl. I WAS on the verge of asking you to meet up in real life. I was going to introduce you to my dog. Was I wrong?*

Still furious about my failed lunch idyll, I typed some bold words—*I hate dogs*—a confession that, if emblazoned on social media, would plunge me into pariah status, even here at Hone. A significant percentage of my coworkers often broadcast pics of their fastidiously shampooed lapdogs, perching them on high-end design objects in crude displays of conspicuous consumption. I went further:

—Let me guess, a black lab? You want to be a solid dude, but a little
edgy, so no blond retriever for you.
—How did you know? Have you been stalking me in real life?
What kind of woman hates dogs?

Like a flood overtaking a wastewater treatment plant, a foul
mood surged within me, a typhoon of stormwater and raw sewage.

—Look, I don't want some sycophantic wolf watching my every
move.
—Um. WTF? OK. Bye.

Having more venom to spew, I felt disappointed that Vrog
had given up so easily. I slumped in a post-adrenalin funk. But
then, remembering the message from Krothor, I pounced and
clicked.

—Krothor here, reaching through the tech wormhole to say hi in the
dystopian future. But seriously, I just wanted to let you know
that . . .

Hearing a familiar lamblike gurgle behind me, I minimized
my Time Travel Dating screen. I took a deep *ujjayi* breath and
turned to face Ila. Swathed in golden mohair, she stretched
with ostentatious detachment in an otherworldly shaft of
sunlight.

"What's up with Client 67A?" She smiled.

"Finally smoked him out," I said. "As the demo crew rips
out his eight-foot ceilings, he's safely entrenched at a Hampton
Inn."

"Good work."

~

In my cave I mumbled over rat bones, tossing them into different formations to see what the future held. But clouds blocked the moon and my visions were murky. I saw Zlegtha in birth throes. I saw faceless men fighting in fog. I viewed a misty vista from great heights. Depleted from divining, I ate a piece of elk jerky and fell upon my skins.

I woke before dawn and walked through darkness to the Great Tree, sat with my back against her scaly bark and felt ancient spirits moving through me. As dawn filled the forest with yellow light, butterflies spewed from bushes, and birds burst into raucous song. An elk fawn leapt in brush. A dark bear loped through deeper forest gloom. And then a huge snake came twirling toward me, its spotted back parting the long grass—a gorgeous creature that sparkled with silver scales. It stopped before me, lifted its neck, and assessed me with cobalt eyes. And then the serpent coiled up the Great Tree. I could see it way up on a high branch, eating the purple fruit. When the snake returned to earth, I thought it was dying. It twitched in the grass and whipped its tail. But then it scooted off, depositing a turd that glistened with black seeds.

Thinking I might take the scat and pound it into a potion, I squatted over the tiny mound. One of the seeds wobbled and cracked open. Out shot a pale green shoot. I thought of elk humping in the tall grasses, cougars caterwauling in the underbrush, snakes intertwined and writhing.

With a thick stiff leaf, I scooped up the seedling and rushed toward my cave. I planted it in a sunny spot nearby, where the soil was black, rich with the red gleam of earthworms.

Later, when Zlegtha's first contractions took her, and the clan gathered in front of my cave, I slipped off with Krothor to show him the tiny sapling.

"From the Great Tree?" he asked.

"Yes." I told him the story of the snake. "Maybe we should climb the Great Tree and harvest its fruit and plant a secret grove."

"Remember what happened when I tried to get my hands on that fruit?"

"Yes." I smiled. "We'd better get back to Zlegtha."

Zlegtha squatted in my cave, gnawing a black snakeroot and crying for her mother.

"She's not even close," said Gronid, "and making a fuss already."

The men drank bark juice outside by the fire, Slonz and Vrog already wasted, yelling crudities at the moon.

I unrolled the elk skin that hung from a branch over the cave's mouth. I lit torches and pounded sacred herbs. I stuck my fingers inside Zlegtha and found her womb still closed.

Zlegtha paced and squatted. Zlegtha ate raspberry leaves and beseeched her ancestors. At last, her contractions quickened, and we painted her belly with snake blood and clay. We chanted ancient words—*zunga grago linguim vra*—scraps of lost language from the Old Ones.

"What's going on in there?" shouted Slonz. I could tell by his voice that he'd ventured out of the Man Zone, that he'd crossed the circle of sacred stones and stepped too close to my cave's door.

"Get lost," I said. "You'll contaminate this place."

"I have a right to know."

"Cool it, Slonz," said Krothor. "Slith, the moon goddess, is watching us."

"Fuck Slith," said Slonz.

"I'd sure like to," said Vrog, aiming his words at me. "A bright round piece, better than any woman on earth."

I could picture him by the fire, humping air, his face contorted with fake pleasure—an expression that resembled rage.

At last the clot-smeared skull emerged, splitting poor Zlegtha fore and aft, but I knew just the herbs to heal her. I cut the cord and tied the knot and jiggled the infant until it screamed, a long pure squawk of fury. I noted its purple man-root and swollen stones, dark hair jellied to its small skull, thin wide lips that looked like Slonz's.

Gronid went out to the fire to warm water while Zlegtha passed her afterbirth.

"They're muddled out there," Gronid said when she came back. "Slonz and Vrog, I mean, though Krothor has done his best to keep the wolves out of them."

We washed the child, wrapped it in fawn skin, and coaxed it toward Zlegtha's nipple.

Just as the infant got the hang of suckling, Slonz ripped off the curtain that kept the night demons out of my cave, the Wicked Ones that rollicked in smoke and vapor and guided mosquitoes to young blood. Vrog stumbled behind Slonz, while Krothor fretted in the moonlight, beyond my circle of stones.

"I want to see my baby," slurred Slonz.

"*Your* baby?" said Zlegtha. "That's numbskull talk."

"Go on," urged Vrog. "It's your right, remember."

Slonz blundered through my cave, kicking over herb pots. Slonz broke through three concentric circles of sacred bones and snatched the infant from Zlegtha's arms.

The poor woman shrieked and wailed.

"It's mine," Slonz hissed. "I can see it in its mouth and eyes."

When he dangled the baby before Vrog, its fawn skin slipped off.

"A boy!" Slonz cried, dancing so hard he whipped up dust. The baby's head wobbled on its delicate neck.

"Watch it, Slonz," I warned, trying to keep my voice from breaking. "You're going to hurt him. You've got to hold him the right way."

"What do you know? You're a scam," he spat. "Moon Witch, Moon Witch," he chanted sarcastically, and Vrog joined him in his taunting.

Laughing, Vrog rifled through my cave for tree bark, slashing sacks of herbs with his flint.

"Easy now," said Krothor, who'd stepped into the cave.

Wearing the new antlers he'd polished with bear fat, Krothor held his spear aloft. "Hand the child back to Zlegtha."

That's when Vrog slipped up behind Krothor and pressed his flint against his throat.

"Drop the damn spear," Vrog hissed.

Krothor dropped it. When Slonz stooped for the spear, the baby swung head-down like a slain rabbit and howled, its lips rubbery with rage. It oozed black shit that dribbled down Slonz's thigh.

"Fuck," said Slonz. "Clean this up, Zlegtha." He handed the child back to his mother.

"Off you go, numbskull," Vrog said. "And take the damn Moon Witch with you."

They marched us out of the cave. They marched us around the Great Tree and down the forest path. They marched us through the meadow and into the Strange Woods, which smelled of wolf musk and fresh carrion. There they left us, wolves yowling as they caught our scent, whirling in circles around us.

I watched Client 67A's Reveal on my screen at Hone. Simplicity Consultants never attended Reveals, only trained Hospitality Liaisons, fake festive people with blinding TV smiles and the sharklike bonhomie of pharmaceutical reps. Since the Hone cameras didn't pop on until the clients were out, I'd never seen Client 67A, whom I'd pictured as a bald sweaty dumpling of a man. I was shocked to see a tall man with a flop of gray bangs, an aging hipster in a rumpled vintage suit. Most of his clothes had been curated and dry-cleaned, meticulously arranged in a so-called closet that was really a small room for clothes.

Client 67A clutched a dented Samsonite that held the last vestiges of his squalid life, and I winced as I watched Ophelia, the female Hospitality Liaison, coax it out of his grip.

"We'll get these in tip-top shape and return them to you tomorrow." She smiled.

"But," muttered Client 67A.

"Don't worry. All medications and essential toiletries will be removed first."

"Groove with the flow state," said the male Hospitality Liaison, "and unshackle your mind." His name was Blaze. His suit was Armani. His eyes matched his ocean-blue tie.

The Hospitality Liaisons led Client 67A into his dazzling new living room—exposed rafters of salvaged heart pine, the sunny glint of huge windows and glass patio doors, a soaring stone fireplace emblazoned with the client's meticulously polished Darth Vader mask. A bottle of Roederer Cristal Brut chilled in an ice bucket. The client's refinished Eames chairs hobnobbed with a de Sede sectional that curled around a brutalist coffee table. With a spasm of smile, Client 67A collapsed into a postmodern lounge chair. He gazed at the Darth Vader mask as though waiting for it to command his next move.

"I think a glass of bubbly is in order," said Blaze, nodding at Ophelia, who strode over to the Knoll credenza and opened the champagne with a festive pop.

I couldn't watch another minute. I closed my computer window and opened a fresh one. Only once had I made it to the end of a live-streamed Reveal, to the part where the Hospitality Liaisons left my client standing on a floating boardwalk that wove through a Zen garden. She'd struggled not to cry. And then the screen went dark.

After glancing around for the prowling, feline presence of Ila, I logged into Time Travel Dating and clicked my message box, where I found a new message from Krothor.

—*Well, that was harsh, though I did enjoy running from wolves with you. I might as well tell you that in real life, I'm a migration engineer. Are you interested in meeting up in our ruined old world or should we try another module (I don't think we'd fare too well with the Stone Age set again)?*

Oh, how I wanted to meet the real life Krothor, whom I pictured as a healthy man with an earnest face and a tasteful field jacket. Athletic, but not a jock. Sensitive, but no wuss. Cognizant of gender politics without being a smarmy faux feminist who lectured me on Judith Butler while rhapsodizing about his threesome fantasies (two women, one man). But I wasn't ready for that first encounter in a safe space, probably an overheated coffee shop where I'd consume too much caffeine and overthink every remark and worry about my weight and the visibility of my skin flaws. And if I wasn't attracted to him (which would become apparent immediately, as it always did), every minute would be excruciating, the blight of disappointment hardening my heart like sclerosis as I made distracted small talk and plotted my escape.

—*Let's try a different module—another time, another place. Anything except the future.*

∼

A stone house upon a hill. A fringe of cold, dark wood. A dead meadow below, full of waist-high tawny thistle.

I wore a fur-fringed wool gown that weighed twelve pounds, its hem dotted with burrs, for I'd been gathering herbs in the meadow. In my hearth, I had a rabbit on a spit, an iron cauldron bubbling with a tonic. My sideboard boasted an array of wooden bowls, each brimming with a species of herb. I had a brindled cat and a husband dead in the ground six years. My parents, keen to be rid of their willful old maid, had pushed me into marriage to the village schoolmaster. Though I'd recoiled at the tufts of gray hair in his ears and the cheesy funk of his body when he cast off his woolens, he was neither libidinous nor cruel, but bookish and absent-minded, prone to tippling and dozing his evenings away. When he died, I felt sad but calm.

Now I had good silver, wine in my cellar. Three hundred books filled my library's oak shelves. Having spent the last decade studying the flora and fauna in my midst, I knew the ways of wolves and butterflies. I followed the cycles of plants and trees, their blooms and fruit and seasons, and understood their uses for pleasure and medicine.

I had little need for town, hitched my two-seater gig to the mare myself and rode to the shops twice monthly, immune to the leers of men, the whispers of churchwomen, the snickers of slouching lads. Last week I received a letter—excellent penmanship, an impressive command of vocabulary, an earnestness that shone forth from the taut cursive.

My name is William Cantey. I believe we are second cousins twice removed. I am a student of entomology, specializing in lepidoptera. I am writing a monograph on moth mimicry and am currently gathering over-wintering eggs. Imagine my delight when I called upon your father, and he joked that you wasted your time chasing butterflies. I will be staying at the Green Monk Inn for a fortnight and would be delighted to make your acquaintance.

I would serve him coffee and scones, but the roast rabbit would be there if he lingered until suppertime. And if I opened a bottle of poor dead Harry's French Bordeaux, so what? Who would know to judge me?

I glanced out the high kitchen window and spotted William Cantey rounding the Lancasters' wheat field—black coat, black hat, black stallion. As he trotted his horse up the hill, I noted dark whiskers and pink cheeks. He stabled his horse in the barn, just as I'd instructed in my letter. He came strolling up my walkway with a purposeful stride, neither cocky nor sheepish. When I opened my door, the first thing I saw were his curious eyes—one brown, one green, shining with an uncommon level of animal magnetism.

"Cousin William," I said, extending my hands to be squeezed. "Do come in."

Another Frequency

During the Christmas rush, deep in exurbia, wind-ing along Wolf Thicket Road, Schnittke's Sonata for Cello and Piano went dead like a tooth with a traumatized root. Just like that, Viv couldn't feel the music in her blood anymore, as had happened recently with Lindsay Cooper's *An Angel on the Bridge* and *The World of Harry Partch* and Miles Davis's *Bitches Brew*. Every day she drove from early morning into the night, through new developments that had once been woods, the lawns garish, the trees bare, the houses tall on razed lots. Bradford pears, crape myrtles, palmettos. Boxwoods, red tips, azaleas. Fake stones hiding sprinkler valves. Solar landscaping lights. Security system yard signs. Trellises. Gazebos. Pools and Jacuzzis. Koi ponds flickering with golden carp.

Viv delivered smart TVs and talking microwaves, French country cottage bedding and faux-fur throw pillows, mid-century accent tables and handloomed rugs from India. A thousand kitchen gadgets, Zappos shoes, the latest tech—tech for toddlers and tech for teens, tech for adults and seniors, tech to amuse pets or lure songbirds or keep nuisance animals away.

Ultrasonic deer repellers. Pole-mount raccoon baffles. Hawk drones to scare squirrels.

Stout and sturdy with a graying pixie cut, Viv could still haul a hundred-pound flat-panel screen without grunting or pulling a muscle. But if the homeowner happened to be lurking in a dim garage or waiting behind the door, her breathing quickened. Sometimes her vision went splotchy. She nodded and accepted their thanks. Rushed back to her truck, to the music, to the map on her DIAD, telling her to turn right on Running Fox Road, right on Brook Pebble Lane, and right on Wolf Glen Circle—no left turns.

But now Sonata for Cello and Piano no longer moved her. Perhaps she needed something electric, something proggy— Gong or Magma or Cos—to get her heart pumping again. She tried *Angel's Egg*; she tried *Attahk*; she tried *Babel*—all to no avail. She thought maybe some early electronica might work, some Kraftwerk, some Delia Derbyshire. Krautrock, maybe Can. But all the music seemed muffled, distant, worn. Next, she played palate-cleansing pop, old favorites from her new-wave teens— Yaz, New Order. She thought the simplicity would refresh her, would revive the girl buried inside her middle-aged body, the taut synth player with a mushroom cloud of hair. The girl who'd sneered and quipped in smoky clubs. The girl who'd twitched and tranced on stage. The girl who could both shriek and croon into a microphone, filling its pores with spittle.

When new wave didn't do it, Viv ventured into stuff from the nineties, stuff she'd listened to in college—My Bloody Valentine, Broadcast, Stereolab, Pram. But nothing did the trick that morning, so she drove in silence until noon, her heart feeling off-kilter and swollen, as though slipping out of its fibrous sac. After lunch she veered wildly, hoping that something would catch. The Residents, Yma Sumac, Soft Machine. The Platters, Bauhaus, Sun Ra. She listened to her own bands, which always made her cringe, riding it out until her last tepid solo release on Bandcamp, *Wire Mother*. And then she found herself weeping on the roadside for no good reason, her truck empty except for a crib mattress and a set of shower grabs for a McMansion's mother-in-law suite. *Cradle to the grave*, she said aloud, perhaps to herself, perhaps to her DIAD or some other surveilling corporate entity that happened to be tuned into her inconsequential existence.

She'd raised a successful child with a woman whom she still loved. Their love was a comforting sofa imprinted from habitual use. Their love was a soft and durable set of linen sheets, washed countless times and hung in the sun to dry. Their love was a sweet old spaniel or patinaed teak or antique silver that sparkled when polished for special occasions. Their love was not the problem at all.

Still, each night when she came in late, depleted as though some ogre had sucked marrow from her bones, Stella jumped up from the sofa, jittery with anxiety. Sensing Viv's distraction, misinterpreting it as something sexual, a new primal restlessness that could be satisfied only by another person, she circled Viv with her cup of herbal tea, asking about her day in a false, bright voice. The last thing Viv wanted was another person.

Each day, as Stella worked at home teaching college classes online, she stockpiled her thoughts, things she would have said to Viv had Viv been home. Now she exploded into nervous chatter—the burning forests, the leaking pipe in the bathroom, plagiarizing students, their son's difficult chemistry professor. Viv didn't mention that she wished to descend in a submarine to the bottom of the sea, to feel the black pressure of deep ocean, to peer through a porthole and observe a vampire squid opening its spiked cloak. She sat on the sofa and ate soup. Like a cat presenting slain rodents, she gave Stella anecdotes from her day, striving to sound light. The retired nudists who lived in the hinterlands of her route, who received a package every week, making a point to meet her in their yard, emerging naked even in freezing conditions. The homeschooling Christian mother with six young children who reminded her of the goblinish kids from *The Brood*. The cagey man who had a suspicious number of ramshackle sheds on his property, each containing an imprisoned sex slave, maybe, or body parts in rusting refrigerators.

"Or tools," said Stella, for Viv had veered toward darkness again. "Outmoded tillers and broken lawn mowers."

Viv pictured a masked villain from a slasher film wielding a weed eater. She imagined a fleshy machine with a slick Cronenbergian mouth—plucking weeds with an anteater's moist tongue, shredding them with bizarre interior teeth, rings of razors that fluttered in the depths of its membranous throat. Such images came to her frequently during the holiday delivery delirium. Santa Claus seemed particularly sinister, gluttonous purveyor of the surveillance state, his gaudy chalet equipped with a thousand monitors. Awake, always, in the endless arctic night, munching on cookies, he watched children sleep, zooming in on their little skulls, penetrating their brains to parse their tender longings. Meanwhile, enslaved woodland elves toiled in his sweatshops, their tuberculoid chests sunken, their faces pocked with acid scars. Squinting, they tweaked circuitry under bare fluorescent tube lights. The elves dreamed of lush forests, riding foxes bareback, sipping nectar from flowers. Their pagan magic, blocked in this place, festered within them like abscesses.

"What are you thinking?" asked Stella.

Viv did not share her thoughts on imprisoned elves.

"Christmas," she said.

"Yes. I know you hate it, and I don't blame you, considering."

"I mean, what it used to mean. The solstice. Evergreen trees. Wreaths that symbolized the eternal cycles of nature." She pictured Dionysus, torn apart and eaten. Dead grapevines, sap sunk down to the roots.

"Wine and blood," she said, yawning.

"I know it's hard this time of year."

"Yes, but I'm grateful for the hours, the money."

"We both are," said Stella, who signed a yearly contract for her adjunct gig. They could always use more money.

And then Viv fell asleep, a new habit that startled Stella. Still holding her soup bowl, Viv slumped, chin to chest. She dreamed she was a forest animal, fleet and clawed. Though a hideous industrial roar pursued her, she saw nothing when she glanced back. She leapt over creeks and slipped through the narrow spaces between trees. In the depths of the woods, she found a cave, its mouth fanged with icicles—a blackness inside, a pulsing dread into which she longed to walk.

~

She listened to Schoenberg, The Fleetwoods, Messiaen. She listened to Os Mutantes, The Family, Salt-N-Pepa, and Radiohead. She listened to Billie Holiday, Komeda, Gnarls Barkley, and Curved Air. Bach, Portishead, Aphrodite's Child. Nina Simone, Burl Ives, Patsy Cline. Third Ear Band, Thomas Adès, Benjamin Britten.

Nothing pulled her. She couldn't get the volume on her portable speaker right. She always seemed to be driving toward the low morning sun, no matter how many times she turned, her eyes dripping from the burn.

She stopped at an enormous Arts and Crafts reproduction, the grounds bare except for freshly planted saplings mulched with shreds of red rubber. She wore her uniform without a jacket, for the day was freakishly warm and humid. She scanned the packages with her DIAD, her magic wand, revealing the contents of three (smart trash can, motorized roller shades, a set of Snuggle-Pedic Ultra-Luxury memory foam pillows). Two packages remained obscure, sealed with unfamiliar blue tape. Her scans marked her location, her progress. She hauled the packages into the open garage in two trips, sensing the presence of a human behind the door. She knocked and rushed away.

"Come in," a voice called. Viv glanced back, saw an older person. "I'm sorry. I didn't mean *come in*." The person laughed. "Force of habit."

Toward noon, Viv drove down Beaver Dam Road, the sun directly overhead, her skin and eyes safe from slants of burning light—a nice time for music. But she listened to NPR, an interview with a general, his thoughts on the war. She hoped that the interview—sober, bleak—would reset her brain, making it receptive to music again. Just to be safe, she listened to a stupid quiz show after the war talk, her jaw stern, unlaughing—like the general's, she imagined. And then she went back to her playlist. Donovan, Fats Domino, Gerry Rafferty, TEEN. The Crystals, Roedelius, Klaus Nomi, *Éthiopiques*. The Cure, Bat for Lashes, John Taverner, Funkadelic. Aksak Maboul and Brian Eno. Daria Zawialow and Wendy Carlos. Devil's Anvil. Deerhoof.

She'd read articles on the mental effects of music. She suspected that her brain was not producing enough dopamine, the happy neurotransmitter that had, in the past, pulled her from doom with a melody, sometimes sweeping her to ecstatic heights. Now she drove grimly in silence, thinking about how music had relieved her from the tedium of her job, dulling her alienation. Yes, music was opium for the masses—she'd always known that. It had gotten her through the long days. But she'd never realized how brutal a day's unfolding would be without it. She'd taken for granted those times when, emerging from her truck at night, she'd linger to catch some movement or refrain while staring up at the stars, feeling a stupid connection to distant balls of burning gas. Now she felt their distance, the coldness of their light.

The last house on her route hopped with children, children in the trees and shrubs, children bouncing basketballs in the stark security light, children inundated with their yearly round of toys and gadgets, a heap that required a hand truck. They danced around her as she trundled packages into the garage, sarcastically calling her Santa Claus. A man came out, tipsy and smiling, and wished her a Merry Christmas. She nodded and hurried back to her truck, thinking of her son, Josh, who'd always asked for books and art supplies.

~

Stella had made a rich beef stew, had opened a bottle of red wine. Stella's hair smelled of vanilla and damp bark. Her hands were soft, freshly moistened with cream. Behind her breastbone, Stella's heart was a hummingbird, red and pulsing fast.

"You seem distant," Stella said, covering her accusation with a smile.

"It's the work," said Viv. "The so-called holiday."

Viv imagined the weeks after Christmas, the sparse deliveries and scheduled returns, the roadsides strewn with dead conifers. She imagined vast tree farms, acres of stumps, roaring industrial mulchers.

"I love you and always will," she said.

"Why did you say that?" Stella pursed her lips.

"It's not untrue."

When she kissed Stella, her wife's body didn't soften, didn't stir. They sat on the couch and ate stew.

"Josh will be here tomorrow," said Stella.

"I wish I didn't have to work."

"He understands."

~

On Christmas Eve eve, a cold front came in, and Josh was half-way between Pennsylvania and South Carolina, driving too fast in his Honda Fit. Viv wore her puffer coat, had the heater on full blast. But by noon she was sweating, stripped back down to her uniform.

After lunch, she listened to her old portable radio, freshly installed with AA batteries, thinking that music might sound different if transmitted by waves—lusher, fraught with ambient static. Maybe commercials would make the songs seem more precious.

She tuned into the local college station and listened to a goth show called *Dark Entries*. She switched to a new oldies station, which played some surprisingly obscure fifties tunes. z93 The Lake aired a 1989 episode of *Casey's Top 40*. Kasem's familiar voice emerged from the void—avuncular, chirpy, pedantic. Though the show was distracting enough to burn through three hours of deliveries, Viv didn't feel the queasy pleasure of true nostalgia. She had no urge to linger in her truck to hear the crescendo of Erasure's "A Little Respect." She felt old, humorless, anthropological.

She fiddled with the radio dial and followed her DIAD route, right turn after right turn, until she found herself at the edge of exurbia, before a mock-Tudor house built perilously close to a floodplain. From a swell of static came chanting—brutish, mystical—as though Gregorian monks had been turned into bears by a witch. The music, wild yet meticulous, gripped her. And then a melody wove through the incantations, an instrument she couldn't place, an electronically altered voice, perhaps, something between howl and theremin. A swell of katydids, an echo of whales. Pricks of violin like shrieks of foxes.

She didn't realize how deeply she'd sunk into the music until a surge of static had her clawing at the dial, frantic to follow the next movement. She lost the signal and then found it again—stark oboe and ambient synth, the combination odd and perfect. And then: warped cello, muffled gongs, a woman's deep voice singing in a language she couldn't place. The melody shifted from low to high pitch, trembling between major and minor scales. Viv's mouth went slack, her eyes wet. Listening, she watched the sky darken, caught the streak of a meteor, the blinking of a plane. The exquisite music faded, and a voice surfaced from a soft fog of static.

That was "Star Thistle" by Humming Wood. You are listening to Dim Shapes. Join me in the ether again, on another frequency—you never know where, never know when.

"Pirate radio," Viv muttered, her whole body warm and throbbing.

Googling "Dim Shapes," she found nothing of consequence. "Star Thistle" was a thorny winter annual. According to the internet, there was no musical ensemble called Humming Wood.

"Excuse me," said a voice.

Viv looked down, saw a tall woman in a black coat.

"Do you have something for me? A delivery?"

"Of course. I'm sorry. I had a phone call, an emergency."

"Hope everything's okay."

"I'm fine. A false emergency. Just a scare."

How long had she been parked there on the road in the dark? Her DIAD would leave a record. She might need an excuse, depending on how long the gap between scans was.

She fetched the woman's package—an indoor putting green, a Sisyphean device that normally would have depressed her. But she could still feel the strange music in her blood, her nervous system tingling, making the night rich, the stars uncanny. When she looked up at the moon, she thought of the word *lunacy*, which seemed, suddenly, enchanting.

She came home late—buzzing, glowing—as though fresh from a tryst, as though galvanized by a new lover. Josh and Stella sat on the sofa drinking wine, supper cooling on the stove.

"We saved you some," said Stella, striving to sound light. "Josh cooked his famous vindaloo."

"Mutter," Josh uttered the sacred nickname, the one he'd started using when learning German in elementary school, the sobriquet that referenced the quiet patter of Viv's speech. He stood, opened his arms.

As Viv embraced her gangly son, she felt a rush of love for Josh in his current form: silky dark hair, huge green eyes, exuberant hand gestures. But she also pined for the boys he'd been over the years. Her mind zoomed back to the bald newborn she'd nursed while cocooned in a blanket, sleep-deprived and watching surreal Soviet films. *Solaris. The Color of Pomegranates. Hedgehog in the Fog.*

"Mutter," Josh smiled. "There's something different about you."

"Exhaustion, maybe?" she said.

"A kind of radiance," he said. "I promise, I'm not being sarcastic."

"Well, holidays on the truck are a real workout. It's like I just came in from the gym, I guess." Viv flexed her bicep and smirked.

"And you're late," said Stella, a catch in her voice.

"Yes," said Viv, simply. How could she explain the music, the delicious darkness of it, the way it had put her into a trance that obliterated her sense of time? She longed for her portable radio. She wanted to sit quietly on the sofa, searching for the mysterious frequency—somewhere between 99.9 and 100.3. But her son was home, at last. The house smelled of curry. And Stella had built a fire of aged cherry, wood she'd bought for the holiday.

Just like old times, Josh did his impressions: the mobster president, their goon of a governor, celebrities—a skill he'd had since he was very young. Whereas Viv normally laughed along with Stella to the point of tears, this time she stared in intense fascination, waiting for the moment when Josh became possessed by the alien personality. When he imitated her dead father, Viv had the eerie sensation that her son was channeling a spirit, speaking in code. Though Josh kept it light, voicing the late man's comic obsession with lawn care, Viv felt a presence in the room. She remembered the dreams she'd had right after her father died, how she'd always asked him how he was doing "there."

"It's all right, I guess," he'd say, his voice tinged with petulance.

In one dream, after Stella had complained of a foul smell oozing from the air-conditioning vents, Viv had found her father sleeping in a coffin in their crawl space. Though he'd looked cadaverous at first, he soon reverted to his normal form: an active old man with ruddy cheeks.

"How do you feel?" she'd asked.

"Not bad, considering."

Considering.

In dreams they never uttered the words. *Dead. Death.*

~

Christmas Eve was rainy and warm, a rhythm of downpours and drizzle, radio static in the truck. More people than usual rushed from their houses, stricken, panicky, ill-prepared for the weather.

"Are all of them there? Three packages?"

Sometimes, a package didn't make it. Sometimes, customers shouted or wept. They spoke of ruined Christmases, devastated children, the broken promises of corporate entities. Even the lucky ones, who had their Christmas arsenals loaded and locked, complained about the unseasonable weather, the skittish storms. Some joked about snow, white Christmas, Santa sweating in his fur coat. Sometimes, Viv mentioned that a cold front was supposed to sweep in soon. Sometimes, she mumbled *climate change* or *deforestation*. Other times, she stuck to affirmatives, nodding as agreeably as she could.

She felt the pull of the radio, the allure of static. As she wound along the woodland-themed roads, she noted variations in pitch and tone, thickness and volume. Fog floated above drainage ditches. Birds flocked in naked trees. They'd followed warm weather, but soon it would be cold again. She wondered if the birds would fly south or stick it out.

She recalled Josh as a precocious seven-year-old, reading a book on colonial America, repeating a phrase that had obsessed him: *Vast flocks darkened the sky.* She pictured Stella in the Congaree swamp, armed with her Peterson field guide and a new pair of binoculars, pointing out birds to their small son.

Pileated woodpecker. Belted kingfisher. Mourning dove.

Viv delivered digital picture frames and carry-on luggage. Waterproof cameras and pop-up play tunnels. Chargeable miniature Land Rovers and cashmere throws. She worked through lunch, wolfing down a sandwich after one o'clock.

The voice surfaced late that afternoon during a fresh squall—hypnotic, deep, vaguely feminine. *Welcome to Dim Shapes. Imagine me at the top of a fire tower, enveloped in a cloud. Imagine me on a wooded hillock, tucked into a rusted camper. Or floating along the river on a barge. I'm nowhere. I'm everywhere.*

Viv pulled to the roadside.

The first sound she heard seemed to come from the woods, a canine howling—coyotes, feral dogs, wolves—that lapsed into women keening, a rhythmic mournful collective wail, so intense Viv couldn't fathom how it came from her old portable radio with the missing battery plate, the AAs secured with black electrical tape. The lamentation quickened, shifted to chanting, and then morphed into percussion—primal and spare. She imagined a whale skeleton on a beach, a woman dressed in deerskins, tapping the rib cage with bone mallets. She thought she could hear the ocean. A mechanical hum in the background thickened and thinned. An exquisite cello melody emerged and faded away. And then an intimate voice—masculine, baritone—sang in a language she didn't understand. Nestled into this language was another language, one she thought she knew. *Kaanana*, a woman sang, *cemjo*. Viv heard a knock on the window, looked up, saw rain-blurred woods.

Kaanana, the woman sang. *Come into the trees.*

"I'm a lunatic," Viv whispered as she opened her door, "a child of the moon."

She got out of her truck and stood in the drizzle, listening.

Women sang in the forest, a ravishing harmony that reminded her of early radio quartets, medieval masses, bacchantes romping on a green hill.

Probably Christmas carolers, she thought, singing in Latin. She pictured them on the porch of a house nestled into the woods.

Viv slipped through wet brush into old-growth forest that would soon be razed for houses, strip malls, high-end chain restaurants. She touched the wet mossy bark of a live oak. Smelled some winter flower, devilwood, perhaps, the wild cousin of tea olive. She followed the music into darkness untouched by streetlamps.

Though she didn't find a cabin, she discovered a clearing, a trace of melody still echoing there. But the women were gone.

Viv stood still, listening to the drizzle, to the wind whipping through wet leaves. She remembered her DIAD, her deliveries, her little radio with the worn plastic dial. She was lost, she realized, but she had her phone in her pocket. She had GPS—over seventy-five navigation satellites in orbit, helping people find their way. Josh had once informed her that there were over two thousand satellites circling the earth, the exosphere crammed with them, the air whirring with a zillion invisible signals.

~

Viv came home wet, late, feverish. She came home to Stella and Josh tipsy, supper still simmering, overcooked.

"We couldn't start without you, Mutter," said Josh.

"You're wet," Stella observed dryly.

"The weather is weird," said Viv.

"Mother Earth is doomed," said Josh. "But have some wine." He poured her a glass of merlot.

"Don't be nihilistic," said Stella.

"More Buddhist, actually," said Josh. "Accepting impermanence."

As they squabbled cheerfully about philosophy, Viv slipped back to the bedroom she shared with Stella.

"Give me a sec to get out of these wet clothes," she called.

She changed into dry sweats, her house uniform, though Stella was wearing a cashmere sweater, Josh a snazzy cardigan. But these were her people. They knew her as well as she could be known.

"That's solipsism," said Stella.

"More like subjective idealism," said Josh.

"How many philosophy classes have you taken now?"

"They're addictive," said Josh, "albeit pointless."

Viv sat at the table and stared at a bouquet of camelias.

"Flowers," she said, "the ultimate ephemera."

The edges of the blooms were already browning. The leaves were sooty from a fungus that fed on aphid honeydew.

"Viv," said Stella. "Are you well?"

"I might be coming down with something."

She shivered.

"Do you want to sit under a blanket on the couch? We can eat there."

"No," she said. "It's Christmas Eve after all."

They raised their glasses in a mock toast, but it was still a toast.

"To overcooked beef," said Josh.

"To mushy potatoes and limp asparagus," said Stella.

"To Trader Joe's merlot," said Viv, playing along, envisioning women singing in the forest, bacchantes in bull masks dancing in an ecstatic frenzy, dismembering a fanatical king.

Viv woke to pattering feet in the hallway, to little Josh, manic with seasonal excitement, running to wake them up. He'd jump into their bed and badger them until they rose. The ritual of opening gifts would begin, the child's excitement stoked by the process more than the things themselves—one unveiling after another. There would be more gifts to open at her parents' place, keeping up the momentum of acquisition, an abstract arc, the culmination of a holiday positioned to prevent winter despair. Then they would feast, stuffing themselves with starches and gravies and soporific fowl, after which their spirits would sag, and the gifts would be idly tested. While some would be incorporated into their lives, holding their worth, others would dip in value, molder in closets, find their way to Goodwill.

There was still the New Year holiday to anticipate. But after that, winter would show its face—all bone and sinew and toothless snarl, scant white hair stripped back from the skull by frigid wind. Scientists had identified January twentieth as the nadir of the season, so-called blue Monday, the day when disappointment, vitamin-D deprivation, and the relentlessness of winter took the collective mood to its lowest point. Even her child was not immune.

But the day was warm and rainy again, and Josh was no longer a child, Viv realized, sitting up, her head spinning. Her father was dead, her mother spending Christmas with her sister in Atlanta.

"You're burning up," said Stella.

Viv hadn't seen her wife standing beside the bed.

She allowed Stella to take her temperature (101) and assured her that this was no flu, just a very bad cold.

"I should remain quarantined in bed, however," Viv said.

"Absolutely not," said Stella. "Josh is home. And besides, we've already been exposed to whatever it is. We'll bundle you up on the couch. We'll coddle you."

For the last decade, they'd agreed to cut down on consumerism and exchange fewer gifts. They had bought Josh a set of Copic markers, and he'd gotten them a Bodum French press. Viv gave Stella a pair of gardening boots, and Stella gave Viv a book called *Music: The Definitive Visual History*. Sipping coffee and eating quiche, Viv stared at a rock painting of a "Stone-Age dance" dated 60,000 BCE. She flipped forward and regarded chamber musicians dressed in velvet and frills, a woman at the harpsichord, her hair adorned with flowers. Recalling her chamber music stage, an obsession that had burned through a whole winter several years ago, she ached for her radio, for the shroud of static, music emerging, entering her body through the portals of her ears, activating brain zones—a miraculous internalization.

"I need to take a walk," Viv said.

"Are you crazy?" said Stella. "You're sick."

"I swear, a brisk walk will sweat out toxins."

"She might be right," said Josh.

"At least it won't hurt me," said Viv. "It's not cold outside."

"Drizzly," said Stella. "You'll get wet."

"Misty, really. And I have a serious raincoat."

"We'll go with you," said Stella.

"I'll be back in twenty minutes."

As though Viv were embarking on an epic journey, Stella saw her off at the door with a fierce kiss. Viv knew what the online articles said. A partner having an affair was often late, restless, always looking for excuses to leave the house, even if not for a tryst—just to get away from the suffocating domestic clutch of the old partner, the one they'd abandon when the brutal truth came to light.

"Everything is fine," said Viv, kissing Stella's soft cheeks, lovely full cheeks that Stella described as chubby. They felt like silk and smelled like vanilla, and Viv felt a tug in her gut, a desire to linger in the warm house, lounge on the sofa with her wife as Josh drank too much coffee and his wit revved into high gear.

"Why would you say that?" Stella pulled away.

"You seem worried."

"You seem distracted."

"I'll be right back," said Viv.

She took her radio to the river walk, three blocks from their bungalow, the park nestled into a floodplain forest. The river, named after an extinct Native American tribe, contained toxic levels of bacteria, pharmaceutical and agricultural chemicals, surprising concentrations of DEET. Still, she found a lovely primordial spot, a sycamore grove, a fallen oak overgrown with moss. She sat on the tree trunk and looked out at the river— muddy and high, churning from recent rain.

Drizzle hissed. Mist floated. When she turned on her radio and found the staticky zone between 99.9 and 100.3, she imagined that the mist was an emanation of this zone, a substance spilling from her radio speakers, a kind of ectoplasm. It didn't take long for the voice to come to her, dissolving and flaring, settling, at last, inside her head.

We meet in the ether again. Dim Shapes here, released into the forest, a voice in the mist, a voice in the mind, bringing you new music from Nether, Chthonic, Troll. I float beside you. I float inside you. Close your eyes. Let me take you into a cave. The floor is damp. Roots curl from your bare feet, tuning you in.

Viv felt the music in her feet first, pulsing from the cave floor like the heartbeat of a giant beast. She felt animals stirring in the darkness around her, purring, panting in intricate rhythms. The snore of a hibernating bear. The twitter of small mammals. The thump of furry tails. She heard insect stridulation, soaring like a string quartet. The percussive drip of sap. The shrilling of mushrooms. Crystalline tones of sand.

Tune into the soil. Tune into the air.

She lay down on the cave floor and felt herself sinking.

Hooded beings loomed over her, gnomic and musty, snouted and fanged. She felt their chants in her blood. One of them, its head floating high on a supple, scaly neck, sang in the most exquisite soprano she'd ever heard.

❧

She looked like she'd fallen into the river. She looked like she'd fucked someone in a mudslide.

"What the hell happened?" hissed Stella. But then her voice softened with worry. "Please tell us what happened."

"The river walk was slippery. I lost my footing, fell into a mud puddle. I'm an idiot."

"Oh my God, Mutter."

Josh loomed over her. He'd grown even taller while she was away.

But no. She was lying down in the bedroom.

"Did you hit your head?" Josh asked. "She could have a concussion," he said to Stella.

"No," said Viv.

Stella massaged her scalp, looking for bumps.

"I don't feel anything," Stella said to Josh.

"At least she's talking now," Josh said to Stella.

"I think she's depressed," said Stella.

Viv remembered a time when she and Stella, green to motherhood, had fussed over Josh, a four-year-old with flu. In hushed panicky tones, they'd discussed his temperature and blankets. Food, meds, water intake.

"I can hear you," Josh had said. "I'm here too. I'm a person, even though I'm small."

❧

Viv lay in bed for two days, falling in and out of dreams, catching scraps of conversation like a child. Stella said, "It all started with the holiday rush." Josh said, "Do you think she should see a therapist?" Her father said, "It's not bad here, but I'm ready for the other place."

Viv dreamed of forests so deep and tangled that the animals there had never caught a whiff of human. Viv dreamed of icy mountains so tall that she couldn't see the valley below, only clouds and sky. She dreamed of tunnels lined with luminous fungi, of underwater caves where tentacular cryptids dwelled. She dreamed she had wings, gills, antennae, compound eyes. When she woke up, it took her a while to remember Stella and Josh. But then they came gushing back to her, the rush of love like a convulsion, a shock to her heart and brain. She loved them as much as a human could love other humans. They made her soup, forced her to drink homemade kombucha, draped her with the comforter she'd kicked to the floor.

"You growl in your sleep," said Stella.

"I do?"

Sometimes Viv woke up and thought Josh was small, hiding under the bed.

"Josh?" she'd cry. "Where are you?"

"I'm here, Mutter," he'd call from the living room. When he appeared beside her bed, shockingly tall, the missing years whooshed back.

Sometimes Viv looked at Stella and saw the girl she'd been—impish and spry, with tangled black hair. Other times she saw an old woman, skin and bones, baggy eyes that had seen it all.

Everything existed at once. Everything slipped away.

∾

One night, Viv woke to singing, canticles in a strange tongue. She saw women at the border of a dream, circling her bed—goat-headed, naked and sinewy, their breasts smeared with green mud. Clatter of hooves. Smells of wet fur and musk. The bed sinking, zooming down.

When Viv sat up, the vision faded. Stella slept, sprawled on the love seat, her feet dangling off the edge. Stella was fresh baked bread, a warm bath, the hearth where Viv's heart burned. Viv wanted to kiss her wife, but Stella was exhausted, asleep at last.

3:30 AM. The time Viv always seemed to wake up. Usually, she managed to get back to sleep, but tonight she felt a surge of energy. She got up, paced the house, spotted her old radio on the end table. It looked strange, like a facsimile made of matter from another planet.

Viv picked it up, noted an odd heaviness, and turned it on. Static. Humming. Chanting.

Come to the forest. Come to the night river, dark as wine.

She found the women in the woods, naked, goat-headed— masked, she realized. Two of them unclasped their hands, breaking the circle, inviting her in. Their hands were cold as river mud, their horns adorned with wreaths of moss. The mud on their bodies twinkled with flecks of quartz. Viv sang with them, an ancient song she remembered from her childhood, a tune passed from kid to kid like a virus, a primal language her body knew. It was a secret song, she remembered now, hidden from adults and older children, sung around forbidden fires in the woods behind her subdivision.

"You'll forget this song when you turn six," a girl had told her.

"It comes from the womb," said a boy.

"From the time before you were born," said a girl.

"Smaller than a speck."

"Nothing."

"Everything."

Now, the song filled her lungs again, knocked against her rib cage, and pulsed through her throat. She felt the song in her heart and bowels, her blood and nerves. The song zipped along her spinal cord, vibrating her tongue and teeth. The song moved her limbs, clumsily at first, but soon she was in sync with the other women, raising cupped palms to the moon as though receiving a bowl of light. Together, they walked to the river and waded in, feet sinking into silt. Together, they swam out to a deep place where the water was still.

The women swam in circles, making ripples that sent moonlight spinning around them. When, at last, they went under, they pulled Viv into the deep, a warm red place flickering with minnows. As water gushed into her throat, she panicked. But then she felt gills fluttering on her neck—they'd been there all along, sealed with skin. As they opened, oxygen flowed into tender membranes.

Viv heard a steady throbbing. She heard a sweet and mournful bellow coming from the depths of the river, where catfish dozed in the silt. Down, down she swam, sinking into soft mud, searching for the river bottom. There was no firm ground, she realized, no such thing as solid matter.

Let the music flow into you.

She could no longer differentiate between herself and the music. The red bulbous convulsion of her heart. The small spasms of arterial valves. The peristaltic pump of her gastrointestinal tract. Oxygen danced through her bloodstream. Neurotransmitters flowed between synapses. Cells divided and regenerated.

When she opened her eyes and saw the leviathan—copper-scaled, iguana-faced—she was not afraid. Its great mouth parted. Its black throat pulsed.

Come in. I'll take you deeper into the song.

She longed to be enveloped, ingested, longed to be devoured by something greater than herself, to explore the belly of the beast—an old story, told in many tongues. But her gills no longer seemed to work. She felt a burning pressure in her lungs.

Hurry, said the leviathan in a gruff voice, which spooked her toward the light.

Viv crawled naked from the water and crept down a littered stretch of river beach. Dogs barked in the distance. She found her sweatshirt in the shallows, stuck on a stick. She found her leggings, pounded into damp sand. She couldn't find her shoes. She heard voices calling her name—Stella and Josh. She waded out, snatched her sweatshirt, and stared at the river. Today the water was red, the color of rum. Quickly, she got dressed.

A flock of geese flew over. A cardinal called in the brush. The day would be warm again, breaking another record.

She'd tell them she fell into the river, that she fought for her life.

I'm sorry. I haven't been myself. I love you more than life itself, whatever that means.

She'd tell them she felt better. Take a long shower. Let them feed her soup.

She would go back to work, hide her old radio in the attic, behind crates of albums and boxes of CDs, behind her old Korg keyboard with the broken stand, behind the theremin Josh made when he was fifteen—a science fair project. She wouldn't allow herself to go up to the attic for a long time.

One spring evening, the first year that Josh was in Virginia at grad school, Viv sat in the yard with Stella and another couple, Tim and Gyeong. The yard was a paradise of daylilies and grackle. Lightning bugs swayed up from the creek.

Their guests were clever and kind, bursting with stimulating conversation. They discussed obscure horror films, quantum entanglement, the impending extinction of bees. They discussed black holes, kombucha fermentation, the educational progress of their children. Trips to Vietnam and Iceland, the history of codpieces, the trials of caring for aging parents. War photography, artificial intelligence, new forms of green energy.

Gyeong told them how to keep vine borers from destroying their squash. Tim shared a hilarious anecdote about the time in high school when he told a French exchange student that "pepperoni" was American slang for "nipples." Stella laughed, looking young again, her head tossed back, eyes squinting at the pink sky.

Viv walked back to the house to fetch another beer. In the kitchen, she detected a hum in the air, the collective buzz of appliances, the drone of the air-conditioning system, and some other sound—high and tingling, as though a bell were ringing in another dimension, sending waves into the human frequency range.

She walked to the hallway, pulled down the attic stairs, and climbed up into the darkness. She turned on the stark light.

Viv rummaged until she found it at the bottom of a crate of old CDs, lighter than she remembered, the metal strangely cold. She held it in her lap, fingered knobs and buttons. The electrical tape she'd used to secure the batteries was sticky, melted from years in the hot attic. Though half-corroded, the batteries somehow worked.

When Viv found the static, small gauzy flies rose from cardboard boxes, filling the space with a dusty whir. Faintly luminous, the flies hovered, thickening the air.

She would listen only for a minute, she thought, just to see if the voice was still there. Then she'd go back to Stella, back to the yard, to birds and flowers, beer and laughter, the setting of the sun and rising of the moon, time rippling through her flesh, leaving wrinkles and spots, driving her red blood.

The Gricklemare

She's been up for an hour when the children come scampering and giggling. But the mist is still thick, crickets still chirring a nocturnal song. By the time she steps out onto her porch, the imps have slipped off into dusky woods.

"Gricklemare Gricklemare," they chant—nonsense language, some bit of Appalachian folklore, a meme, maybe, or something from a kids' Netflix fantasy series.

She spots one of them, crouched behind a mountain laurel shrub, a blond child so pale he seems half-dissolved into the mist. And then another, tittering above her in a cedar—a girl perched on the highest branch. How did she climb up there so fast?

"Gricklemare Gricklemare," the girl croons, birdsong needling around her voice.

Sylvia wonders how many children are hiding in the forest. Dizzy, she sits on the old rattan chair that came with the cabin.

"Gricklemare Gricklemare," the children taunt, halfway down the mountain now.

"Gricklemare!" Sylvia shouts back, the word sticking in her throat when she sees the egg smashed on her porch step, blue-shelled, the meagre yolk still intact.

"Little shits," she hisses. She fetches a bucket and rag, cleans up the mess. She might have slipped on it and tumbled into the ravine that's unnervingly close to the cabin she rents, battering her body against tree trunks.

Sylvia goes back into her study, sits down at her laptop, reads through the words she wrote before sunrise: *Using an Ecojustice education methodology to engage rural communities with Indigenous knowledge systems and Western scientific traditions, thereby deconstructing the imperialist hegemony of traditional ecopedagogy* . . .

Darkness stirs inside her like a roused flock of grackle. But really, it's more like a sap, a fog, *a humor*—the archaic medical term fits best, her body tainted with black bile, melancholy vapors floating up from some foul green gland to cloud her mind. While she writes gibberish, the world burns. As Alex used to remind her, by the time her useless theory is put into practice, bees will be extinct, the polar ice caps melted to filthy slush, coral reefs bleached white as bone. She half wishes the children would come back, for she longs to talk to someone, anyone.

She will not think of Alex. She will keep him contained, down in some festering fold of her frontal cortex, where, according to a recent article she read, bad memories go.

But Alex slips up from the murk. Alex with his blue eyes and black hair. Alex with his womanly lips, his stark rib cage fit for a pietà. Alex cocking his head like a hen as he considers something she has said. Alex sneering, claiming that science will save the world, not gibberish. Alex delivering a sharp retort. Alex lingering in the air of her apartment a week after his body is gone—scent molecules, dead skin cells, dirty socks in the closet, pulsing with disturbing energy. She'd thrown the socks in the trash, but one night, like a starved racoon, she'd dug them back out again.

"A walk in the woods." She speaks the words aloud to summon the act.

Alex gone shockingly fast, like the chestnut ermine moth, like the purple-faced langur, like the Kalimantan mango. She does not know exactly where he is—studying slime mold in some dwindling forest. What she misses most is not the sex but the mammalian warmth, the everyday hum of their parallel lives, when they were kind to each other.

"A walk in the woods to get my serotonin levels up."

Sylvia lives on the edge of a national park—a great privilege, she reminds herself, because she's white, writing a grant-funded dissertation. She was raised in a nuclear family funded by a nuclear engineer who used to laugh at her when she told him, as a child, that trees could talk to one another. She holds grudges, dwells on things. Years ago, when her father was in the hospital having kidney stones removed through an incision in his back, she left an article about mycorrhizal networks on his night-stand, along with the toxic chocolate shake he'd requested from McDonald's.

"Trees *can* talk," she whispered as he came out of his anes-thetic haze, and then she slipped from the room, leaving her ghostly words behind her.

Now she feels sick about this, remembering the look on her father's face when he saw her outside the SRS Badge Office, a green-haired teen in combat boots, protesting all things nuclear. She'd protested the nukes but had no problem taking nuke money, jumping to snatch her generous allowance from her father's hand.

What a little hypocrite she was.

She turns to the window, focuses on wind in the trees.

Since she moved to Black Knob, memories surface in the shallows of her mind like stingrays rising from the ocean floor. She'd imagined herself in nunnish seclusion, making peace with herself, learning to live alone, enjoying epiphanies during wood-land walks, and rushing back to the cabin to type furiously into the night.

Walking along an old logging trail fringed with lush poison oak, Sylvia relishes the feel of fog on her skin. She breathes in the scent of spruce, sugar maples, dewy mountain laurels. But she tenses up again when she passes the rusted trailer, a kudzu-smothered Holiday Rambler from the 1970s—abandoned, she hopes. She can see the roof of a collapsing cabin behind it—the red gleam of wet heart pine. She's surprised it hasn't been dismantled by carpenters from Asheville, hungry for reclaimed wood.

She feels the uncanny allure of the trailer, its door ripped off, its opening fringed with vines—a cave mouth. As a child, she could never resist creeping into derelict buildings, even after stepping on rusted nails, getting clawed by feral cats, breathing in asbestos, lead dust, toxic mold. Even after enduring a hundred lectures from her parents, who'd always circled her as they preached, cigarettes fuming in their hands.

Sylvia veers off course, steps inside, smells mildew, the prefab walls speckled with it. A scattering of cockroaches. A grubby sofa, dolloped with bird droppings. A red Formica dining table, rusted aluminum legs, no chairs. Wads of clothes on the putrid shag—vintage polyester, rayon, acrylic—cloth spun out of oil through the sorceries of shut-down mills. Holding her breath, she tiptoes down the narrow hallway, the flimsy subfloor creaking beneath her. When she hears a strange cackle, she freezes. There is something—alive, human, animal, other—in the dim back bedroom. Whatever it is could kill her, but she can't stop herself from peering into darkness to catch the witch at her work, the monster feeding, or the psychopath reveling in the exuberant spatter of his kill.

Two windows, no glass, plastic blinds, one half-open.

A particleboard dresser with missing drawers.

Soiled mattress on the floor.

A chicken—*a fucking chicken*—squatting in a nest of twisted sheets.

The chicken squawks again, but doesn't flee, sitting as though tranced, beak open, red eyes gleaming.

But then it jumps to its feet, flutters up to the dresser and out the window, a flurry of black feathers.

The hen has laid a small egg, reddish and speckled.

Recalling the bits of blue shell she cleaned from her porch stoop that morning, Sylvia picks up the egg—still warm—and slips it into her jacket pocket.

When she emerges from the trailer, the mist is gone, the day stark and blue. No clouds.

Though she finds the warm egg vaguely repulsive, she taps it on the counter, cracks it open, and deposits a dollop of unfertilized goo into a skillet slicked with hot oil. The dark yellow yolk, tainted by a tiny drop of blood, quivers. She picks the red out with a spoon, washes it down the sink. She puts bread in the toaster, mashes an avocado into paste with a fork.

Alex would have eaten the egg as it was, blood drop and all. Alex would have said she was squeamish. Once, in the thick of sex, when she'd reached the soaring point where she'd forgotten that Alex was the person affixed to her, despite his characteristic arrhythmic panting, he'd uttered a crass phrase that she'd always hated—*Let's make a baby*—pulling her out of her trance.

"Why did you say that?" she asked, afterward.

"I don't know, but it seems only natural, when you think about it."

"If we lived naturally, I'd have a dozen babies by now, my bladder and uterus prolapsed from multiple births. I'd probably be dead."

"You're afraid of the body, the flesh," he said dramatically, like a poet in a play.

"You might be too if you had to give birth."

"You evolved to give birth; I evolved to knock you up."

She cringed again. *Knock you up.*

"I might have a baby one day, just not now."

"I didn't mean now."

"What did you mean, then?"

After that, the air grew stagnant from his sulking. Winter came to their northern college town, slithering like a great, white dragon around their apartment building. Alex, immersed in his dissertation on slime molds, became reticent, moody, searching kitchen cabinets, scattering litter wherever he moved, growling so quietly that the hum of the electric heater almost effaced his beastly language. She detected a pungent scent on his clothes, sweet and pissy with a note of onion, full of signals she couldn't decipher. He staked out territory near the TV, cocooned himself in a comforter, cluttering his environs with books and crumbs and bits of gristle. He darkened the air in the living room.

She kept to the study they used to share. Stepping into the room each morning, she felt herself descending, as in a shark-proof tank, into the depths of ecopedagogy, the intricate theories difficult to decipher, like the language of whales. There was so much to read before her comps in May. She spent hours scrolling through luminous texts, processing words until her eyes burned.

One dim day, the light ambiguous, Alex followed her to the bathroom. He dropped his blanket on the tile. He bit his lip. His cheeks were flushed. She was about to turn away when she noticed his erection, keening from his body like an exuberant animal, pressed against damp thermal cotton.

Wet sparks shot from his eyes. His smile made her think of summer—humid air, green mountains. Alex smirked and removed his sweatshirt. She was shocked by the luster of his pelt, how pretty and soft his naked skin looked next to the hair. She couldn't stop herself from sinking her hands into it. She caressed his starveling ribs.

In the bedroom, she waited in the dark as he rummaged for a condom, remembering the thrill of her youthful exploits, a time when the reek of a Trojan had filled a parked car like an explosion of napalm.

"We're out," he said. "It's been a while."

"Let's just be careful," she said.

"Let's not," he huffed into her ear, his weight upon her again.

"You have to be." Her words—stark, loud—punctured the mood, but they kept going.

The egg smells gamy, like the chicken giblets her mother used to fry. The egg glistens, so oily that it seems to quiver in the light. She moves to the shadowy side of the table, takes a bite, gags on the rich flavor—nutty, fishy, off. Pinching her nose toddler-style, she gulps it whole, barely chewing it, like a seal swallowing a fish. The egg leaves a film of grease in her throat, unwholesome and metallic, like something from a can with a label she cannot read.

The children chant in the forest.

Higgledy, piggledy, my black hen,
She lays eggs for gentlemen;
Sometimes nine, and sometimes ten,
Higgledy, piggledy, my black hen.

Perhaps the children followed her along the logging trail. Maybe they saw her take the egg. Now that school is out, they have nothing better to do than to spy on her. One of them whips past her window, a streak of pale hair. Another—long-snouted, weak-chinned—peers from the brush like a meerkat. Others jump in the branches, sending down drifts of leaves.

Perhaps they expect her to offer them treats. Maybe she could ward off their pranks with cookies, but she's no good at baking—she has no sugar in the house.

At last, they flit off, rustling through brush like low-flying birds.

In the evening, she sits on the porch with a glass of dark wine, enmeshed in the thrumming of katydids and crickets, wondering if their love calls change her heart rate, the rhythms of her blood, tiny valves spasming open and shut. *An unscientific thought,* Alex would say, *but a charming one.* He'd lick her neck, massage her toes, frankly press his beautiful bony hand against her crotch. She stretches in the humid air. The temperature has not dropped off yet but will soon. The moon floats like a scrap of gauze in the pink sky. When the sky darkens, an owl screams, so loud she thinks it must be a siren signaling a state of emergency—flames sweeping through the woods, bombs falling, some deadly chemical spreading through the atmosphere, odorless, invisible. The owl swoops from a spruce, its wingspan shockingly small.

Every time she sees the sweep of stars appearing in the dark sky, she pictures Alex, stumbling around the campus quad with his Star Chart app. *There was an ancient astronomer who fell into a ditch,* she thinks. *Or was it an astrologer, a well?* She breathes in the mystical moist night air. She sips her wine, watching fireflies sway out from the woods, still thriving in this protected ecosystem. She senses the hum of a body moving near her, turns, sees nothing. Perhaps a deer has passed in the dark.

Her phone throbs in her pocket, the ringer always off. She looks at the screen, sees an unfamiliar number, and then a voicemail signal. She listens, hearing only static, bleeps, and then the word *Alex* in a garbled voice. She returns the call, gets voicemail immediately—a stock, impersonal greeting.

"Yes, you called me," she says. "I'm not sure if I know who you are. Is this Alex? Do you have a new number?"

Sylvia wakes to the startling certainty that someone is in her house, a small person pattering, opening drawers and slamming them shut. One of the children, she thinks. She slips out of bed, pulls on her robe, tiptoes to the living room. Two windows— heavy, difficult to open—gape. Wet night air blows through the room, fluttering scattered papers, clumps of white fluff that she identifies as pillow stuffing, the gutted pillow flaccid, draped over a sofa arm. Whoever has done this is in the kitchen now, searching through drawers in the glaring light. By the time she steps into the kitchen, the vandal is gone, the window left wide open. The ancient fluorescent overhead buzzes. Flatware is scattered on the counters, broken dishes on the floor, an entire roll of paper towels unfurled and strewn.

"Little shits," she hisses, imagining herself snatching a child up by the scruff of its neck. She has no idea how old these children are, how strong, how wild.

"Tomorrow," she says.

Tomorrow she will buy bolts for the windows and doors. Tonight, she will call the police.

She reaches into her pocket for her phone, feels a small lumpish thing—warm, clammy. She plucks it out, tosses it into the dim living room. She sees something—bald, grayish pink like a newborn mouse—slithering under the sofa. Her phone is in her other pocket. She swipes on the flashlight and peers under the sofa: a sock, a book, a withered apple core.

The policewoman is small, elfin, with a neat cap of nut-brown curls, large eyes, a pointed chin.

"Can you describe these children?" Officer Simmons yawns.

"I've only seen flashes. There's a pale one with blond hair— boy, girl—I don't know. Also, a dark-haired girl."

"About how old?"

"I don't know. They hide in the woods."

"No children live up here, as far as I know. So they must be from town. How do you know they're children?"

"As I've told you, they've been stalking me."

"Stalking?"

"Pranking, following, spying. They smashed an egg on my doorstep yesterday morning."

"Those are heavy windows. I don't see how a child could open them."

"Perhaps this is an unrelated incident. Or maybe the children are older."

"Teenagers?"

"Maybe." But Sylvia knows they are children—slight, willowy, quick.

"Anything else?"

"Not that I can think of."

Sylvia doesn't mention the thing she found in her pocket, the damp, warm heft of it, the way it wriggled across the floor like a salamander with rudimentary legs.

"Mind if I take some pictures?"

"Of course not; please do."

When the officer is gone, Sylvia checks the locks. She falls into fitful sleep, a carving knife stashed under her bed. In a dream, she presses a raw lump of beef to her ear and hears the voice of Alex.

"Where are you?" she asks.

"In the air," he says. "Look out your window."

She sees him, hovering in the mist, his skin glowing damply like luminescent fungus.

"Are you dead?"

"I don't think so." He huffs out an angry laugh.

"Are you sure?"

Alex looks stricken, and then a fury comes upon him. He whirls in the mist, sending gusts of damp air into her house. He sucks her out of the window, whips her up into the sky.

Sylvia wakes, thinks she hears the children in the cabin again, but it's only a tree tapping a window, the ice maker rattling, the creak of the old house settling deeper into the earth.

The next morning Sylvia finds dirty plates in the kitchen sink: two chipped atomic dishes from the 1950s—the ones that came with the cabin—congealed with dark fat. She vaguely recalls eating in the middle of the night, something from a can, mashed meat, crunchy with cartilage—she thought it was salmon, but it must have been something else. She finds a pile of dirty laundry on the bathroom floor, her clothes musty, as though fetched from a basement. Green scum rings the bathtub. A congealed skin of urine coats the toilet bowl. Mold has grown on her leather shoes. Moisture oozes from the cabin's plank walls.

"Little shits," she hisses, for the children opened her windows and let mist float through her house. The cabin has no air-conditioning. Ancient spores, ignited by moisture, have come back from the dead. Immersed in her dissertation, she has not noticed the mess.

She spends the day cleaning with vinegar, ammonia, and bleach—cleaning in a frenzy like her mother used to do, dizzy from fumes, jaws clenched, mop brandished in her white-knuckled fist like a weapon. The vacuum roars; the washer rumbles. She scrubs with sponges, scouring pads, and course-bristled brushes, rooting out muck from nooks and cracks. Pulsing with adrenaline, she pulls the stove from the wall and stares in horror at the filth behind it. But she obliterates it all. Buried for decades, green linoleum resurfaces. She washes clothes, towels, bedding, bath mats. She dumps bucket after bucket of gray water into the sink. When she finishes, it is late afternoon, she has forgotten to eat, and she feels she might levitate when she steps out onto the porch and looks at distant mountain peaks. She floats through the clean house with a glass of wine, enjoying beautiful views, forgetting that she should drive to town to buy bolts for the windows.

The light is too delicious, soft green, crisp, no mist in the air. She relishes the silvery sound of crickets, the soft fuss of birds. At the top of the mountain, she feels like a woman in a turret, caught in an ancient spell. She scans the forest, half hoping that someone will appear. She drinks more wine, falls asleep just after dusk, exhausted, breathing in the smell of sun-dried sheets.

She wakes with a fever at 3:36 AM, the house quiet, wisps of mist floating in the lamplight. Did she leave a window open? Did the children come back? Dizzy, clutching her head, she walks through the rooms. Her eyes itch and leak. She has trouble bringing objects into focus—the brown blur of a chair, the dark blot of a shoe, quivering window frames. In the bathroom, she rifles through the medicine cabinet, pulling bottles close to her squinting eyes: NyQuil, Tylenol, Robitussin. She can't remember which concoctions she bought, and which were in the cabin when she came. She finds a brown bottle of Aspironal, an aspirin product, she guesses, and takes a sip—licorice, rust, mud. It leaves an oily residue on her lips.

Stumbling back to the bedroom, she sees pillows on the floor, strewn books, loose sheets of legal pad paper drifting in the breeze. She's too tired to pick up the mess, too dizzy to find the open window.

Back in bed, her sheets smell sour. Maybe they were still damp when she took them off the clothesline. Her head throbs. She sinks into sleep and resurfaces again.

"Sylvia," someone whispers, the voice painfully familiar. *Alex.*

"Alex?" She squints into the dimness. "What are you doing here?"

He slips into bed beside her, smelling of sweat and smoke.

"Why didn't you call?"

"I did."

She remembers the weird phone call, the static, the feeling of wind in her head.

"I've come a very long way," he whispers. "Through forests and storms, along winding roads and through the air."

"I can't see you," she says.

"It's dark, but I'm here."

His breath, hot on her cheek. His arm, heavy on her belly. His toenails, too long, pricking her ankles.

He kisses her. His tongue, longer than she remembers, probes the depths of her throat.

She gags, pushes him off her, sits up.

"I'm sick," she says. "Can you turn the light on?"

He flicks the lamp on. In the brief flare of light, she sees Alex, naked, sitting on the bed, his spine knobby, each jutting vertebra coated in downy brown hair that she doesn't remember. And then it goes dark again.

"Bulb's dead," he says.

"You're too skinny," she says. "Where have you been?"

"In the forest."

"Vague answer."

He slips on top of her, stabbing her thighs with sharp pelvic bones. He smells of mushrooms and soil, damp brown leaves, the sharp mineral odor of corroding vitamin pills. And then she breathes in something intoxicating—warm kitten fur, summer grass, cinnamon, custard.

Alex slides his strange tongue up her left thigh.

She wakes up, still feverish, her joints sore.

"Alex?"

She hears him, rattling in the kitchen, opening and closing drawers. He must be making breakfast. Her bedroom window is open wide, pink fog outside, the hiss of rain.

"Can you please close the windows?" she calls.

He doesn't answer. She hears glass breaking, a dish crashing against the kitchen floor.

She gets up, pulls on her robe, moves to the window, attempts to yank it down.

"Alex, can you help me with this window?"

She walks into the living room, which is filled with fog. Cumulus clouds ooze through her house.

Touching the damp wooly upholstery of the old sofa, she feels her way toward the kitchen, finds it empty, dish shards scattered across the floor, pieces of broken glass on the counter, the trash can overturned, a brown smear of coffee grounds on the linoleum. She remembers the apartment she shared with Alex in Pennsylvania. She remembers bickering over the messes he made. Probing for neuroses, he'd analyzed her desire for order, pronouncing her fear of chaos excessive, irrational.

"Alex?"

The door hangs open. She steps out onto the porch, thinking he must've gone to town to get light bulbs and beer, for wine gives him migraines.

"Gricklemare, Gricklemare," children chant from the forest.

They are back again, lurking in the mist, crackling through brush, stirring in the branches.

She pulls out her phone, scrolls through contacts, almost calls Officer Simmons. But the children have already fled, down the mountain toward the old logging trail. And Alex will be back soon, to help her with the windows, to clean up his mess.

It's just like him, she thinks, pacing the cabin, fists clenched. Just like him to deem her irrational and arrive unannounced in the middle of the night, to slip into her bed after all this time. Just like him to wreck her kitchen and then vanish before she wakes up. And the bathroom, too—soggy towels heaped on the floor, dark hair thatching the drain, toothpaste smeared all over the counter. She still has his old number in her phone, even though he's changed phones, still has playful texts she hasn't deleted, a furious voicemail that she listens to every now and then to vanquish her desire for him—a tirade that breaks off after three minutes (though she knows he kept thundering long after the beep). She remembers the call she got yesterday, the word *Alex* blooming from the static. She searches her recents but can't find the number.

Why didn't you call? she'd asked him last night.

I did, he'd said.

If he comes back, she will tell him to go. She'll do it calmly, rationally.

This will be best for both of us, she'll say, casually sipping from a cup of detox tea. In the meantime, she'll carry on with her life, forge ahead with her dissertation, wring sense from abstractions, deconstruct sacred binaries and formulate new paradigms. Her words will glow with meaning. Her arguments will jar people out of their complacency and inspire them to act, to press against the intricate cages of their bureaucracies like clever rats, to stop mass extinction, to save the dying oceans, to get out there with roaring jackhammers and break up pavement, free the stifled soil, plant a million tender saplings. But when she sits at her desk, she goes straight to Facebook. When she and Alex broke up, they agreed to end their virtual "friendship," for, as they admitted to each other, they'd both be compelled to stalk and spy—not a healthy situation.

Privacy settings in place, all she can see is his profile picture— Alex, squatting in the forest beside a slime-mold-yellowed log. The picture, dating back a month ago, inspired thirty-one likes. She sees only one comment: *Where are you, man?*

She pulls herself away from Facebook, attempts to read a PDF called "Building a Partnership Ethic for Ecopedagogy in the Segregated Rural South." But she squirms in her task chair, finds herself pulling on running shoes, rushing out the cabin door, slipping down the footpath that descends to the old logging trail. Finds herself near the uncanny trailer.

She enters the cave mouth swathed with vines.

The hen clucks in a back bedroom, and Sylvia moves slowly down the narrow hall. But she doesn't find the bird on the mattress this time. It's in another room, at the end of the hall, where the flooring is starting to give and the air smells so musty that she cups her hand over her nose and mouth. She opens the flimsy door, steps into a room filled with sunlight. Two windows glint, no curtains.

An ancient person sits in an olive vinyl chair, so shriveled and shrunken that Sylvia thinks of the Cumaean Sibyl, withered down to a mite, spending eons brooding in a jar. The person is bald, dressed in a gray polyester pantsuit—feet bare, sallow-nailed, dangling. The elder holds the black hen, pets its closed wings, peers with clammy eyes. The elder stiffens and sniffs.

"You," the elder rasps.

"I'm sorry," says Sylvia. "I didn't know you lived here. I mean, assuming that . . ."

"You ate the egg."

"Yes."

"And the Gricklemare came."

"Gricklemare?"

"Now you want to get rid of it."

"I'm not sure what a Gricklemare is."

"Lure it with blood and wild honey, lead it to a hollow tree, trap it in with moss. You can give it a task it'll never finish, befuddle it. Make it fetch water with a busted bucket. Make it pick up straws. But it will always be there."

"Where?"

The elder releases a wheeze of laughter and falls asleep. The black hen stands, squawks, flutters her lustrous wings.

Back at the cabin, Sylvia wonders if she should call Adult Protective Services, have them look in on the demented old person who lives in a trailer that would probably be categorized as condemned. But then they might confine the elder to some dismal reeking institution in town, the smell of woods and fresh air far away. Sylvia recalls an article she read about abuse in nursing homes, a bleak piece of investigative journalism that had turned her heart black and confirmed her worst suspicions about the world. Maybe she should just check in from time to time, take the person food and water, a first-aid kit, warm clothes when winter comes.

"Gricklemare," she whispers—the same word the children chant. Maybe the old person has heard the children's taunts. Maybe the children have listened to the ravings of the elder. Perhaps they've gossiped about the odd woman on the misty mountain. Maybe they've conspired against the stranger—for that is what Sylvia is, perched in her rental cabin, ignorant of the people in the town below, spending her days typing what most people would read as nonsense.

"Gricklemare," she says.

Finding the word addictive, she utters it a third time.

"Gricklemare."

And then she sits in the stillness, branches tapping the tin roof.

Sylvia pours herself a glass of red wine, for she is cold, even though it's summer. Her fever has returned, though she felt fine all day. On the couch, she burrows under a comforter, keeps the wine bottle near, reads a Gothic novel, a paperback copy she found in the cabin, the cover and title page ripped off, the spine dusty with disintegrating glue. A countess dressed in dark brocade spirals up a stone staircase, traverses torchlit hallways, attempts to unlock the iron latches of heavy timber doors.

Sylvia's eyes ache from reading. When she looks up from her book, the world has gone blurry again. But she can still see something oozing through the keyhole, a dark wisp of curling fume. She smells sulfur, an odd aerosol scent. *The children*, she thinks, playing another prank, setting off a smoke bomb on her porch. Now someone is in the kitchen again, rattling through the silverware drawer.

But it's only Alex, leaning in the doorway, wearing nothing but a pair of dirty cutoff jeans, his skin pale from months of forest dwelling. His mouth twists into a smirk that she some-times hates, sometimes adores, depending on the context.

"Where have you been?" she asks, forgetting about her plan, the insouciant dismissal, the cup of herbal tea.

"In the woods," he says.

"Vague answer."

As he moves toward her, his feet leave black footprints on the rug.

He massages her shoulders, kisses her wrists, guides her into the dimness of the bedroom.

When she lies down, she feels a surge of dizziness, the pres-ence of the fever like a gas shifting inside her.

"I'm sick," she says.

"That's okay." Alex slips on top of her, strangely light, almost hovering.

She doesn't realize she's naked until his bony finger slides inside her. She reaches for the meat of him, cool in her grip, like metal.

"You're cold down there," she says.

"Only because you have a fever," he says.

This seems reasonable, for her body burns. She is slippery with sweat.

He pushes himself inside her, cold at first but then warm.

"Be careful," she tries to say, but her words come out as moans.

She squints at the face above her—dark, blurred. Her limbs feel heavy, hard to move.

"Wait," she tries to say. "Stop."

She sleeps into the afternoon, the day garish and loud with birds. The light from the window burns her eyes, but she's too weak to get up and lower the blinds.

She hears the shower running. Alex. She has yet to see him in sunlight. He is shadow and detritus, elusive odors and scant words. Today she will tell him to go. Today she will get back to work. Today she will forget about him for good. She manages to sit up, manages to stagger to the window and close the blinds. She makes it to the bathroom, hears someone puttering in the steam. But when the vapor clears, Alex isn't there. Sylvia groans at the sight of wet towels piled on the floor, stubble in the sink, wads of toilet paper everywhere. Determined to make him clean up his mess, she moves toward the kitchen.

"Alex?"

Trash strewn across the linoleum. Cabinets ransacked. Food boxes clawed open. Rice and cereal scattered.

Racoons, she thinks—a mundane epiphany, a dull flare in her brain, followed by a gush of relief. That makes perfect sense. Racoons are notorious for their cunning. They can traverse heating vents, squeeze through holes in the floor, climb into attics and claw their way through rotting ceiling plaster. She will get Alex to drive to town and buy a trap. Together, they'll search for holes, passages through which a wily mammal might slither.

Alex has left the door open again, and his green Honda is not in the driveway. Though she hasn't seen it since he arrived two days ago, Sylvia can picture it there, its hatchback plastered with bumper stickers. *I ♥ Slime. I Brake for Mushrooms. Morel Majority.* And then a paranoid thought works its way into her mind, like fungus into the brain of an ant. *Alex is camping in the Pisgah forest with his research team, a girlfriend among them. He cannot resist sneaking away in the night and slipping into Sylvia's bed. That's why he always takes a shower—to wash away the smell of her.*

There was a similar overlap when they started dating in grad school, an entomologist he claimed was brilliant, a woman who wore a pheromonal perfume that drove Alex mad but smelled like insect repellent to Sylvia. Their first month together, Sylvia would sometimes smell it on his clothes. Just before they moved in together, he confessed at a teahouse. Looking constipated with piety, he claimed he was coming clean, that he was over the entomologist, that he was ready to move in with Sylvia.

When Alex creeps in tonight, he'll be shocked to find Sylvia on the couch, the overhead light glaring. Wearing what he calls her "Joan-of-Arc martyr's face," she'll tell him to get his ass back to his fucking tent, to never come near her again. She'll get a restraining order if she must.

But now her joints ache. Her head swims. Now she needs rest, a swig of cold medicine, and an Advil. A glass of wine to calm herself, a dim room, a warm blanket. Sleep.

She wakes to the clatter of racoons, tiny paws rifling through cabinets and drawers. She gets up, thinks of the countess from the novel as she moves through the dim cabin, her long robe fluttering behind her. The noise seems to be coming from the kitchen, but when she turns on the light, she sees only the racoons' mess—scattered macaroni, a flour bag clawed open, a jar of homemade jam broken on the counter, dripping black gelatinous clots onto the linoleum. The preserves were here when she came, along with a few jars of unidentifiable vegetable matter, fleshy green nodules that look like polyps.

Sylvia cocks her head, listens, hears the hum of the fluorescent light, the chirping of crickets, something scurrying down the hallway toward the bathroom. The vermin have wrecked the bathroom too, opened toiletry bottles, smeared fruity shampoo and almond-scented lotion onto the floor.

"Little shits," she hisses.

Now something stirs in the linen closet at the end of the hall, a musty space she never uses, packed with mismatched sheets, threadbare towels, tattered wool blankets. When she opens the door, a cloud of moths flutters out, hovering for a spell before floating off into the dimness. Sylvia smells musky urine. She scans the closet with her phone light, searching for holes in the ceiling, walls, baseboards, and floor. To get a better look at the floor, she pulls out a cardboard box filled with cloth scraps, shines her light, sees nothing.

Maybe the animal is hiding in the box of rags.

Sylvia picks through scraps, pulling out pieces of vintage cloth, remnants saved for quilt making, she guesses. Admiring the quaint patterns, she wishes she could sew. She dips her fingers in, sifts through cotton and silk, feels something cold and fleshy—*probably dead*—and jerks her hand out.

Slowly, she unburies it—a writhing, mewling thing that stares with lumpish mole-like eyes. Its flesh is pink and transparent, mottled with clusters of fine black veins. Its dark vital organs pulse—visible, invisible, visible, invisible. Sylvia counts: eight sets of rudimentary limbs, squirming.

Opening its whiskered mouth, baring rodent teeth, the creature hisses. Sylvia drops her phone, fumbles for it, catches the animal bellying its way down the dusty hallway toward the kitchen.

The animal keeps quiet after that, tucked away in some secret nook.

Sylvia sits in the dark living room, listening, waiting. She thinks of species that don't fit neatly into the so-called phylogenetic tree. The duck-billed platypus—half-mammal, half-reptile. The sea anemone—half-animal, half-plant. The eusocial naked mole rat, with its grotesque and swollen queen. She drifts off, dreams she's back in her childhood bedroom, suffering some horrible disease. Her feet, black and swollen, drip green liquid into a tube that fills a drainage bag. She calls for her mom to change the bag, but her frightened mother won't come into the room.

When Sylvia wakes up, her fever is worse—throbbing, psychedelic. Her joints and muscles ache. Her eyes ooze, blurring the lamplight. Her body seizes up, and she releases a violent sneeze, a haggish hack that reminds her of her grandmother. She remembers the strong smell of the closet, fears she breathed in toxic spores, the evil black stuff that seeps from your sinuses into your brain, causing insomnia, anxiety, memory loss.

When she sees Alex perched on the sofa arm, she feels relieved. Maybe he'll make her soup, as he used to do in Pennsylvania—warm steaming bowls filled with foraged fungi. In the summer he'd sauté fresh mushrooms in butter; in the winter he'd hydrate freeze-dried toadstools, withered gnarled things kept in a dark cupboard, brought back to fleshy life with moisture.

Alex flits from the sofa arm to the chair, from the chair to the window—agitated, as though trapped. Now he hunkers on the floor, his eyes huge and orange, spinning like whirligigs. When he floats up into the air and bumps his head against the ceiling, she realizes that this person is Alex, yet not Alex. She wants to run to her car, but her limbs won't move. Watching her arm muscles twitch, she remembers the Latin etymology of the word *muscle: little mouse.* Mice, restless inside her skin. Racoons, scampering through the heating ducts. A tiny creature—half-arthropod, half-rodent—hiding in cupboards and boxes of rags. Alex (not Alex) roaring, laughing, braying as he moves naked toward her, a flurry of claws and fur.

She resurfaces in the early morning, her body sore, bruised, and scratched. She feels a weight on her chest, the cold flick of a tongue against her neck. Something is licking her.

"Alex?"

She squints—sees the dim fleshy eyes of the creature staring into her own. Its maw is wet, dark. Its buckteeth drip. She flails, swats it off her, sends it flying. It thumps against the wall, leaving a damp stain. Squeaking, it slips under the bed.

"Gricklemare," she whispers, feeling dense, like the last person in English class to understand that Dr. Jekyll and Mr. Hyde are the same person.

Lure it with blood and wild honey.

She gets up, slips on her robe, hurries to the kitchen.

Ten years from now, honey will be extinct, but today Sylvia has a jar of buckwheat honey—dark, almost black, purchased at the Asheville farmers market from a couple who capture wild swarms—authentic stuff, food for larvae, nectar transmuted by enzymes in the crops of endangered bees, regurgitated, sealed in wax cells, stolen, harvested.

She pours honey into a bowl. With a paring knife, she cuts into the center of her palm, just as she did over twenty years ago when she and her best friend, Emily, became blood sisters. She'd lain in bed that night, rubbing her bandaged hand, wondering if Emily's blood was flowing through her veins and hers through Emily's.

Sylvia thinks of Emily as she squeezes the cut, dripping blood into the bowl. She mixes the concoction with a teaspoon. Spattering sticky dollops across the floor, she makes a trail from the kitchen to the bedroom. She goes back to the kitchen, finds a dented aluminum colander, sits crouched in the pantry, holding the sieve, leaving the door ajar.

At last, the creature moves into the kitchen, squirming across the floor, slurping up honeyed drops with its long, sticky tongue. It squeals and coos with pleasure. Glowing like a bioluminescent jellyfish, it rolls onto its back and wallows in ecstasy, smearing gory honey across the linoleum. Sylvia can see the organism's black heart beating in its chest. She can smell its body, a urinous floral smell, with a sharp note of kerosine. She has a perverse desire to pick it up, to stroke its belly, feed it honeyed blood with a dropper, just as she'd once fed milk to an orphaned squirrel. But she remembers Alex (not Alex) squatting on top of her, rocking on his hairy haunches, pinning her arms to the bed with his paws.

The Gricklemare, lolling in an opiate daze, is easy to catch. She pokes it with a wooden spoon, rolls it into the colander, turns the colander upright, and slaps on a pot top. Though the creature squeaks mournfully, it cannot move, still stunned from gorging on honey and blood.

Sylvia secures the makeshift cage with duct tape, pulls on her sneakers, hurries down to the creek, where green moss grows in stunning velvety clumps. She fills a plastic bag until it bulges and then returns to the cabin.

The Gricklemare is still in its cage in the pantry where she left it. Squeaking, it gnaws weakly at the aluminum walls of its prison. Sylvia drops the cage into a cloth shopping bag, grabs her bag of moss, and takes the footpath to the old logging trail.

Nearly every day she has passed it, a gnarled oak with a hollow at its base, the perfect cozy nest for a woodland mammal, the perfect nook to trap the creature. Though she fears it will wriggle through the moss, slither through dead leaves back to her cabin, and haunt her all over again, she reminds herself that normal rules of logic don't apply to this situation—a kind of spell, she realizes, something she used to believe in when she was a child, a feeling that comes surging back, a reckless sense of wonder that she has forgotten.

She works quickly, peeling off duct tape. And then she stands before the tree, holding the colander, securing the top with her hand. Unleashing a high-pitched whistle, the creature thumps against the walls of its cage. Sylvia inhales, regards a clump of cumulous clouds—breathes, breathes—and then she dumps the Gricklemare into the hollow, where it flops onto its back. But now it's squirming again. Now it lurches half-upright, sniffing, straining to see with its nubby eyes.

She snatches handfuls of moss and stuffs them into the hollow, burying the Gricklemare, cramming the space so thickly that the creature will surely suffocate or starve before gnawing its way out.

~

Sylvia does not return to the tree until autumn, when the air changes, when the walnuts are golden, when the black gums are ablaze. She has settled back into her work habits. She has written another chapter of her dissertation. She has learned to split a log in half with one strong stroke of a gleaming sharp axe—an axe she bought at the hardware store in the town. She has more than enough wood to get through the winter. She will feed the ravenous potbellied stove, keep it burning so that she may write three pages a day. At this rate, her manuscript will be finished by the time the daylilies bloom. She will not remain to savor the miracle of spring but will vacate the cabin and never come back.

The local children have lost interest in her. Perversely, she misses their taunts, their patter, the way their wild glossy hair caught the light when they stirred in the forest.

As she takes the thin trail down to the oak tree where she trapped the Gricklemare, she scans the brush, the trees, the sky—looking for children. When she reaches the tree, she thinks she has made a mistake—for the moss is gone, the hollow closed up with a smooth bulb of fresh wood—sappy, dripping. She presses her hand against it, half expecting it to crumble. But the wood is solid, sticky, warm from a slant of fall sunlight.

When the wind stops rustling through the dry foliage, when her heart settles down, when her hands stop shaking, Sylvia can hear it twittering inside the tree: the Gricklemare.

"Still there," she whispers.

She imagines herself hacking through new wood with her axe, finding the sickly organism nested in leaves and crumbs of moss, scooping it up with her bare hands, taking it back to the cabin, and releasing it. It would slink through its secret burrows again, marking them with its scent. Mist would ooze through her house once more, infecting her sinuses, seeping into her brain tissue. Feverish, she'd feel like she was living inside a cloud. Alex (not Alex) would emerge from the fog, a whirl of fur and claws and hungry eyes, a prospect that both thrills and sickens her.

She has seen him at dusk, lurking at the wood's edge, looking confused. Lost and shivering, barefooted, dressed in shorts and a threadbare T-shirt, he's not prepared for the sudden temperature drop. Alex (not Alex) always stares at the cabin as though he doesn't quite remember it, gazing longingly at the fairy-tale smoke that puffs from the stone chimney. Feeling a mix of pity and repulsion, Sylvia always turns off the lights and watches by the window until he slips back into the cold forest.

And then she puts another log in the stove, pours herself a glass of wine, pulls her chair close to the fire. She opens an old paperback novel, starts to read, feels the release of atmospheric pressure when, at last, she gets lost in the words and forgets, for a spell, who she is.

All the Other Demons

A week after our vacation in a budget beach house, when summer lost its promise and turned rank and wild, vines snaking up from the sewage-scented patch of swamp behind our house, a censored version of *The Exorcist* was scheduled to air one Primetime Saturday. The previews sent demonic currents through our house, inspiring our dad to hiss and spit, faking possession, attempting to build up to the terror, our initiation into true horror. We were old enough to finally watch it, he said—the twins ten, me twelve. Our baby brother, Cabbage, caught the fever too, running through the house screaming, *The ex-sa-sis is comin'*, shrieking when he heard the preview, the dark croak of Regan spewing from one of our TVs: the grainy black-and-white relic the twins had scavenged from a shut-in's roadside trash; the console color Zenith we'd scored from Granny Mab.

That summer I grew cystic breast buds. That summer Old Testament thunderstorms ripped through our shit town at least twice a week. That summer our mother cut her gleaming black hair into a no-nonsense pixie cut, hissing *fuck beauty* when Dad told her she'd made a terrible mistake. That summer our father, a high-school teacher with months on his hands, smoked a hundred cigarettes a day and splashed Jim Beam into his coffee most afternoons, nattering on about the Mad Monk Grigori Rasputin, Fighting Dick Anderson of the Confederate Army, and *The Sorrows of Young Merlin*—the scaly, slippery beast of a novel with which he wrestled every day—the novel that kept him up at night.

We were all twitchy from too much caffeine—sweet tea with two cups of Dixie Crystals sugar, Mountain Yeller, and Mr. Pig—and the twins had started scavenging Dad's cigarette butts, smoking them back behind the shed, where spooky clouds of mosquitoes floated up from the creek. I stole my cigarettes straight from the carton, entire packs that my parents didn't miss, and slipped out to the magnolia tree to smoke. Our unkempt Boykin spaniels scratched up the grass to cool their bellies in damp dirt. Little Cabbage, obsessed with digging to the Devil, was always squatting in Superman Underoos, hacking at the earth with a rusted trowel. The twins yodeled in the treetops or fought each other with the boxing gloves Dad bought them so they wouldn't break each other's noses. Inside, our huge, rangy father, once a high-school football star, stomped around the house, filling it with his moods, while our tiny mother played solitaire, smoking her share of Dorals.

The Devil was what brought us all together. Whenever an *Exorcist* preview came on, we huddled in the den, with its shag carpet and dark wood paneling, marveling at the astonishing vileness of Regan, her face cracked and blistered, pea-green vomit dolloping her chin, her sulfur-yellow eyes glowing with otherworldly light. Dad, expert on all things, explained that the entity possessing the girl was not Satan per se, but Pazuzu, a Babylonian demon of wind and storms.

"I'll kill Pazuzu too," said Cabbage, whose hellhole was now three feet deep, surrounded by rocks and bricks and steak knives. "First I hit him with a brick, then stab him in the heart."

"Assuming he has one," said Mom.

"What about all the other demons?" said Dad, who went on to list the multitudes that cavorted in Hell—Beelzebub, Moloch, and Belial among them.

"I'll get 'em all," said Cabbage, who went out to the shed to hunt for more weaponry.

The twins, scared shitless, trembled and hugged each other on the plaid couch.

Mom went to check on the chuck roast she had thawing in the sink.

"I myself am Hell," muttered Dad, walking to the kitchen to refresh his drink.

I drifted out to the magnolia tree to smoke, haunted by Regan's knowing smirk. As a storm blew in from the east, I imagined Pazuzu descending, smelling of car exhaust. I'd studied his statue in *A History of Mesopotamian Mythology*, a library book Dad had checked out. Pazuzu, the Hell King's firstborn, brought famine and locusts, but weirdly, he was also a domestic spirit who protected homes from malicious guests. He had a horned head and canine snout, a scorpion tail and serpentine penis, two sets of shining wings. I imagined metal music blaring as the demon whirled down, Pazuzu squalling AC/DC's "Highway to Hell," lightning bolts shooting from his red claws. In my fantasy, Pazuzu morphed into Tommy Lee, the most beautiful member of Mötley Crüe—his mane resplendent, his makeup perfection, his cheekbones more exquisite than Cleopatra's.

"Sometimes the Devil turns to smoke," said Cabbage, who lurked in the shadows of the magnolia. Born premature, Cabbage had spent his first month steeped in the warm moisture of an oxygen tank, and he still resembled a bleached frog—small and pale, with a potbelly and jutting ribs.

"Other times the Devil is skin and bones," he said, "muscles jumping, red and slick. That's when you stab him. That's when you get him in the head with a brick."

Cabbage seemed more fidgety than usual, dark circles under his eyes.

"Daddy says the Devil can melt to shadows. The Devil can scatter into a hundred snakes and slither off to hide. He can be wind or thunder, jackal or wolf, a nest of screaming spiders under your bed. The Devil can be a gentleman in a rich-man suit, smoking a long cigar."

Cabbage took a swig of Kool-Aid from a plastic cup and returned to his hole to dig.

The storm blew over without erupting, and I felt bereft, stuck in the sticky humid day. Instead of thunder, I heard the insipid drone of my best friend Squank's moped. A plump, clammy boy with silky black hair and skin the blue-white of skim milk, Squank was the only other weirdo at my school. In the first throes of puberty, he squawked and oinked, hence his nickname. Every time he committed what he thought was a sin, he pinched himself on the tender undersides of his arms, where his amphibious skin was dotted with bruises. We'd experimented with kissing, but feeling no love spark, settled into easy companionship.

I ran out to the driveway, where Squank idled on his Puch Sport.

"I got the you-know-what," he called, referring to the sake he'd promised, an exotic Japanese liquor we'd seen on the *Shōgun* miniseries. I hopped onto the back of his bike, barefooted and dressed in a polka-dotted romper, and off we rode, past the elementary/middle school, past the armory, past Sky City discount store, past the juvenile detention center, out into the green boondocks—dismounting, at last, at the edge of a pond fringed with gnarled live oaks. There we found a stump that resembled a low table.

We'd been obsessed with sake since April. Back when azaleas still bloomed, we'd imagined ourselves in a Japanese garden, sipping from tiny cups with an air of worldly sophistication. While

Squank's parents were churchy teetotalers, my dad swigged Jim Beam, the cheapest whiskey on the planet. After tasting the nasty swill once, I swore I'd never get drunk on bargain bourbon. Squank swore he'd never get drunk at all, but there he was squatting on the ground, a solemn look on his face as he pulled an unmarked plastic bottle and two large thimbles from his backpack.

"Closest thing to sake cups," he said.

When he poured the clear liquid into the thimbles, his eyes flashed, the silver gray of sharks feeding in shallow surf. A mourning dove moaned. The day glimmered with possibility, the throbbing forest rich and deep. I recalled my father raving about Russian cognac, Lord Byron on laudanum, a book called *Confessions of an English Opium Eater*. When Dad got drunk, his good eye sparked with double energy, as though about to jump out of its socket. While his right eye was perky, blue as the Caribbean, his left seemed to droop, its pupil displaced, its iris a murky olive brown.

"Kanpai," said Squank, taking a swig. "That's the Japanese word for cheers."

The second he swallowed, Squank was pinching his arms, reciting his litany: "I'm punishing myself. I'm punishing myself."

"Where did you get it?" I asked.

"I have my sources."

I picked up my thimble. Cicadas chanted in the mystic heat. I pictured Bacchus wreathed with poppies, accompanied by maenads and prancing satyrs. Keen for intoxication, for Dionysian abandon and ecstatic revery in the mythic woods, I downed the liquid.

"It tastes like salt water," I said. "Plus, I don't feel anything."

"It takes some time," said Squank. "Let's have another round."

We slammed back two more shots, and I gazed up into the boughs, listening to the old trees creak in gentle wind. Did I feel anything? Perhaps—an enticing tingle, a whisper of mystery. Squank reached for my hand, his palm weirdly damp. I recalled the time we kissed, the tentative probing of his pointy tongue, the sickly curiosity I'd felt before pulling away.

After Squank removed his hand, we did another shot. And then my friend's cool smile erupted into a taunting sputter.

"I'm punishing myself. I'm punishing myself." Croaking, sniggering, he pinched his arms. "I'm punishing myself—not for drunkenness, not for gluttony, but for lying."

"It's not sake is it?"

"Nope."

"What then?"

"Saline solution for my sisters' contact lenses." Squank fell onto the ground, seized by a laughing fit. He had older sisters, tall, cool girls as pale as the moon, opposite in every way to my small, dark, spastic brothers.

"Gross," I spat. "You turd."

"I'm punishing myself. I'm punishing myself."

New bruises bloomed on Squank's tender arms.

The day was hopeless, stagnant, drained of magic. I refused to speak to him the whole way home, refused to hold on to him, leaning back on the moped, clutching the back of the seat. When he dropped me off, I darted inside without looking back.

In our hot, smoky kitchen, Mom was singeing the chuck roast. Dusk fell, and Dad switched to Beam and Coke—no more sly splashes into his coffee cup. It was cocktail hour, and my father held forth on the mystery of young Merlin's paternity.

"Merlin was sired by an incubus," said Dad. "And his powers flowed from his demonic side. Incubi are associated with sleep paralysis and dark, erotic dreams."

Mom hefted the five-pound shoulder steak to inspect its underside. "This roast weighs more than Cabbage did when he was born," she said.

"Do you know how to identify an incubus?" asked Dad.

"Something every woman needs to know," said Mom.

"Their penises are unnaturally large and cold."

Mom laughed, eased the roast back down into the cast-iron skillet, and lit a fresh cigarette.

They didn't see me standing there, mortified in a shroud of smoke, trapped and panicky, still seething over Squank's trickery. I was about to make a beeline for my room when I heard the growl of Regan emanating from our sunken den. The den, a renovated garage, was semisubterranean, five degrees cooler than the rest of the house, carpeted in ancient, lichen-colored shag. It boasted one small window, knotty-pine paneling, stained-glass swag lamps the color of flames. The room smelled of mold and smoke and some obscure chemical—carpet glue or termite spray. Water stains darkened the low popcorn ceilings. In one corner where the carpet was peeling up, a swarm of millipedes flourished on dewy concrete.

I stepped down into the atmosphere and beheld the marvel of a demon-powered girl talking smack to an exhausted, vomit-spattered priest. I kneeled before the television, immersing my body in its eerie light. With her luminous eyes, Regan seemed to gaze right into my soul.

Squank did not call to apologize, and I spent endless days shut up in my hot room, flipping through outdated fashion magazines, pining for the lavish hair of impossibly beautiful models who glared with expressions of lofty boredom. After a week of harassment, Mom finally agreed to give me a Rave home perm. I sat on the bathroom toilet as she toiled with rod rollers, fantasizing about returning to school with big hair, my limp strawberry-blond tresses transformed into a riotous mass of spiral curls. I'd tease it into a heavy-metal mane and spray it with toxic gusts of Aqua Net, the brand Dad used to shellack his comb-over into a crisp wing that covered his clammy and enormous forehead. I'd somehow acquire a leather miniskirt, expertly apply moody eye shadow, grow a foot taller, and blossom into succulent womanhood. Nobody in seventh grade would recognize me. I'd remain aloof, dark mysteries stirring inside me like nocturnal birds. I imagined Squank squinting at me, thinking I looked vaguely familiar, his dumbass eyes widening with astonishment when he finally figured it out.

"You'll have to suffer for beauty," said Mom, hotboxing a cigarette as she prepped the bottle of solution, making the bathroom smell like a chemical weapons lab. As she doused each roller, I struggled to breathe, swabbing the flesh-scorching runoff with a washcloth. I closed my eyes lest the concoction blind me, trying to hold on to the image of myself as a femme fatale coolly strolling into homeroom, my hair as formidable as a nuclear mushroom cloud.

"Forty minutes," said Mom, setting her kitchen timer. "Call me when it goes off."

I fished a cigarette from Mom's pack and smoked while gazing into the mirror. My reflection was like a sip of vinegar. I had Dad's mega-brow and big nose, swarms of freckles that had leapfrogged from odd lineages on both sides of the family, but my lips were full and pouty like Mom's. I turned away from the window, bit my nails to the bleeding point, and blew a hundred smoke rings.

At last, the timer went off, but Mom did not appear immediately with the neutralizing solution. When she finally unfurled my tresses and rinsed my hair, I rejoiced to see wet corkscrew curls. I went to work with a curling iron and blow-dryer, sculpting and teasing until I resembled a cotton-top tamarin. Though my scalp was hot pink and damaged hair ends fluttered to the floor like dying moths, I felt that sexy *je ne sais quoi*, the eternal power of the femme fatale surging through my veins. I slipped Mom's cig pack into the pocket of my shorts and walked out into the hot day. Cicadas sang their mating dirges. Our spaniels grunted like swine in their muddy nests. The plaintive whine of Squank's moped wove through the afternoon song like a minor melody.

I strolled out to the carport and lit a cigarette, channeling the ennui of an heiress on a terrace, unmoved by the exquisite mountain vistas stretching into distances without end, not one shitty ranch house or split-level in sight.

"Wow," said Squank, but then he tittered—the nervous laughter of a boy out of his depth. I imagined the creepy pressure of his damp hand holding mine, the weird meld of longing and repulsion I felt when he touched me. Though I wanted to hop onto the back of his moped, I restrained myself. Recalling the thimbles of saline solution he'd served me, I chose not to speak to him. Studying the clouds, I remained coiled within my own mystique.

"What did you do to your hair?"

I did not deign to answer him.

"Okay. So you're giving me the silent treatment. Look, I'm sorry about the sake."

It was not sake, I resisted uttering.

We'd spent three months fantasizing about Japanese gardens—the slow geometry of bonsai trees, the tranquility of trickling water, the eternal dignity of stones. Though we knew we'd never visit such a place, sake was an elixir with the power to transport us. And Squank had turned our mutual longing into a cheap prank.

"I guess I deserve this." Squank pinched his arms, reciting his masochistic incantation: "I'm punishing myself." Though he attacked himself with unusual ferocity, I did not stop him. I tossed my cigarette butt onto the concrete, stamped it out, and stalked inside, where I took refuge in our living room, a room we seldom used, a space fetishistically maintained by Mom and Dad lest some hifalutin visitor drop by and observe the shame of the true caves in which we dwelled: the smoky kitchen with its maggot-hued linoleum and chipped Formica countertops, the dank den, where one might discover a month-old pork-chop bone moldering beneath the sleeper sofa.

The living room boasted a powder-blue velveteen sofa, floral wingbacks, and a gilded mirror that echoed the glory of saffron wall-to-wall carpet—the only new carpet in the house. In the hushed sanctuary of the living room, an elegantly curved mantel clock ticked above the cold hearth. I sat in the tranquil space, plotting revenge. I'd feed Squank brownies that contained subtle traces of dog poop. I'd invite him to picnic in the sticks and then steal his moped, leaving him stranded in the wilds. I'd tell his choir-directing mom that he sometimes took puffs off my cigarettes, an infraction that would get him whipped and then grounded for a month.

I lit a Doral and strolled around the lovely room, pausing at each revolution to study my new hairdo in the gilt-framed mirror. I imagined that I was alone in a mansion at the edge of the sea, waiting for my lover, who resembled Tommy Lee. The fantasy was set in the eighteenth century. Tommy Lee would arrive on a black stallion, bearing a bouquet of wildflowers he'd picked in some gloomy glade. When I closed my eyes to summon this image, I heard a jazz of insults blaring in the summer night.

I walked to the kitchen, where Mom and Dad's idle bickering had caught fire. Sneering, my tiny mother hacked up a chicken with a boning knife, attesting that Dad's sister was a melodramatic hypochondriac who subsisted on pork and cake. Circling the cramped space, my gigantic father declared that Mom's brother was an illiterate leprechaun who wore size five shoes, cheap shiny loafers that resembled a fairy's light footwear. Mom said Dad was a lazy boozer because he was raised by rich drunkards. Dad said Mom came from a tribe of redneck elves, that her father was a simpleton who hadn't graduated from high school.

The fight was just gearing up. They had at least a dozen relatives to belittle before reaching the rage they craved—an ecstasy of fury that would purge them of human emotion, leaving them light as fasting saints, practically levitating, their faces incandescent. But now they snarled and jeered. Now they stomped on the dingy linoleum, working to unleash the transformative hor-mones into their blood.

Taking refuge in the den, I turned on the television to find Regan tied to her bed, writhing and groaning as two exhausted priests flung holy water at her, scorching her pale, pubescent skin. The preview seemed to possess our television, coming on multiple times each day, filling the den with unholy light. As the familiar red font of the film's title surged to center screen, Cabbage screamed, the strange high-pitched screech of a rabbit. He crouched in the darkness behind the sofa, shielding himself from Regan's demonic face. When the teaser was over, and a commercial for Secret deodorant came on, Cabbage inched out into the light.

Cabbage wore his oxygen tank, two plastic Mr. Pig bottles strapped to his back with a complex array of ropes. A segment of green hosepipe ran from the tank to his mouth, and Cabbage took deep breaths through the tube as though his life depended on it. At last, when he'd had his fill of imaginary oxygen, he pushed the tube aside.

"How did the demon get inside the girl?" he asked me.

"I don't know," I said. "We'll have to watch the show and see."

"Can't," said Cabbage, "'cause I'm just a little child."

My parents, worn out from raging, slumped at the kitchen table before a feast of fried chicken, potato salad, and canned green beans. The twins gnawed drumsticks while idly arm wrestling. Cabbage picked the breading off a thigh. Dad carved at his breast like a bored king. Mom always ate the giblets, those dark crunchy innards, saving the deep-fried heart for last, devouring the bird's small soul, absorbing its power to fortify herself for conflicts to come.

We ate in a communal stupor, lulled by rich food, our fingers slicked with grease. With no prelude of thunder, soft rain fell as night came on. Dad flicked ash onto his pile of bones. He sighed and fixed himself another drink.

"How does a demon get inside you?" Cabbage asked.

"A mystery," said Dad, perking up at talk of demons. Lighting a cigarette, our father held forth on possession.

"In the Bible, they tied a possessed man down, but he broke his shackles," said Dad. "Jesus found him outside a cave, his skin cadaverous, his eyes lit up like the sulfurous flames of Hell. When Christ asked who inhabited him, the demon spoke in a deep, gravelly voice: *My name is Legion, for we are many*."

Cabbage shuddered. The twins gasped.

"Don't listen to your father," said Mom, getting up to clear the table. "He's an idiot bullshitter who comes from a long line of idiot bullshitters. I don't know how he talked me into marrying him."

"You, a hick from the sticks, married me for my money."

"What money? Your drunken father lost it all."

Dad winced and turned back to demonology. Hungry for occult knowledge, we hung on to every word.

"The demons begged Jesus not to send them back to Hell," said Dad, "so he cast the evil spirits into a passel of swine. The pigs oinked and squealed, bucked and brayed. Their eyes rolled back in their skulls, and froth dripped from their muzzles. The pigs stampeded through the village, trampling a toddler to death. They passed out of the town and entered the wilderness, where they ran over a cliff and plunged into the sea."

"Where did the demons go?" asked Cabbage.

"Demons are eternal," said Dad. "They go this way and that, riding the wind in search of empty souls to fill with their evil."

Cabbage whimpered and sucked his thumb. The twins embraced. I bit my ragged nails. Drunk on the powers of terror, Dad tittered. And then he swayed off to the dining room, where his typewriter sat on the table, a Brother electric that beeped every time he misspelled a word, which was frequently, for his novel contained long passages in medieval English: tomb engravings, poems and spells, the weird muttering of spirits and elves.

The week before *The Exorcist* aired on Primetime, Squank didn't call, nor did he appear on his Puch Sport, revving his small engine, tempting me out into the sprawling summer day. I hadn't seen him since the day I got my home perm. I refused to call him, for he'd betrayed me, mocking the fantasy we'd hatched during the tender month of April, when we first started cruising on his moped, fleeing our shitty neighborhood for the fresh green woods. I flung my restless body around our mosquito-infested yard, smoking cigarette after cigarette. Each afternoon the humidity swelled to unbearable pressures. Thunder grumbled, but the relief of rain did not come.

Little Cabbage, intent on slaying Hell's array of demons before the possessed girl inhabited our television, disappeared into his hole. When the cicadas paused their pulsing song, I could hear the steady hacking of my baby brother's trowel. Down in the wet clay, Cabbage gibbered nonsense spells Dad had taught him to keep demons at bay.

Each day after lunch, when the day's promise slumped, Mom and Dad started bickering, which soon flared into full-fledged brawls. Mom called Dad's novel a childish fantasy, said our family couldn't afford his summer off. Dad called Mom an unlettered fool who'd never tasted the sublime—said she'd eat her words when she saw *The Sorrows of Young Merlin* on the bestseller list. Mom said if she ever heard the word *Merlin* again, she'd scream bloody murder, commit herself to a lunatic asylum, or chop off my father's head. Dad said Mom's haircut made her look like a dour little man, an accountant who balanced checkbooks and counted spoons. He said he'd divorce her when he became a famous author. At this, Mom laughed—a high mocking titter that filled the house with disturbing energy, as though emitting a dangerous electric charge. Toxic gasses seemed to flow from my parents' venomous mouths, and we children stayed outside lest we suffocate on their hatred.

On the morning *The Exorcist* was due to air, Mom went on cooking strike, refusing to make breakfast, shouting, *Fend for yourselves!* We fed on off-brand cereals—Cocoa Nuggets, Fruity Freakies, Crispy Chunks, and Pranks. When Dad poured himself a second cup of coffee and started up on Merlin, Mom dashed for the utility closet and pulled out our ancient vacuum cleaner, which resembled a small, battered military tank. Just when Dad launched a monologue about Merlin's time of madness, when the young magician ran off into the Caledonian Forest to subsist on grass and wild fruit, Mom went into a frenzy of vacuuming, filling the house with the machine's rattling roar.

"I'll suck up every speck of filth in this fucking shithole," Mom shrieked, her eyes lit with unholy fires that we could not comprehend. So we fled the house—first the twins, then Cabbage, me next, and, at last, our father, stumbling out into the garish day in his red velour bathrobe, clutching a sheaf of papers to his chest. Dad set up camp at the picnic table, fortifying himself with a carton of Dorals, a thermos of coffee, a bottle of Wite-Out, and his dog-eared copy of *Vita Merlini*. Dad fussed with his manuscript, making marginal notes, wincing every time the twins hollered. He popped a Valium, splashed Jim Beam into his coffee, and read snippets of his novel aloud.

> *Merlin envisioned his wife Gwendolen, decking herself in*
> *jewels. Vanity, thy name is woman.*

> *The naked succubus floated in a cloud of pink mist. Her breasts,*
> *voluptuous yet firm, could be glimpsed through the vapor.*

When morning passed into the torpor of afternoon, the twins descended from the treetops. Heat-dazed birds rasped in the shrubs, and Cabbage emerged from his hole.

"Daddy," said Cabbage, "I'm hungry."

Exhausted from digging, Cabbage stood shirtless in a beam of sunlight, the stark contours of his newt's rib cage cast into high relief. When my father surfaced from the Caledonian Forest to regard his scrawny son, a shadow passed over his face.

"Your mother is neglecting us," he said. "She's a gadabout, a wench of no consequence."

"We want lunch," said the twins.

"I'll cook up a sportsman's feast," said Dad.

We followed our father inside to discover that Mom had wandered off somewhere, probably to the neighbors', swanky old alcoholics who owned a wet bar and a Jacuzzi.

"Don't worry, children," said Dad. "I have game in the freezer, fish I caught with my own hands."

From the depths of the freezer, Dad wrested bass and bream, which he'd cleaned and gutted long ago, storing them in knotted bread bags for the long freeze. He peeled the plastic away from frozen clumps of small fish, piled them onto a plate, and put them into the microwave to thaw. Spinning in the microwave light, the game popped and steamed. When the fish had thawed into a gelatinous mass, Dad opened the microwave and unleashed smells of stagnant swamps, of drainage ditches and backwaters haunted by moaning ghosts. Retching, we staggered out into the backyard, where Dad had set up his propane fryer, its aluminum pot filled with recycled oil he'd saved in mason jars.

Soon Dad joined us with a heap of breaded fish, singing "Hang Down Your Head Tom Dooley." A Jim Beam bottle bobbed festively in his bathrobe pocket. In the shade of the magnolia, he unfolded a lawn chair and got to work.

As Dad plopped fish into the sputtering oil, he turned to the topic of Hell.

"In Hell," said Dad, "three-headed dogs dismember beggars and kings. Dragons swoop to feast upon the organs of the gutted damned. Demons teem—Beelzebub and Hypotenuse, Belial and Mumblebeast, also Darkling, Draco, and Scab.

Dancing merrily, they cast grappling hooks to pull sinners from rivers of boiling blood."

Nattering on about Hell, Dad expertly wielded a set of tongs, pulling crisp fish from the fryer, piling them onto a plate fortified with paper towels, and plopping fresh batches into the sputtering grease to cook. The air seemed to swim with unwholesome oils, a substance that left a film on the skin. The spaniels romped in the thick air, begging for food, nuzzling our legs, smearing us with fur and filth. The humidity destroyed my hairdo, turning carefully sculpted bangs into a sticky mass of clotted curls. I felt weak and limp, dirty and hopeless. Disturbing images flickered through my head: Squank cackling maniacally as he downed a thimble of fake sake; Mom opening her mouth to release the roar of a vacuum cleaner; Regan levitating in the strange gusty air of her bedroom.

By the time Dad set the heap of fried fish down on the picnic table, it was late afternoon, and Mom was still gone. Dad served the fish with a bag of white Sunbeam bread and a bottle of Texas Pete. According to Dad, the bread would prevent us from choking on bones.

According to Dad, our family could live indefinitely on wild game if our mother never returned.

"We'll shoot doves from the power lines if we have to," he said.

We ate the fish on cheap paper plates that soon became limp and soggy with grease. First, we nibbled off the crunchy fins and tails, which resembled potato chips with bones. Starved for protein, we gnawed through breading to get at the white tufts of meat, spattering on hot sauce to quell the freshwater funk. We nibbled around spines and rib cages, spitting stray bones onto our plates.

By the time we finished eating, our plates had disintegrated into greasy pulp. Clouds of flies hovered, darkening the air around the picnic table, creating an atmosphere in which we seemed trapped, a cursed miasma of our own making, composed of our breath and gastrointestinal emanations, the stench of fried fish and unkempt dogs, plus the cigarette smoke that perpetually flowed from the moist charred tissue of Dad's lungs. I was about to retreat to take a shower when I heard the wistful whine of Squank's moped, the sound of escape, the sound of adventure in distant backwaters, wildflowers swaying along country roads that led to secret swimming holes.

I decided to forgive my oldest friend. I'd climb on his Puch Sport and let him whisk me away to some other place.

Not bothering to hide my eagerness, I ran out to the front yard. After all, Squank and I had been best friends since third grade. Our friendship had survived that long awkward afternoon when we'd experimented with French kissing, clinically inserting our tongues into each other's mouths. We'd laughed afterward, wiping our mouths and gobbling Tic Tacs, swearing we'd be best friends forever.

Though Squank drove by slowly, he did not swerve into my yard. What's more, an unfamiliar girl perched on the back of his scooter. Though she had the face of an Ewok, her hair was glorious—honey-blond and sun-streaked, frosted and whipped—effortless big hair with natural waves that could not be tamped down. The turbulence of the moped ride had only improved it, and she preened like a Wella Balsam model. Squank, dressed in khaki shorts and an Izod the hue of golf-course grass, simpered. The fool was wearing his older brother's Ray-Bans. He'd made a mess of his hair with his sisters' L'Oréal mousse.

The thought of Squank kissing the girl didn't bother me. But when I pictured them speeding down Lake Warren Road, heading toward the green gloom of dense forest, I felt an ache in my gut. I imagined the girl's hair fluttering in wind, her face serene as they moved through dappled light.

Though Squank pretended not to see me, standing defeated with my deflated hair, he cruised back and forth down my street three times before darting off into the wild summer yonder. I longed to run after them, to push the girl off Squank's moped and climb onto my rightful perch, kicking her in the face as we drove away. But I slumped back into the house, into the cramped kitchen, where my parents were bickering again. I discovered that Mom had spent the day sipping vodka tonics and lounging in our neighbor's Jacuzzi, floating in an ethereal daze while listening to classical music, *forgetting*, as she put it, *that she was married to an idiot.*

Now she stood in the kitchen with clenched fists, surveying the wreckage—strewn cornmeal and spattered grease; bowls full of sallow, malodorous juice; scattered globs of raw fish stuck to the microwave interior. Flies buzzed ecstatically amid the mess, for Dad had forgotten to close the back door.

"But I fed our children," said Dad. "While you left them to starve."

This sent a shudder through my mother, a convulsion that worked its way through her body joint by twitchy joint. At last, she opened her mouth to release her fury, spewing barely intelligible words. My parents resumed their dance of rage, stomping and lunging, waving their arms, spitting out insults to punctuate each gesture.

Just when I was about to flee the house and run out into the gathering darkness, I heard the weirdly ethereal theme song of *The Exorcist*, a bewitching combo of synths and bells. The twins had already nestled into their corner of the sofa. Cabbage hid behind Dad's gun cabinet, hoping to catch a forbidden glimpse of the possessed girl. I stepped down into the cave-like atmosphere of the den, with its dark paneling and cool, damp air. I smelled mold and smoke and that elusive chemical akin to insecticide or superglue. I sat on the sofa and watched the opening credits roll.

At an archeological dig somewhere in the Middle East, a Catholic priest unearthed a small statue of Pazuzu. Just when the priest encountered a larger statue of the demon, my parents stopped arguing and slipped into the room. Silently, they sat down—Mom on the sofa, Dad in the vinyl wingback chair. And so it began—our introduction to Father Karras and his crisis of faith, to Regan and her mother, to Ouija-board shenanigans and mysterious rumblings in the attic. By the time Regan peed on the floor at her Mom's party, we were in, forgetting our humble surroundings, dwelling in the Georgetown manse with Chris and Regan and Sharon, a sprawling matriarchal space where estranged fathers forgot to call on birthdays and annoying boyfriends got hurled out of windows. Even in the garish hospital light, where Regan endured a carotid angiography, we knew the demon was inside her, evading the most invasive of X-rays.

Even the commercials seemed sinister. A demented-looking Uncle Sam ordered Americans to chew Dentyne gum as their patriotic duty. An authoritative male voice urged a woman, represented only by her lipsticked mouth, to eat a moaning carton of yogurt. A preview of a documentary called *The Body Human: The Bionic Breakthrough* promised a future of grim-looking cyborgs. My family endured these breaks in silence, rising only to use the bathroom. The twins did not squirm or plunder the kitchen for snacks, but sat holding hands, breathing in unison. My parents did not exchange light insults or snide remarks. Though I had no idea where Cabbage was, I sensed his presence, an anxious energy lurking outside the nimbus of television light as we waited for full-fledged possession to kick in.

We did not have to wait long. Soon Regan was flailing and spitting vomit, breaking out into boils, doing something mysterious with a crucifix that cut out the second the procedure started. Soon she was croaking in a guttural voice, insulting her mother and the two hapless priests who labored with all their souls to squelch the powers that surged through her adolescent body. Demonstrating superhuman strength, Regan made her bed bounce like a carnival ride. Grinning with panache, she rotated her head 360 degrees. The girl talked astonishing smack to Father Karras, weaseling her way inside his head, shapeshifting into his bleating dead mother and taunting his pathetic faith.

As the priestly fathers flung fake holy water and *the power of Christ*, Regan levitated serenely, her arms spread wide, performing a feat commonly attributed to saints, rising toward the claustrophobic barrier of her bedroom ceiling. I recalled endless evenings lying in bed, gazing at my popcorn ceiling, feeling like a boxed doll. I longed for Regan to blow the roof off her house, morph into a winged demoness, and soar up into the stormy sky, where multitudes of fallen angels swirled, howling at the edge of some mysterious abyss.

When the words *help me* appeared, etched in scar tissue on Regan's pale, childish stomach, I had the gut feeling that her appeal was not for the fathers who labored to subdue her fearsome energies, but for the world that did not offer her the vistas she craved. She was trapped in an adolescent body defined and contested by society. Terrified of its transformative powers, the priests tied this body down, stalked around it, and scorched its flesh with fake holy water.

After discovering Father Merrin's corpse in Regan's room, Father Karras grew desperate and finally attacked the girl, punching her in the face, attempting to strangle her. Bereft of the Holy Spirit, fed up with his own impotence, Karras begged Pazuzu to enter him, craving the uncanny stir of the supernatural inside his mortal body. Purple-faced, yellow-eyed, he suffered some terrible epiphany before leaping out the window. At the end of the film, when Regan appeared bruised but demure, I felt weirdly deflated, searching for some sign that the demon might return.

As the credits rolled and the haunting theme song returned, Cabbage rushed weeping from the dim margins of the den and flung himself into Mom's arms.

"Shit," she hissed. "Did you just watch the entire movie? I thought you were in bed."

"I didn't see much," he protested, but the child could not stop sniveling.

Repeating the phrase *Jesus Christ, save us*, the twins made the sign of the cross.

"Pretty scary, huh?" said Dad, attempting to deescalate the situation with a wry tone. But there was a tremor in his voice. He looked unkempt and sweaty, as though a demon had just vacated his body.

"Come on, children. It's just a movie. Look, you can all sleep together on the fold-out couch. That way, nobody gets possessed." Dad forced a laugh—a deranged chuckle that sounded like a cough.

In rare harmony, our parents worked together to prepare the sofa bed, folding out the thin, musty mattress and covering it with sheets, retrieving an assortment of pillows from our rooms.

And then they abandoned us to the endless night.

Still in shock, the twins crawled into bed. Embracing, they murmured a steady stream of prayers—appealing to God, the Lord, Jesus Christ, Jehovah, the Virgin Mary, and the saints.

Though I hated sleeping with my brothers, I could not bring myself to leave the den, where mysterious energies seemed to flow from the dark television. The thrill of the movie still hummed inside me, and I wanted to lie down and savor the forces that remained.

After I settled into my side of the bed, Cabbage squirmed in beside me, moaning and trembling, smelling of metal and damp earth.

"Let's turn on the TV," whispered Little Jack.

"Mama said not to," Cabbage whimpered.

"This is an emergency," said the Runt.

When Jack flicked on the television, a US flag rippled in the wind as the crescendo of the national anthem blared its final notes. And then the screen lapsed into hissing gray static. It was midnight, the Devil's hour, when television stations closed shop for the night and blood-smeared witches danced naked under the moon. The static sounded like locusts thrumming in the desert. The mass of gray pixels resembled throngs of demons swarming, flapping their black wings, obliterating the sun. Mesmerized, we stared at the TV.

After the boys fell into fitful sleep, I stayed up for hours gazing at the screen. Black-and-white faces strobed—Pazuzu and Regan snarling and smirking. But then Regan surged into color, her face three-dimensional. She inhabited the television—her eyes aglow, her cracked lips oozing some glistening goo.

"I've been waiting for you," she croaked.

"Why?"

"I have secrets to tell," she taunted. "Secrets that will change your life."

I kneeled before the screen, electricity flowing from the wet carpet into my body. When I touched the television, I felt a stronger current, which intensified as Regan told me astonishing things—ravishing truths that would make normal life impossible. And then the screen went dark. I fell into dreamless sleep.

When I woke up, I remembered nothing the girl had said, only the giddy feeling of possessing vast wisdom. The clock radio glowed: 3:00 AM. Soon my brothers were awake too, groaning and writhing. They'd suffered nightmares so horrifying they could not speak. Every time their bodies jerked, the mattress bounced on rusted springs, and all three boys cried out, certain that Pazuzu was among us. Soon they were in a hysterical huddle—weeping and twitching, pressing themselves together as though longing to fuse their souls so the demon could not detect them.

I lay down and closed my eyes. As the bed shook, I pictured the ancient Syrian statue of Pazuzu hovering over me, the one that appeared in Regan's bed just after she descended from her levitation. I imagined the demon shattering his stone prison to emerge, a shimmering creature with emerald eyes, a golden mane, and lustrous fluttering wings.

A metal ballad blared, dreamy and operatic.

I stretched my arms toward the spirit and whispered, *Come in*.

Notes

"Bride"

p. 8: "Man is a rational, moral animal, capable of laughter" is a translation of "homo est animal rationale, mortale, risus capax" (Notker Labeo, monk of St. Gall, 11th century; quoted by Michael George in "An Austere Age without Laughter," *Medievalists.net*).

"Erl King"

p. 41: My title "Erl King" is a reference to Angela Carter's short story "The Erl-King" (*The Bloody Chamber*, Harper and Row, 1979) and Johann Wolfgang von Goethe's 1782 poem "Der Erlkönig" (Verlag Das schlaue Schaf, 2019).

p. 41: The following line is from an English translation of the book *Venerabilis Agnetis Blannbekin* (transcribed by a monk in the 13th or 14th century and published in Latin in 1731): "And behold, soon she felt with the greatest sweetness on her tongue a little piece of skin alike the skin of an egg, which she swallowed" (p. 35, Agnes Blannbekin, *Viennese Beguine: Life and Revelations*, translated by Ulrike Wiethaus, Boydell & Brewer, 2002).

p. 44: "She looked at me as she did love and made sweet moan" is adapted from lines 19–20 of "La Belle Dame Sans Merci" by John Keats (first published in Leigh Hunt's *The Indicator*, 1820).

p. 44: The line "I am certain of nothing but of the holiness of the Heart's affections" is from a letter John Keats wrote to Benjamin Bailey (dated November 22, 1817, *British Literature Wiki*, University of Delaware).

p. 45: The phrase "willing suspension of disbelief" is from Samuel Taylor Coleridge's *Biographia Literaria; or, Biographical Sketches of My Literary Life and Opinions*, Volumes 1–2, Chapter XIV (Leavitt, Lord and Company, 1834).

p. 57: The phrase "drowsy with the fume of poppies" is adapted from "Drows'd with the fume of poppies" from line 17 of the poem "To Autumn" by John Keats (*Lamia, Isabella, The Eve of St. Agnes, and Other Poems*, Taylor and Hessey, 1820).

p. 63: The line "I'll make you beds of roses" is adapted from line 9 of Christopher Marlowe's poem "The Passionate Shepherd to His Love" (1599) (*Poetry Foundation*).

"The Maiden"
p. 67: The phrase "young and easy under the locust boughs" is a reference to the line "young and easy under the apple boughs" from line 1 of the poem "Fern Hill" by Dylan Thomas (*Deaths and Entrances*, J. M. Dent and Sons, 1946).

p. 74: "Laughing with full-throated ease" is a reference to "Singest of summer in full-throated ease," line 10 of the poem "Ode to a Nightingale" by John Keats (*Lamia, Isabella, The Eve of St. Agnes, and Other Poems*, Taylor and Hessey, 1820).

"Flying"

p. 93: This version of "A Wise Old Owl" is from *Punch, or the London Charivari*, Volume 68, April 10, 1875.

p. 102: This version of "Hey Diddle Diddle" appears in *Hey Diddle Diddle and Baby Bunting*, a picture book by Randolph Caldecott (George Routledge and Sons, 1882, *Smithsonian Libraries*).

"Arcadia Lakes"

p. 112: The description of the picture book about an overfed fish is based on my childhood memory of reading *A Fish Out of Water* by Helen Palmer, illustrated by P. D. Eastman (Random House Books for Young Readers, 1961).

"The Mothers"

p. 127: The quote here is adapted from a line in chapter 12 of Marina Abramović's *Walk Through Walls: A Memoir*: "I began to feel more and more strongly that art must *be* life—it must belong to everybody" (Crown, 2016).

p. 129: The phrase "Hell is other people" is from Jean-Paul Sartre's 1944 play *No Exit*, adapted from the French by Paul Bowles (Samuel French, Inc., 1958).

"Moon Witch, Moon Witch"

p. 151: The line "A house is a machine for living in" is from Le Corbusier's manifesto *Toward an Architecture* (p. 151, translated by John Goodman, Getty Publications, 2007).

p. 151: The adage "If one's life is simple, contentment has to come" is often attributed to the Dalai Lama.

p. 158: The maxim "The root of suffering is attachment" is commonly attributed to the Buddha (Pali Canon, 1st century BCE).

p. 159: The line "Decay is inherent in all compounded things" is commonly attributed to the Buddha (Pali Canon, 1st century BCE).

p. 159: The phrase "You must have chaos within you to give birth to a dancing star" is a variation on Friedrich Nietzsche's line from *Thus Spoke Zarathustra*: "I say to you: one must still have chaos within, in order to give birth to a dancing star" (p. 15, translated by Graham Parkes, Oxford University Press, 2005).

"Another Frequency"

p. 188: *Music: The Definitive Visual History* is a DK Smithsonian book from 2015.

p. 195: "Driving her red blood" is adapted from the phrase "drives my red blood," which appears in line 7 of the poem "The force that through the green fuse drives the flower" by Dylan Thomas (1934) (*Poets.org*).

"The Gricklemare"

p. 203: This version of "Higgledy, Piggledy" is from *Favorite Nursery Rhymes* ("Pictured by Ethel Franklin Betts") (Frederick A. Stokes Company, 1906).

p. 204: The phrase "the mystical moist night-air" is adapted from line 7 of Walt Whitman's poem "When I Heard the Learn'd Astronomer" (*Drum-Taps: The Complete 1865 Edition*, New York Review Books, 2015).

"All the Other Demons"

p. 225: "I myself am Hell" is an adaptation of Satan's lament, "Which way I fly is Hell; myself am Hell," from line 75, Book IV of *Paradise Lost* by John Milton (1667) (Anchor, 1971).

p. 241: These descriptions of television commercials are based on ads that actually aired during the 1981 CBS Primetime version of *The Exorcist* and can be viewed on the website *Internet Archive* (CBS *Primetime 05-09-1981 The Exorcist WOC*, see: archive. org/details/vts-01-1_20201011). This includes the ad for the 1981 documentary *The Body Human: The Bionic Breakthrough.*

Acknowledgments

I would like to thank my ingenious and steadfast agent, Madeline Ticknor, at Janklow & Nesbit, and my brilliant and supportive editor, Elizabeth DeMeo. I am endlessly grateful for the Tin House team: my visionary book designer, Beth Steidle, and also Masie Cochran, Nanci McCloskey, Jacqui Reiko Teruya, Becky Kraemer, Isabel Lemus Kristensen, Meg Storey, Lisa Dusenbery, Justine Payton, and Mariah Rigg. I am indebted to all of the writers, magazine editors, and anthology editors who have published and/or endorsed these short stories, including Bradford Morrow, Stephen Corey, Michelle Wildgen, Gerald Maa, Jeff VanderMeer, Carmen Maria Machado, Brian Evenson, Anthony Doerr, T.C. Boyle, and Bill Henderson. Thanks to the University of South Carolina for supporting this book with a Creative and Performing Arts Provost Grant. I could not survive without my group of weirdo friends, including Libby Furr, Genovina Bestoso, Steve Taylor, Dan Hendricks, and Cathy Warner. Thanks to my late parents, Frances and Joseph Elliott, who nurtured my freakish imagination throughout my life. Thanks to my husband, Steve Dennis, and my in-laws, John and Sybil Dennis, for their support and loving attention to Eva. I would not be the person I am today without my daughter, Eva, a voracious reader, amazing writer, and marvelous artist who astonishes me every day.

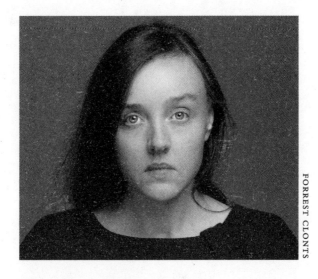

Julia Elliott is the author of the story collection *The Wilds*, a *New York Times Book Review* Editors' Choice, and the novel *The New and Improved Romie Futch* (both from Tin House). Her work has appeared in *The Georgia Review*, *Tin House*, *Conjunctions*, and the *New York Times*. She has won a Rona Jaffe Writers' Award, and her stories have been anthologized in *Best American Short Stories* and *Pushcart Prize: Best of the Small Presses*. She teaches English and Women's and Gender Studies at the University of South Carolina and lives in Columbia with her husband, daughter, and five hens.